Wisdom

by
Amanda Hocking

First Paperback Edition: September 2010

For information:

http://amandahocking.blogspot.com/

Wisdom – Book IV

ISBN 9781453816981

For Eric and my mom — for tirelessly believing in me and supporting me.

Without you, none of this would be possible.

For Pete — fellow Aardvark., and for the rest of the Clique — Valerie, Greggor,

Bronson, and Fifi - for loving me when lesser people would've stopped.

To Kalli — my number one fan.

Terror ripped through me.

I had no idea where I was. I woke up expecting the familiarity and safety of my bedroom, and this wasn't it. It was hot, almost unbearable. Sweat soaked my skin, but I shivered. Disoriented, I stumbled out of bed.

I tripped over my own foot and fell onto the floor with a heavy thud. Cursing myself, I rubbed my knee, even though the pain had stopped. I'd been training hard to work on my strength and grace, and I hated when my clumsiness returned.

The light flicked on in the room. I sat on the floor and squinted up in the brightness to see who turned it on Peter stood in the doorway, wearing only ripped jeans, and he stared down at me.

I finally remembered where I was, but I still couldn't shake the panic. My heart pounded like crazy, and that's what summoned Peter.

"What are you doing on the floor?" Peter asked.

"I tripped."

"Are you okay?" He walked over to me and bent down so he could help me up.

I took his hand, and when he pulled me to my feet, I noticed the sweat gleaming all over his chest and his arms. If I hadn't been so distracted by my own terror, I might have taken the time to hate how perfect and gorgeous Peter looked. Every time I saw him, I wished he would get less attractive.

"What's going on?" His voice had taken on a protective edge that I was unaccustomed to hearing from him. He'd been working on showing me his gentler side, but it still surprised me.

"I don't know." I shook my head.

"Alice, you're terrified." He heard the panicked racing of my heart and no matter what I did, I couldn't slow it. "What happened?"

I bit my lip and pushed my hair behind my ear. He put his hand on my arm, and his bright emerald eyes managed calmed me a bit. I wanted to tell him everything, but I couldn't explain what freaked me out so much.

"It was like a bad dream," I said. "But it wasn't a dream. It was more of a … *feeling*."

"What kind of feeling?" Peter asked

"Just fear, this really intense fear."

"You were just sleeping, and then you were afraid?" He dropped his hand from my arm and studied my face. "No images that went along with it?"

"No." I furrowed my brow, trying to remember what exactly woke me up. "There weren't images, but I felt paralyzed. Right before I woke up, I felt really scared, and I couldn't move." I shook my head again, this time to clear it. "It's over now, and I'm done talking about it."

"As long as you're okay." Peter sounded reluctant to let the topic die.

"Yeah, I'm great." I forced a smile. "Except I'm really hot. Why is it so hot in here?"

"The central air is broken. I've been out back trying to fix it, but the sun is really getting to me. And, as it turns out, I know nothing about air conditioning units," he sighed. That explained the grease stains all over his jeans and the smudge that ran just above his naval, on the hard contours of his abdomen.

"That really sucks," I said and looked away from him.

"I'll call a repairman, but I don't know how long it will take them to get here." Peter ran a hand through his dark hair. He'd been wearing it shorter since he moved, probably because of the continuous heat. "It's the drawback of living out in the middle of nowhere."

"Yeah, I bet," I said. "I think I'm gonna take a shower."

"It's only noon."

"I doubt I can sleep anyway," I shrugged.

"I'll see if I can find a fan for you," he offered and stepped towards the door.

"Alright. Thanks," I smiled at him. He nodded, then left me alone in the room.

I went over to the closet to look for clothes. It was mostly bare since I hadn't packed that much for my ten-day stay. As soon as we'd gotten here, Mae insisted on putting my things away and doing my laundry.

I would've been fine with living out of a suitcase, but Mae wouldn't stand for it. With Daisy around, her maternal instinct seemed to be in overdrive. Really, I wasn't sure how Peter tolerated it.

After Mae had gone against Ezra's wishes and turned her great-granddaughter into a vampire, he'd given her three days to get out. They'd left in two. Peter chartered a private plane, and he, Mae, and Daisy had escaped to the Australian outback.

Even though they were gone, Mae still kept in contact with us, particularly with Milo. She'd been sad we spent the holidays apart, and after Christmas, she began plotting to see us.

Milo started school next week, so he decided now would be the best time to visit. Jack didn't think it'd be good for him to come with because he didn't really want to see Mae or Peter. He didn't even want me to go, but he didn't try to stop me.

It was just my younger brother Milo, his human boyfriend Bobby, and me spending a week and a half with Mae, her child vampire Daisy, and Peter. With a broken air conditioner.

Milo told me that January was summertime here, but if I had understood exactly how hot that could be, I might've put off visiting until July.

Peter bought a huge farmhouse about an hour away from Alice Springs in Australia. From what I'm told, it's a nice town, and Sydney's supposed to be divine, not that I've seen much of either of them. Sydney's a four-hour flight away, but that's not what stopped us from going. Daisy can't go out in public. She's only five and has almost no control over her bloodlust.

Milo'd tried to spin this as a trip in celebration of my eighteenth birthday last week, and in a way, it kinda was. Mae threw a little party for me, with a cake that only Bobby could eat. She gave me a lovely dress, and Daisy made me a card.

I got in the shower, and the cold water did wonders for me, but I couldn't shake the trepidation. Something was off, and I couldn't put my finger on it.

I thought about calling Jack back in the States, but I hardly ever got any reception. Besides, I didn't want to alarm him. He'd been convinced that this trip was a horrible idea, but it hadn't been that bad. A little dull, maybe. Jack's real fear, of course, was Peter.

When I got out of the shower, I went over to the dresser and pulled open the top drawer. Amongst my bras and underwear, I'd hidden Peter's present to me. A beautiful diamond encrusted heart-shaped locket. I loved it, but I had no idea how to explain it to Jack.

Nothing was overtly wrong with Peter giving it to me, but Jack wouldn't approve. For my birthday, Jack had a Muppet specially made to look like me and had taken me scuba diving with the sharks at the aquarium. They were pretty awesome gifts and I loved them, but they weren't the same caliber as expensive jewelry.

Then again, Jack had also given me immortality, so he kinda had Peter beat.

"Is it cooler in here?" Milo opened my bedroom door without knocking, and I dropped the necklace in the drawer and slammed it shut.

"Um, I don't know," I said, taking a step away from the dresser.

"I think it's hotter in here," Milo groaned but walked into my room anyway. Like Peter, he had decided that shirtless was the way to go. "It's got to be at least a hundred degrees here!"

"Have you tried the pool?" I asked.

"Yeah, right." Milo wrinkled his nose and flopped back on my bed. "The sun's still out, and even if it wasn't, you've seen the pool."

Something was wrong with the filtration system, so skeavy green moss covered the pool. There seemed to be something wrong with everything in the house. Apparently, it had been even more rundown when they bought it, but Peter and Mae were fixing it up. But the pool didn't work, the air went out, the wrap-around porch sagged, and the roof needed replacing.

I went over and pulled back the heavy curtains, looking outside. The sun stung my eyes, and I stared out at the emptiness. They didn't have a neighbor for miles, and everything looked dry and faded. I slid open the window and a hot breeze wafted in, but at least it was better than nothing.

"I'm starting to think this was a bad idea," Milo said wearily.

"It's not that *bad*. I mean, other than the heat." I sat on the bed next to him. Beads of sweat stood out on his chest, and he looked up at me, his big brown eyes dejected. "You've had fun seeing Mae, right?"

"Kinda," he shrugged and looked away.

Milo had been the baby, the one that had garnered all of Mae's attention until Daisy came along, and she required a lot more than he did. He wasn't a real jealous person, but this struck a nerve with him.

Being ignored by our real mother had been bad enough, let alone her replacement.

"What's Bobby doing?" I asked, hoping to cheer him up by talking about his boyfriend.

They'd been together for four months, and they weren't "meant for each other," not the way vampires are, but there was still something there. Bobby made Milo happy, and he was a good guy.

Bobby mostly lived with us back in Minneapolis, and despite my initial hatred of him, he'd really grown on me. Some of that probably had to do with the fact that I'd bitten him, bonding us together slightly. It tended to drive Milo nuts, but we couldn't do anything about it.

"He's sitting in front of a fan in our room," Milo said, scratching absently at his arm. The spiders here were crazy about him. The bites didn't really hurt him, but they left irritating, itching bumps for hours. "Even the heat is getting to him, so you know it has to be bad."

"He's probably just used to living in our climate," I yawned. We hated being hot, and we constantly kept our house at frigid temperatures. Plus, we had just come from winter in Minnesota. "Ugh! It's too hot sleep!"

"Tell me about it." Milo looked up at me. "What time is it back home? Maybe Jack's up."

"I don't understand the time difference. You tell me."

"I don't know what time it is here," he said and made no effort to find out. "Have you talked to Jack lately?"

"The other day. The reception here is so shoddy, it's hard for me to get through."

My heart ached at the thought of him. I was bonded with Jack, so it was painful to be away from him. It had lessened a bit over the last few months, but it still wasn't anything where I'd enjoy not being around him.

"How are things there?" Milo asked.

"The same, I guess. Ezra is moping around the house, and Jack can't wait for us to get back."

"I still can't believe that Ezra hasn't talked to Mae," Milo looked a little wide eyed over it, and I felt the same way.

No matter how mad or frustrated I might get with Jack, I couldn't imagine going *months* without talking to him. It would be like going months without eating.

Bobby shrieked from his bedroom down the hall, but Milo and I were slow to react. Spiders had been infesting their room since we arrived, and Bobby screamed like a girl every time he saw one. Admittedly, some of them could actually kill him, but most of the time, he'd already stomped on them by the time Milo or I came to the rescue.

I heard a door slam, followed by a bizarre clawing sound. Bobby's heart beat frantically, but his wasn't the only one. Another heart pounded hard and fast, but it was quieter and not as rapid as a human.

It was the sound of a vampire's heart. A very small, very hungry vampire.

By the time Bobby yelled again, Milo and I were already running out of my room. His room was way at the other end of the hall, but we could see Daisy, clawing at the door with her bare hands. She was strong enough to tear the wood, leaving bloody trails as it splintered out around her fingers.

Before we had a chance to reach her, she managed to tear a hole in the door big enough for her little body to wriggle through, and Bobby started screaming like hell.

- 2-

Bobby had locked the door behind him to keep out Daisy out, but that didn't help us rescue him. Milo got to the door first and tore into it.

Bobby kept screaming, and Milo dove through the hole before it was big enough. He sliced open his side pretty bad, but he wouldn't have noticed at all if it wasn't for Daisy. The scent of blood made her even crazier.

I reached through the hole and unlocked the door, deciding that seemed faster. Bobby stood on the bed with his back pressed against the wall. A nasty bite on his arm dripped blood all over the sheets, but he just stared wide eyed at Milo wrestling with Daisy.

When she wasn't crazy with thirst, she was an adorable little girl with chubby cheeks and downy blond curls. But when she gnashed her teeth, trying to get at the blood running out of Milo's side, she looked evil.

Her face contorted with a deep snarl. Her lips pulled back, revealing her sharp teeth, unnaturally large for a child. Her eyes blazed, and she moved like lightening.

Milo couldn't move fast enough, and she kept biting him as he tried to pin her down. When she bit him, she wasn't even trying to drink his blood. She just snarled and snapped at anything like a crazed animal.

I pushed Milo out of the way, and Daisy was instantly on her feet. I wrapped my arms around her before she could dive at Bobby, who still seemed to be her main target.

The way she wriggled made it impossible to hold her in my arms. She turned her head and nearly bit my shoulder, but I grabbed a clump of her hair on the back of her head.

She twisted around, pulling out chunks of her hair, and I had to take more drastic measures. I slammed her head down onto the floor, pressing her face to the hard wood, and I knelt on her back.

I felt guilty about it because this was a five-year-old kid I was fighting, but it felt a lot more like pinning down a piranha.

"Are you okay?" Milo jumped onto the bed with Bobby, but other than being freaked out, Bobby looked alright.

Daisy kept trying to bite me and clawed at the floor. Her pudgy little fingers bled, but she didn't notice.

Abruptly, she stopped. She lay perfectly still and silent, just long enough for me to think that I had killed her, and then she started crying. Not like a whiny brat that didn't get their way, but like a scared little kid that had gotten hurt.

I looked to Milo for help, unsure if I should get off her and risk her attacking again.

Within seconds of Daisy crying, Mae appeared in the bedroom.

"What the hell are you doing?" Mae shouted and pushed me off Daisy. It was much harder than she needed to, and I went flying into the wall, cracking my skull on the plaster.

Mae scooped Daisy up off the floor, and she had gone back to looking like an ordinary little girl. She hung limp in Mae's arms, big wet tears running down her face as she sobbed. Her curls were sticking to damp cheeks, and her fingers hadn't healed yet.

"That little monster tried to eat me!" Bobby said. He held his arm up to slow the bleeding, and Milo stood in front of him on the bed.

"I don't care what she was doing!" Mae held Daisy fiercely to her. Tears stood in Mae's eyes, and she glared at us. "She is just a child!"

"She is not just a child," I said. "She nearly killed us all!"

"Oh, she's just hungry." Mae brushed it off. "And Bobby is a human. She's not used to being around them."

"I don't care what she's used to being around!" I shouted. "What would you have done if she killed Bobby? Or if she kills somebody else?" Mae shook her head, unwilling to look at me.

"I'm going to go feed her." That's all Mae said on the subject, then turned and carried Daisy out of the room.

"That was so ridiculous," I sighed, running a hand through my hair.

Milo inspected the wound on Bobby's arm, but despite the blood, it was fairly shallow. The intoxicating, sweet scent of him filled room, and my stomach rumbled.

It had been months since I'd bitten Bobby, but often times when I was hungry, I found myself craving him. I hungered for Bobby's blood more than any other human. Standing this close to him, smelling him, reminded me that it had been over a week since I had eaten.

Milo had not taken it well when I bit Bobby before. Sharing a human with another vampire is unsettling. For weeks afterward, he'd followed me around like a puppy, causing many a fight between the three of us. Biting intensifies the feelings you already for each other. Eventually it faded, but even now, I felt protective of Bobby.

As Milo looked over Bobby's wounds, he wrinkled his nose in disgust, smelling Daisy on the bite.

"You need to get it washed up and put a Band-Aid on," Milo said, dropping Bobby's arm.

"Alright." Bobby climbed down off the bed. He looked down at his pants, splattered with droplets of blood, and sighed. "I'm gonna have to throw these pants out! Dammit! I loved these pants."

Bobby took the whole "getting attacked by a vampire" thing pretty well, but he actually had more experience with them than either Milo or me. He got involved with them when he was eighteen, so he had two more years dealing with this than we did.

He went into the bathroom to get cleaned up, and I looked back at Milo. "Mae has completely lost her mind," I said in a hushed voice, but Milo didn't say anything. "You can't tell me you're on her side."

He hopped off the bed and wiped off the blood on his side. Using the mirror hanging on the wall, he studied his wounds, and some would've been serious if he wasn't a vampire. The bite marks on his shoulders and arms were nearly healed already.

"I'm not on anybody's side," Milo said at length.

"Daisy almost killed your boyfriend," I said. Milo turned back to look at me, meeting my eyes evenly.

"So did you."

"That's different." I shook my head. "I was dying. She's an out of control child."

"Maybe," Milo admitted. "But what are we gonna do about it? You want me to go kill her?"

I didn't know what I wanted him to do, but Daisy clearly wasn't safe. This was the first time anything like this had happened since we'd been here, but she was crazier than any vampire I'd seen.

I didn't have a good answer, and Milo didn't want to talk about it. I went back to my room to sulk, since there wasn't anything better to do. Peter came up a little while later to fix the bedroom door, and he warned us that Bobby shouldn't be left alone anymore.

I was mad at Mae, so I wanted to spend a long time hiding out in my room. Then I realized that she was mad at me, so hiding would probably please her. To spite her, I decided to get up.

When I got down stairs, Daisy sat in the dining room. Coloring books and crayons were spread out all over the round table. Her hair had been tied up with a ribbon, and she had changed into a frilly pink and white sundress.

Her fingers healed up completely, making it possible for her to hold the crayons as she colored. She sang "Across the Universe" in an angelically perfect voice, and I'm sure that her Beatles repertoire was all Mae's influence.

It wasn't that I didn't understand where Mae was coming from. Daisy had been terminally ill, and if Mae hadn't turned her, she

19

would've died. Daisy was her great-grandchild, and she was an adorable, sweet girl… when she wasn't a terrifying demon from hell. She was just much too young to have any impulse control, and she was going to be stuck looking like a perfect five-year-old for the rest of her life.

"Hi, Alice," Daisy chirped. She kept coloring and didn't look up at me, but she'd stopped singing. Under the table, I could see her legs swinging back and forth.

"Hey," I said stiffly. I wasn't the best at interacting with children, especially sometimes monstrous ones. "Where is Mae?"

"Hanging up laundry on the clothes line. She said I could stay inside if I promised not to go anywhere," Daisy informed me.

Mae had left her completely unsupervised a few hours after she'd nearly killed us. Awesome.

"That Mae sure does love doing laundry," I muttered.

"Do you wanna color with me?" Daisy looked hopefully at me with her honey-colored eyes. She really was a miniature version of Mae.

"Um, no, that's alright." I didn't want to get invested in an activity with her, but I stepped closer to the table to see what she worked on. She had a *My Little Pony* color book splayed out next to her, but she drew something on a blank page that I couldn't decipher. "What's that you're doing?"

"I'm making a card for Bobby cause I hurt him." Daisy held up the paper so I could look at it.

From what I could tell, it appeared to be a poorly drawn pink unicorn with a rainbow behind it. The words "sorry Bobby" were spelled correctly but with letters turned around.

"That's a really nice card." I forced a smile at her. "I'm sure he'll like it."

"I hope so. I didn't want to hurt him." Daisy sounded sad and stared off for a second, then went back to coloring. "I need glitter. Peter says he's going to get me some the next time he goes to town."

"That's pretty nice of him." I rubbed my arms and noticed the heat didn't seem to be bothering her that much. But when I was a little kid, the heat never seemed to get to me either.

The screen door slammed shut behind me, and Mae came into the kitchen. She smiled tightly at me, so I figured she hadn't forgiven me yet. Which made sense because I'd done nothing that I needed to be forgiven for. I subdued Daisy the only way I knew how in order to save Bobby's life, and she hadn't really been hurt. She *couldn't* really be hurt.

"Daisy said you were hanging up laundry," I said.

"I like the way the fresh air makes the clothes smell," Mae replied, her British accent sounding colder than normal. She wore her loose curls in a bun, and sweat dampened her sundress. She brushed past me and went over to Daisy, admiring her pictures and giving her a kiss on the top of her head. "That's a beautiful card, love."

"Thanks," Daisy smiled up at her. "Alice says that Bobby will really like it."

"I'm sure he will." Mae glanced up at me, and some of her anger dissolved. She sat down in a chair next to Daisy and colored a picture of her own. "Daisy ate and took a nap, and she's been coloring just fine all evening. She's just fine when she eats."

"I'm sure she is." I couldn't really argue with Mae. What could I say while Daisy was right there coloring? So I changed the subject. "Have you heard anything about the air conditioning?"

"Not yet," Mae shook her head. "But it's cooled off since the sun went down. Outside, it's not that bad at all." She looked up at me. "Peter's sitting out there."

I wasn't sure if I should join him. Since coming here, I'd tried to spend very little time alone with him. But the heat was still stifling inside the house, and I could really use a break, so I went outside.

The one thing I would say about the outback is that the stars were amazing. Without all the light pollution from the city, they twinkled above me like nothing I had ever seen.

I stepped down off the front porch to get a better look at them. It was much cooler outside than it was in the house, so I let the night enchant me for a moment. I heard a sound to my left and looked back over to see Peter sitting on the end of the porch, his legs dangling over the edge.

"The sky is really brilliant." I took a few steps over to him.

"It is." Peter leaned forward to admire the sky. "It's not something I've gotten accustomed to yet. I've spent too much time in the city."

"Is that why you came out here?" I leaned up against the porch next to him, and he kept looking up. His face was impossible to read, the way it always was.

"You know why I came out here," Peter answered quietly.

22

I dropped my eyes and kicked at a stone on the ground. He had come here because of me, and I didn't have anything to say that.

Shortly before he left, Peter had confessed his love for me, but I couldn't reciprocate. Well, maybe parts of me could, but I refused to. Not when I had Jack, and I loved him. Then everything had happened with Mae and Daisy, and Peter had seen his chance to escape from me. Again.

"So you like it out here then?" I asked. "Away from all the hustle and bustle of the Cities?"

"I don't know," Peter sighed. "The weekly flights to Sydney to visit the blood bank are irritating, but the silence and isolation is nice." He paused, thinking. "I don't suppose I like it anywhere very much anymore." I felt his eyes searching me. "I've been worse places, though."

"Was that some kind of dig at me?" I asked sharply.

"Alice, I'm not trying to fight with you." His eyes glowed green in the darkness, even without any light, and he let out a long breath. "I can't win with you. I'm either being cruel, or I'm asking too much of you. Whatever I say, it's never the right thing."

"You didn't say anything wrong." I shook my head. "I was just asking if you were happy."

"Don't ask me that," Peter said gently. "Don't ask me because you don't want to know the answer."

"How are Mae and Daisy doing?" I asked, changing the subject.

"Not well," he said. "Daisy isn't getting any of her bloodlust under control, and Mae refuses to admit that that's a problem."

"Oh yeah?" I cocked an eyebrow at him. "Daisy has been doing stuff like today?"

"She's never around humans, or it would be far worse." He lowered his voice, in case Mae might be inside listening. "Daisy went after a wallaby or a koala a few nights ago."

"A wallaby and a koala don't look anything alike," I pointed out.

"It was something small and furry and gray-ish," Peter shrugged, not caring what it was. "It was a bloody mess by the time I got of a hold of it."

"You mean she killed it?"

When he said that she went after it, I had assumed that she chased it down because she was a little kid and they were cute. I had chased down hundreds of bunnies and squirrels when I was young in an attempt to make them my friends.

"She tried to eat it," Peter said.

"No way! That doesn't even... I thought animal blood wasn't edible?"

"It's not." He gave me a meaningful look. "She just gets so crazy when she's hungry, she can't even differentiate animal blood from human."

I had been around animals since I turned. Jack has a Great Pyrenees, Matilda, but I never once wanted to eat her, no matter how hungry I got. Her blood didn't even smell right.

"Holy hell," I said. "That's intense."

"She's attacked both Mae and me on several occasions," Peter said. "We feed her every day, but it's not enough. I know she's only been a vampire for a few months, and she was so young to start with, but I would've thought she'd gotten better by now. If anything, it's worse."

"What's gonna happen with her?"

"She's going to live out here forever, and we're going to hope for the best," he said. "There's not much else we can do."

What had happened today with Bobby wasn't a fluke, and as cute and innocent as Daisy looked coloring at the table, she was equally as dangerous.

I stood outside with Peter for a while longer, but a tense silence fell over us, and I escaped back into the house. My bedroom was still too warm to sleep in, so I tried to put a fan in my window. Peter had brought a giant old metal box fan up from the basement, and it had to have come with the house.

Spider webs clung all over the fan, and when I tried to brush one off, I felt the familiar burning sting of a spider bite. It scurried away, not that I would've killed it anyway, and I stared at the red bump on my hand.

"Did a spider get you?" Bobby grimaced and leaned in my doorway.

"Yeah. The damn things are everywhere," I muttered.

I went back to trying to get the stupid fan to fit in my window, and Bobby came in and sat down on my bed, as if I'd invited him in. Once I got it wedged enough where I thought it could work, I turned the fan on, and took a step back as dust sputtered out.

"Nice." Bobby waved his hand in front of his face.

"I had to do something before I died of heatstroke," I said once the dust explosion settled. The fan seemed to be working, so I shrugged and lay down on the bed. "I am so sick of this. It's ridiculous."

"Tell me about it." He leaned back against the wall with his legs crossed underneath him.

His commiserating would've been more convincing if he wasn't wearing purple jeans and a tee shirt. Admittedly, the tee shirt was paper thin, and I could see the black designs of his tattoos through it.

"You're wearing pants." I looked over at him. "You can't be that hot."

"Yeah, but they're *purple* pants," Bobby said as if that that made some kind of distinction. "Hence, I'm awesome."

"Do you even own shorts?" I puffed my pillow up under my head so I could look at him more easily when I was lying down. "I don't think I've seen you wear any."

"Just swim trunks. Shorts aren't my thing."

"How does Jack's wardrobe make you feel?" I asked, smiling sadly at the thought of him. Jack wore Dickies shorts almost every day of the year, regardless of the weather. He was ridiculously awesome that way.

"It works for him, so more power to him." Bobby scratched at the bandage on his arm that covered up Daisy's bite, and he wrinkled his nose at it. When he looked down, his black hair fell more into his eyes, and he brushed it back. "She bit down right into my nautical star! I bet I have a scar that totally wrecks it."

Bobby had a sleeve of tattoos that ran all down his arms, but most of them were black and shades of gray. The only one with color was a green nautical star on the back of his arm, and that was the one that Daisy got.

"She bit the back of your arm?" I raised an eyebrow.

"Nasty little brat," he said. "I don't even know what she was thinking. All the good veins are on the underside of my arm. She doesn't know *anything* about being a vampire."

"She certainly doesn't," I agreed wearily. "You need to stop picking at it, though, or it will scar."

Bobby continued scratching at it, so I kicked him gently in the knee, and he stopped. He leaned back, resting his head on the wall, and sighed.

"Between the spiders and Daisy, this trip is gonna be the death of me."

"I really wish I hadn't let Milo talk me into it." I stared up at the ceiling. "What is he doing anyway?"

"Sleeping. He says it's too hot to sleep during the day," Bobby said. "He's probably right. But luckily for me, I never sleep anyway." Bobby's insomnia had made him a perfect fit for our lifestyle. "I can't believe I'm wasting my last week and a half of winter break here. When Milo asked me to go to Australia, I was thinking Sydney hot spots and kangaroos and coral reef diving."

"I know, right? Mae said they were living off the grid, but I thought we'd at least *visit* the grid."

"And just think, you could be wasting your time here *and* going to school when we get back," Bobby grinned at me, but I shook my head. "Oh, come on. You should at least graduate."

"I didn't let Milo talk me into it, and I'm not going to let you," I said firmly.

Milo dropped out of school at the beginning of his junior year because of the whole turning into a vampire thing, but he'd gotten under control enough and could handle going back. He'd enrolled in some swanky private school in Minneapolis to finish out the eleventh grade, and classes started on January twenty-first. The same day, Bobby started the new semester at art school.

"So you're just gonna be a high school drop out? What are you gonna do with your life?" Bobby asked.

"What am I gonna do if I don't drop out?" I asked. "I mean, it's not like I can do eight years of med school still looking like I'm eighteen."

"You can just pretend you're Doogie Howser or something," he suggested. "Or you can do something you don't need as much school for. Like a dog groomer."

"A dog groomer? Really? You think I look like a dog groomer?"

"No. I just haven't the faintest idea about what you aspire to be." Bobby cocked his head at me. "Do you even aspire to be anything? Or is this the zenith of your existence that I'm looking at?"

"I don't know. I have forever to figure it out," I hedged his question. Lately, the exact same thing had been bothering me.

In high school, I hadn't really been worrying about grades or school because I didn't care. Milo had always buckled down, insisting that an education and a career were important.

Even though Milo was only sixteen and a vampire, he still hadn't changed his mind. He wanted to finish out his high school career at a nice school, go onto college, and get a job. He still planned on having a normal life and doing normal things.

When I first became a vampire, I thought I had it made. But now that I had nothing but time on my hands, I was starting to think that I had misjudged this whole eternity thing.

"Did I just Debbie Downer the whole moment?" Bobby looked apologetically at me. "You're being all quiet and sad now."

"Nah, I'm okay. I was just thinking," I brushed it off and smiled at him.

"You're not supposed to think. We're on vacation!" Bobby said with false bravado. He leaned forward suddenly, looking excited. "We should do something really fun. We could chase down kangaroos or something." His smile widened and his eyes sparkled. "Or we could see if we could get a dingo to take our baby." He said the last part with an exaggerated Australian accent, trying to channel Meryl Streep.

To bone up for the trip, Bobby had rented *A Cry in the Dark* and watched it like ten times. I'm sure there were better movies about Australia, but this one was his favorite. It was the true story of a woman who was accused of killing her own baby, but she insisted that a dingo took it.

So, throughout the last month, I had heard Bobby spout "a dingo took my baby" about a thousand times.

"You're such an idiot," I rolled my eyes, and he laughed.

My phone jingled the first three seconds of "Purple Rain," and I leapt out of bed. For the majority of the trip, my phone had sat discarded on my dresser because I could never get any service.

The "Purple Rain" ringtone just meant that I had a voicemail, but that meant that it had connected with something long enough to register that. I rushed to grab it before the signal dropped.

"Who is it?" Bobby asked, jumping out of bed after me. We had been stranded without technology for so long that he was excited vicariously.

"I don't know." I tried to call my voicemail, but the call immediately dropped. "Damn!"

"Go over to the window!"

When I walked over to the window, a bar flashed on. The closer to the window, the brighter the signal. I was a little fanatical about having a chance to hear someone's voice (in particular Jack's), so I pushed the screen out of the window.

"What are you doing?" Bobby asked.

"Getting a signal!" I leaned out the window, and I finally managed to connect to my voicemail.

I had barely talked to Jack since I'd been here, and I hadn't heard from anyone else at all. Leif didn't have a phone. Olivia had tried to reach me, but we had never been able to get each other on the phone. Jane was supposed to get out of rehab sometime soon, so I expected to hear from her.

"You have one new voicemail," the automated voice told me, and my heart raced.

"Hey, Alice, this is Jack." My heart soared, but even with my happiness, I noticed something wrong with his voice. It sounded sad and faraway. "I've been trying to get you on the phone. I even tried Milo and Bobby, but..." He sighed, and my heart clenched. Something was very wrong.

"I didn't want to do this over the phone. I mean, I knew I'd have to, but I didn't want to leave it on a voicemail..." He trailed off, and Bobby asked something behind me, but I just waved my hand at him.

"I don't know how to tell you this, but... Jane's dead. I am so sorry, Alice. Jane was murdered last night."

- 3-

The last time I saw Jane, she promised she would get out of this life.

Back in November, she had been seriously injured in the fight with the lycans and spent a month in the hospital recuperating. I hadn't really talked to her much after that because I thought it would be better for her if we severed all ties. Besides that, there hadn't really been that much keeping us together anymore.

We had been friends since we were seven, but the older we got, the clearer it became that our priorities were vastly different. Jane was addicted to partying, drinking, sex, and eventually, vampire bites. I didn't want any part of that life, and she didn't know how to stop.

I hadn't heard from her for a long time, until a few nights before Christmas. Bobby had been working his ass off on some school project, and he aced it. To celebrate that, he wanted to go out. Milo, Bobby, Jack, and I headed out to V – the vampire club in downtown Minneapolis. I had been hanging out there more since I started training with Olivia, and despite myself, I kinda liked it.

After hearing a dance remix of "Jingle Bell Rock" far too many times, we decided to leave. It was snowing out, but in that nice way, like it does in movies, all magical and soft. With fresh snow, everything seems to look cleaner and brighter, and since it was after four in the morning, there weren't many cars driving around to muck it up.

I was staring up at the sky, watching the snow fall down. The clouds seemed to glow from the city lights, and the skyscrapers towered above us. For one brief moment, the whole world fell silent, and I felt like I was living inside a snow globe.

The silence was broken by the sound of an erratic heartbeat, reminding me of a scared rabbit. My throat felt parched, a dull reminder that it had been almost a week since I'd eaten. But I didn't go to the clubs looking for food. I didn't even feed off humans. Bobby had been the only person I'd bitten, and I had no choice when I did that.

"Oh my god," Milo said. He stood a few feet in front of me, holding Bobby's hand, and he leaned forward to get a closer look. "Is that *Jane*?"

"What are you talking about?" I brushed past him to see what he was talking about. Jack followed behind me, in case trouble should arise, the way it always seemed to when Jane was around.

When I saw her, I stopped cold. She stood at the corner, waiting around the entrance of *V*. Her legs were spindle thin, jutting out from her short skirt. Her hair was longer than it had been before, but it hung limply around her gaunt face. Shivering like mad, her skin had a bluish tone to it, and her eyes darted all over.

"Jane?" I took a few uncertain steps over to her. Her eyes locked on mine for a split second, then quickly looked away. "Jane, what are you doing here?"

"Nothing." She shook her head and turned around the corner to get away from me.

"Jane!" I repeated and ran after her. Jack, Milo, and Bobby lagged behind, giving us some space.

"What do you want?" Jane stopped but wouldn't make eye contact. A streetlight glowed nearby, and she hid in the shadows of it.

"Aren't you supposed to be in the hospital?" I asked.

When she moved, I tried to see if there were any bite marks on her neck. I didn't see any, but that didn't mean anything. They healed quickly, and she could have fresh ones on her arms and thighs out of sight.

"I came home yesterday," Jane replied flatly, and she twitched. Once, she had been the most beautiful girl I had ever known. Now she looked like she had leukemia.

"What are you doing here?" I whispered.

Another vampire rounded the corner. He didn't acknowledge us at all, but Jane stared after him with a hungry expression on her face. Humans craved vampires just as much as we craved humans.

"I thought you were done with this," I said, pulling Jane from her vampire lust.

"Don't give me that shit, Alice." Her eyes were frantic and nervous, making it hard for her to keep them steady on me. "You left me for dead on the steps of a church. Don't pretend like you care about what's best for me."

"I did not leave you for dead. You were alive, and we thought it would be better if you got professional help instead of living around vampires!" I shouted, and she looked away. "I was almost

35

killed trying to save you! I risked my brother's life because I wouldn't hurt you! So don't tell me that I don't care!"

"Alice," Jack said from behind me, and I realized that my words echoed off the buildings. I was loud, especially considering I was yelling about vampires.

"Fine, whatever, you care." Jane shrugged, but tears stood in her eyes. "It doesn't change anything."

"What are you talking about?" I softened and took another step closer to her.

"Look at me," she laughed darkly. "Look at me, Alice!" A tear spilled down her cheek and she brushed it away. "I'm a junkie!"

"Jane," I said.

"What am I supposed to do?" she asked. "I spent the last month in the hospital, and they couldn't figure out what was wrong with me. They know I'm an addict, but they can't treat it. I mean, what twelve-step program is there for getting bit?"

"I'm sure any twelve-step would work," I said, and she laughed again.

"I hope so." She sniffled and rubbed at her nose. "My dad is sending me to rehab tomorrow. I want it to work. I hope it does. But I just needed one more fix. I know everyone says that. One last time and all that." She smiled thinly at me. "I don't care if it's cliché. I want to feel good one last time, and then I can try and make it through this."

"The last time someone bit you, they almost killed you!"

I know what a hypocrite I sounded like, especially since Milo had almost killed Bobby before, and Peter had almost killed me.

36

Vampires were really dangerous, and I would warn off any human involved with them. Spend enough time with them, and you're gonna end up dead.

"I know!" Jane fidgeted and shook more than she had been before. "God, I know, Alice! You think I am such an idiot! I know how dangerous this is, way better than you! I'm the one that let them feed on me for months! I'm the one that lost all the blood and nearly died, *twice*. Okay?"

"Then why are you doing this?" I asked.

"Because I have to!" She looked at me with this insistent need. It was a hunger I shared, except in reverse. She wanted to be bitten, I wanted to bite. The idea seemed to occur to her as well, and her expression changed from one of panic to pleading. "Alice, if you're really worried about my safety, then you could just do it."

"What?" I scrunched my face up and took a step back. "No. Don't be disgusting."

"No, Alice, listen," Jane moved towards me. "I need just one more bite, really just *one* more. And you know you wouldn't hurt me. Jack is right here!" She gestured to him, and I glanced back to see the uneasy look he gave her. "He wouldn't let you hurt me. Just do this one time, and then I'm going to rehab first thing in the morning."

"No, Jane, no way." I waved my hands and took another step back.

"Fine." She crossed her arms over her chest and looked at me defiantly. "If you won't do it, then I'll find somebody else who will. And they might be dangerous. They might kill me. Who knows?"

"That's emotional blackmail!" I yelled, and I heard Milo mutter something about her playing dirty.

"No, it's a fact! I am getting bit tonight. And if it's not you, then it's somebody else." Jane shrugged and stared at me, as if it didn't matter to her one way or another.

The vampire part of me became aware that we were talking about eating and not just eating anything, but fresh, warm, human blood. My stomach twisted happily, and my mouth salivated. When hunger took over, logic went out the window.

I turned to Jack, knowing that he would be the voice of reason, but he looked at me dismally and shrugged. He wouldn't be mad at me, and my thirst became more dominant.

"You promise you're going to rehab in the morning?" I looked back at Jane.

"Alice, don't be stupid!" Milo shouted. He stood at the corner a ways behind us, and Bobby had to rein him in.

"I promise," Jane nodded, and for the first time in a long time, I saw a glint of happiness in her eyes. The only thing that gave her any pleasure was being bitten.

"I'm never doing this again," I warned her, and Jack sighed loudly.

Jane nodded again, and with that, I swooped in to bite her. I pushed her back against the silver windows of the building, slamming her body harder than I needed to. She gasped, and I sunk my teeth into her neck. It was the first time I had ever consciously bitten anyone, and I was surprised by how natural it came to me.

The instant her blood started coursing through my veins, wonderful heat burned through me. It was an insatiable pleasure that flowed right from her blood and all over me. Her heartbeat echoed in my ears, pounding along with mine.

All her emotions ran over me, and she felt scared and small and helpless. She was out of control and terrified of what she would become. More than anything, she felt alone and unloved.

I snapped back from the bite, which is harder than it sounds. I hadn't drunk from her for very long, and I had a maniacal urge to latch back on. Wiping her blood from my mouth, I took a step back, and Jack's arms went around me to steady me.

Eating always made me woozy. Fresh blood hit me harder, and Jane's sadness and depression weighed down on me.

"Why'd you stop?" Jane slumped against the wall, sliding down onto the snow. Blood seeped from her neck, and the air smelled deliciously of her. If Jack hadn't had his arms around me, I would've gone in for more.

Milo and Bobby rushed over to take care of Jane before she passed out in the snow. I wasn't that far from losing consciousness myself, so Jack suggested everybody get home. Milo knew where Jane lived, so he and Bobby were in charge of getting her there safely.

Jack half-carried me back to the car, and the whole time, I mumbled about how sad she was and that I'd only made everything worse.

Jane called me two days later from rehab. She claimed heroin addiction, because she said that sounded the closest to what she was going through.

On my end, the conversation was awkward. I'd taken advantage of her, like she had been some drunken one night stand, and that made me feel dirty in all the wrong ways. Towards the end, she thanked me for biting her.

"As strange as it sounds, that's the closest I've felt to anyone in a really long time," Jane said. Her voice was tinny from the bad connection with the landline at the rehab center. "I don't mean in a perverse way, but... Everything I did, I was just looking to feel like someone cared about me, I think. And you were the first person that ever did. I could feel it.

"So, thank you." She laughed nervously. "God, that sounds so stupid to say. But whatever. I'm really gonna work this shit, and I'll be out in a few weeks. And then we totally need to go shopping."

After that, we managed to fall into something that felt like what our friendship had been, before Jane went crazy partying and I went crazy with vampires. She called me a few more times when she was in rehab, and she wrote me a few letters.

She was getting better. She was going to be the Jane that I had missed for the past three or four years. She was going to be my best friend again.

- 4 -

We got the first flight out of Australia, and the twenty hours of flying didn't help anything. I felt like some kind of stiff zombie the whole way.

Even Milo had shed a few tears when he found out, but I couldn't muster any. I couldn't seem to feel anything.

The flight had given me plenty of time to try to sort through my feelings of denial. Milo tried to talk about it. When that failed, he tried to talk about anything at all, but I couldn't make myself talk. I felt blank inside.

It just didn't seem possible that Jane could be dead. With all the stuff she had been into lately, I always half-expected her death, but I never really believed it would be real. I talked to her last week, and she was doing so much better. She was *finally* getting her life on track.

Jack waited for us at the airport. He stood at the bottom of the escalator, looking uncertain.

When he saw me, his whole face lit up, but there was still an unusual sadness in his blue eyes. I jogged down the escalator, pushing past people that swore at me, and I dove into his arms. I wrapped my arms and legs around him and let him lift me off the ground.

"I'm so glad you're home," he said into my hair, holding me to him. It wasn't until that moment that I was able to cry.

Milo drove the car back to the house so I could curl up in the backseat with Jack. Jack and I had made plans to move out a few months ago, but once everyone took off, we didn't have any reason.

We decided to stay in the house for as long as we lived in Minneapolis, but it was looking like it wouldn't be for that much longer. Probably just until Milo finished the school year.

It was unbelievable how much I had missed home. I would've cried out of relief if I wasn't already crying. Jack helped me carry my things up to our room. I curled up in his arms on the bed, and he stroked my hair.

"What happened?" I asked when I had myself under control. I'd talked to him once on the phone before we left, but the connection was sketchy, so he hadn't been able to say much about Jane.

"I don't know all the details," Jack said. I had my head on his chest, so his voice rumbled in my ear. "I only read about it in the paper."

"It was in the paper?" I tilted my head up at him.

"Yeah." He hesitated, and his worried eyes met mine. "I heard about it on the news, but I didn't know it was Jane until Olivia called to tell me about it. Then I read about it in the paper."

"Oh my god!" I sat up, and he kept his hand on my back. "What the hell happened where it was in the paper and the news and Olivia called?"

"You remember that girl they found in December?" Jack sat up a little more, but he did his best to remain as calm possible. This bothered him more than he'd openly admit, but I could feel what he felt, so I knew.

"That wasn't Jane. I've talked to her since then," I said quickly. Hope surfaced, but he shook his head.

"No, that wasn't Jane," he said. "But since that girl died, they've found two more just like that. I guess it'd been on the news, but I hadn't been paying that much attention."

"What does that have to do with Jane?" I asked.

"These girls were killed in a certain way, left in a certain way." He rubbed my back, preemptively comforting me. "The police won't give out specific details, but they've all been teenage girls, around your age. And they've all been left out in the open in downtown Minneapolis."

"What do you mean?"

"Usually, killers hide their victims, I guess, but these ones have been laid out on the sidewalks," Jack explained. "Jane was left on the sidewalk on Hennepin Avenue. Olivia saw the police when they found her." *V*, the vampire club that Olivia owned, was right off of Hennepin.

"You mean..." I swallowed hard. The room started to sway, and Jack put his arm around me. "A serial killer murdered Jane?"

"Yeah, that's what they think."

"It wasn't a vampire?" I looked up at him.

"I don't know. Olivia couldn't get close enough to find out but nobody really knows much of anything. The paper had a lot of rhetoric, but not a lot of fact."

"Well what did they say?"

"They were profiling the victims, and the police talked about all the efforts they're making to stop this." He studied me, and I stared down at the bed. "It's not your fault, Alice. Whatever happened with Jane. You didn't do anything."

I had introduced Jane to vampires and brought her down the path with me. It'd be impossible for me not to take some of the blame about what had become of her.

"Did the paper say when the funeral is?" I asked, ignoring him.

"Tomorrow, at four. Did you want me to go with you?"

"I don't know." I shook my head. "I don't even know if I want to go."

"Why wouldn't you go?" Jack asked.

"Because I'm a vampire!"

Just sitting didn't feel right anymore, so I stood up, and Jack watched me. I paced the room and pulled at the sleeves of my sweater. My hair felt greasy and sweaty, and I needed to shower and sleep.

But I wanted to run and move. I wanted to do something that mattered, that could fix what happened to Jane.

"Alice." Jack didn't get off the bed, but he moved to the edge so he could reach out and touch me. He held out his hand towards me, and for a minute, I didn't want to take it. I felt like crawling out of my skin.

44

"I don't know what to do," I said. "I don't even know what to feel. I mean… Jane pissed me off, *a lot*. She could be so vapid and willfully stupid that I'd want to smack her. But she was so loyal. And all the shit she's been going through the past few months, that's my fault. I brought her into this!"

"Alice, no," he shook his head. He took my hand and tried to pull me to him, but I refused. "Jane already had problems. Before this, it was drinking and sex."

"But drinking and sex aren't what got her killed!" I yelled.

"You don't know what got her killed," he said gently. When I tried to turn away from, he took my other hand and forced me to look at him. "I'm not saying that you and Jane were the greatest friends, but you cared about her and did the best you could by her. And she knew that, and she cared about you too."

That only made me cry harder, and I let him pull me onto his lap. Normally, his love overpowered my emotions, but I could only feel my own guilt and confusion. Jack held me in his arms for a long time. The exhaustion of the trip wore me down, and I fell asleep.

Milo woke us up at two the next day, convinced that we should go the funeral. He managed to win me over by crying and talking about the time that Jane had dressed him up and put makeup on him when he was six. She had been the bitchy older sister that I had never been, and he wanted to go pay his respects and refused to go without me.

After I showered, I went into the closet to pick out something to wear. Jane had spent so much of her life dressing me properly, and for her funeral, I couldn't find anything. She'd be so disappointed if I showed up in the wrong outfit.

I sat on the floor amongst a slew of dresses, crying, when Jack came in. He'd just gotten out of the shower, and he looked down at me.

"Alice, what are you doing?"

"I don't have anything to wear!" I sobbed, holding up an ugly pink dress. "I can't wear this to her funeral!"

Without saying a word, Jack walked over and sat down behind me. He wrapped one arm around my waist and pulled me close to him, and with the other arm, he sorted through the dresses. He tossed aside the obvious rejects while I worked on calming myself down. By the time he needed my input, I had myself mostly under control.

We narrowed it down to two dresses; a skimpy black one that would make me look too hot for a funeral but Jane would love, and a simple black dress that was suitable.

"So, what are you gonna do?" Jack asked, resting his chin my shoulder. Both his arms were wrapped around me as I held up both the dresses in front of me.

"There was only one Jane," I said finally and dropped the skimpy dress. "And she would be so pissed if I upstaged her at her own funeral."

I got ready fast, since Milo repeatedly told me we were running late, but both Milo and Jack beat me. They waited outside the bedroom for me, and we rode together to the church in silence.

The sky was overcast, which was the one good thing about the day. I wore gigantic sunglasses anyway, but I figured they were appropriate for mourning.

When we got to the church, Jack pulled into the parking lot, but I wasn't ready to go any further. The lot was already filled with nice cars, similar to or more luxurious than the Lexus. Jane's father was a very wealthy business man, and Jane had been his only child. Most of the people filing into the church appeared to his clientele and friends.

A few of Jane's other friends were there, but once she got involved in the whole vampire scene, most of her other friends had fallen to the wayside. The ones that did show up stood out horribly.

A girl Jane used to party with showed up in a bright red miniskirt and an entourage in tow, and she texted on her phone as she walked into the church. One of Jane's former hookups looked like he was taking it pretty hard, but that could've just been because he was incredibly high.

"Are we going in?" Milo asked from the backseat. I watched all the men in prim business suits and tweaker kids. "Alice?" I didn't say anything, so he sighed in frustration. "It's going to start soon."

"If you want to go inside, nobody's stopping you," Jack looked sharply at him.

"I'm not trying to be mean, but I don't want to disrupt the service." Milo leaned forward between the seats and touched my shoulder. "Alice, I think that you need to go and do this."

"Milo," Jack said.

"No, he's right. Let's go." I opened the door before I lost my nerve and stepped out of the car.

Jack came around and took my hand, and Milo went to my other side. As we walked to the church, I noticed a weather-battered flyer tacked onto a pole. I'd seen thousands of others all over the Twin Cities the past few months. A black and white photo of Daisy took up most of it, with a number to call with any information regarding her disappearance.

Her abduction had been quite the news story. An adorable five-year-old with a terminal illness taken from an affluent neighborhood tended to get a lot of attention. By now, everybody had started assuming she was dead, so it had lost some fanfare.

The church was packed, and it was hot in the way all crowded places were. The heat and the sadness were stifling. The sounds of crying and heavy heartbeats filled my head.

The mahogany coffin sat at the end of the long center aisle, the lid flipped open. Looking at it from the back of the church had the same dizzying effect as looking down from a great height. From where we stood, I couldn't see Jane, only the white lining of her coffin.

My knees felt weak. The moment felt so completely surreal. Jack squeezed my hand, and Milo moved in closer to me.

We slid into a pew in the back because it was the closest, and I felt unsteady. I had expected that strange numbness to come back over me, but it didn't. I was nauseated, and all my emotions felt amplified.

Milo cried softly through most of the service. He had never been a huge fan of Jane, mostly because he thought she was a bad influence, but he'd liked her. She could be very funny and kind, and sometimes she was that way with Milo.

After her cousin delivered the eulogy, the pastor opened it up for anybody to speak, but I couldn't do it. Anything I had to say about Jane felt sacrilegious. I'd let our friendship fall apart, and if I hadn't, maybe we wouldn't be here.

At the end, they called everybody up to say their final respects to her. Jack waited behind in the pew while Milo and I went up. I couldn't have made it by myself, and I was thankful to have Milo next to me, holding my hand. He was the only one that knew her the way I did.

The worst part about seeing her in the coffin was that she didn't look dead. It'd been almost exactly one month since I'd seen her, and she looked much better now. She had put on some weight, in a good way, and her skin had color again. Maybe that was just the makeup, but it didn't matter.

Jane looked more alive than she had in months, and she was dead.

I reached out and touched her hand, her skin cold and stiff. Tears slid down my cheeks, and I wanted to apologize, to say goodbye, just say anything to her, but I couldn't form the words. My mouth wouldn't work. Milo's choked sob was the closest I came to saying anything.

We were the last people at her coffin, and the pallbearers watched us. I'd already taken too much time not saying anything, so I gently steered Milo away from the coffin. I looked away from Jane, knowing that was the last time I'd ever see her.

Milo and I had almost made it to our seats at the back of the church, and I saw something that made my heart stop. Milo had his head bowed, but I looked up to make sure we wouldn't pass our pew.

Our mother stood in the middle of the aisle a few feet in front of us.

I stopped short, and Milo lifted his head. Her mouth fell open when she got a good look at Milo.

We had both changed since we'd become vampires, but his was far more drastic. He'd been sixteen when he turned, but thanks to his pudgy cheeks and large brown eyes, he'd always appeared younger. With the transformation, he'd grown taller, broader, and gleaned off his baby fat.

Mom had last seen him over four months ago, but he'd aged several years, looking like he was eighteen or nineteen now.

Since we'd turned, we'd done everything in our power to cut ties with our mother. Milo still called her on the phone sometimes, but she couldn't see us. It would be much easier for her if she went on with her life without knowing what we were.

For the funeral, Mom's hair was still a frizzy mess, but she had draped herself in some kind of black garment. In an attempt to look nice, she'd put on bright red lipstick and heavy eyeliner.

"Milo?" Mom leaned in towards us, like she didn't believe what she was seeing.

"Hi, Mom," Milo swallowed hard. He squeezed my hand even tighter. His heart hammered in his chest, and so did mine.

"Is that really you?" She reached out as if she meant touch him. When her hand got close, she let it fall to the side and just stared at him. "When you walked past, I thought... You look so much like your father." Mom *never* talked about our father, except occasionally to say that he had done nothing to help take us.

"Thanks?" Milo replied uncertainly.

Behind us, they had closed the casket and started wheeling it out to the hearse. The funeral had officially ended, so everyone filtered out around us, but we didn't move.

"That private school must be sitting well with you." Mom continued gaping at Milo.

"Uh, yeah," Milo fumbled. Mom believed that he was attending a private school in New York, but that was a lie to explain his sudden absence. She thought I had taken off to live with Jack, and that was true.

"You've really grown." Her voice cracked. "You both have. You look really good, Alice. You've grown up into fine young adults." A thin smile spread out across her face. "You did blossom without me."

"Mom, that's not true," Milo rushed to ease her guilt.

"When did you get in?" Mom asked, thinking that he'd flown in from New York for the funeral.

Her tissue was balled up in her hand, and I couldn't believe that she had cried over Jane. I didn't even know what she was doing here. She liked Jane well enough, I guess, but she'd hardly knew her.

"Yesterday," Milo said, continuing the lie. "I was gonna visit-"

"No, I understand," Mom shook her head. "Your sister needed you." She looked away for a moment, then turned to me. "I wanted to call you on your birthday last week, but I didn't think you'd answer."

"You should've called," I said.

"Would you have answered?" Mom asked pointedly, and I dropped my eyes. "I know you have a life of your own now. I didn't mean to intrude on it by coming here-"

"No, you didn't intrude," I said quickly. Tears welled in her eyes, and I had never seen her look so fragile before. Drunk, tired, irritated, those were her three basic moods.

"Jane had been a very good friend to you over the years, and I thought I owed it to her to thank her for taking such good care of you." Mom discreetly dabbed at her eyes. "I am truly sorry for your loss, Alice."

"Thank you," I said, unsure of what else to say.

"I don't need to bother the two of you anymore, so I'll be on my way," Mom said rather abruptly and turned to walk away from us.

"Mom, wait." Milo let go of my hand and rushed over to her.

Before she could respond, he threw his arms around her and hugged her. I was afraid he might accidentally hurt her, but she didn't seem to be in pain when she hugged him back. Fresh tears streamed down his cheek.

"I love you."

"I know you do, sweetie. I love you too." Mom rubbed his back for minute, then pulled away from him.

"I'll come visit you before I leave," Milo promised, sniffling. She put her hands on his cheeks, smiling at him.

"You don't need to do that. You just get back to school," Mom said, her words thick with tears. "You need to get a good education so you can have a life of your own. That's all I've ever wanted for you." She dropped her hands from his face, that sad smile hanging on her face. "Take care of your sister, okay?"

"Okay," Milo nodded.

She pulled her black flowy dress around her and walked away from us. Milo wiped at his cheeks with the palms of his hands, clearing away all his tears, and I walked over to him.

I chewed my lip and stared after our mother as she walked out of the church. I should've hugged her, but when she was standing there, I just didn't feel it in me. I could hardly speak, let alone move.

"Are you okay?" I asked.

"Yeah. Are you?" He was still trying not to cry. "Sorry. I'm being such a baby."

"No, you're being Milo," I forced a smile at him.

The church was completely deserted now. Jack had been hiding in the back, giving us a private moment. Once Mom was gone, he walked over to us.

"That was your mom, wasn't it?" Jack asked.

"It sure was." I took a deep breath to keep from crying again.

"Are you holding up alright?" Jack shoved his hands in the pockets of his suit.

"I'm as good as I can be," I said.

"That was kind of intense, wasn't it?" Milo asked me. "I really didn't think I'd ever see her again."

"Are you glad you did?" Jack asked.

"Yeah." Milo chewed his lip. "Yeah, definitely. I needed some closure. I think we both did."

I'm not sure if he was talking about him and Mom, or him and me, but either way, I didn't feel like I'd gotten any closure. I just felt even more shaken up than I had before.

Milo was in a much better mood on the car ride home, almost to the point of being giddy. All the crying had some kind of cleansing effect on him. I wish it did the same for me.

When we got home, Bobby sat cross-legged on the kitchen island, dipping celery into peanut butter.

"How was it?" Bobby asked.

"Good, in a really weird way," Milo told him.

"Where's my dog?" Jack noticed her absence instantly. He loosened his tie and looked around for Matilda. Every time he walked into the house, she was a giant white ball of fur that attacked him.

"She's outside with Leif," Bobby said.

"Leif's over again?" Jack muttered as he walked to the French doors that lead out to the backyard.

Leif had been a part of the bloodthirsty vampire pack that had come here to kill Peter, and the rest of us in the process. But Leif had disbanded, and he'd almost died helping us.

Since then, he'd become a vagabond. I'm not really sure where he lived or what he ate (although he assured me he didn't kill anyone), but every now and then, he would stop by to shower and crash here.

I could never get a real read on how Jack felt about Leif. Jack didn't seem to trust him, but I think that was only because he couldn't figure out what Leif's deal was with me.

If I were him, I wouldn't get it either. Leif and I had some kinda connection that I couldn't explain. As soon as I had met him, I had felt it. But it wasn't sexual or inappropriate. It was just a bond.

Jack went outside in his suit, and by the time I followed him, he was already rolling around in the snow in it. Matilda barked happily at him, her thick fur packed with dirty snow. As soon he'd come out, she'd lost all interest in Leif, I'm sure. She might be the only thing on earth that loved Jack more than I did.

"You're dressed up," Leif said, looking me over. He stood off to the side of the house, barefoot on the stone patio.

His brown hair was damp from melting snow, so he slicked it back a bit, as opposed to its normal wild look. His eyes were large and deep brown, reminding me of Milo's, and I think that's why I'd always liked him. I couldn't help but trust anybody that looked like my brother.

"Um, yeah, we were at a funeral." I rubbed at my bare arms, not because I was cold, but because talking about it made me uncomfortable.

"I'm sorry," Leif said sincerely. "I hope everything is alright with you."

"I don't know if it is," I shrugged. "But it will be." He smiled at me, and Jack stopped playing with Matilda so he could stare at us.

"Would you mind if I used your shower?" Leif asked Jack, and he nodded. Ezra had already okayed it for Leif to shower here as often as he wished, but Leif always asked Jack anyway.

"You should wash your clothes too," I said as Leif walked towards the house. His jeans and sweater were little more than rags at this point. "Or borrow some of Ezra's. Yeah, do that. Just throw those and take Ezra's."

"Thank you," Leif smiled again.

As soon as he walked into the house, Jack brushed the snow off his clothes and walked over to me. Matilda ran circles around him, not realizing that he had finished playing with her.

"You didn't really wanna play with Matilda did you?" I asked, looking up at Jack.

"What do you mean?" Jack tried to pretend like he didn't understand what I was getting at.

"You just wanted to come out here and take Matilda away from Leif. You're always marking your territory around him." I raised an eyebrow at him. "I should probably be happy that you don't pee on me." Jack laughed, and it sent warm shivers through me. He had the greatest laugh of all time, and it still got to me.

"Maybe." Jack's smile faded a bit, remembering that I was sad. "Sorry. I shouldn't have worried about that as soon as we got back. I'm kind of a jackass."

"No, it's fine. I'm fine, mostly." I forced a smile to prove it. "Will you spend the day with me anyway?"

"I wanna spend every day with you." He looked down at me, his blues eyes soft and adoring, and kissed me gently. His lips were cold from the snow, but I loved the way they felt on mine.

When he stopped kissing me, I rested my head against his chest, and he wrapped his arms around me. If anything could make me feel better again, this was it.

- 5-

The icy wind whipped through my hair, and at this altitude, it was much colder than it was on the ground. The windowed walls of the nearby buildings were like mirrors, reflecting the city lights around us. The skyscraper jutted over fifty stories in the air, and we towered over most of the other ones in Minneapolis.

The iron bar running around the edge felt like ice in my hands, and I gripped it tighter and leaned over the edge of the building. Olivia hated it when I did this, because if I landed wrong, I might not survive a fall of this magnitude.

For me, this was just an extension of my training. I wasn't afraid of heights exactly, but I had to overcome something. My stomach twisted, and I hated how disoriented they made me feel. Headlights dazzled the roads, and people looked like tiny dots walking below us.

"Alice, will you stop that?" Olivia said tiredly.

"In a minute!"

Olivia was a stunningly attractive vampire aged well over six-hundred years, but she didn't look a day over forty, and a very beautiful forty at that. She owned the vampire club *V* located below the building we were in, and she lived in the penthouse suite on the top floor.

Before she retired and bought the club, Olivia used to be a fantastic vampire hunter. A handful of vampire hunters work to keep rogue vampires in order. Some vampires can be particularly dangerous, both to humans and other vampires, and a hunter is necessary to contain them.

When I'd been attacked by a lycan vampire pack a few months ago, Olivia had come to my aide because she'd taken to me. I couldn't be sure how deep that liking really ran, but she knew I was with Jack, so I didn't worry about it.

That attack had left me reeling with how helpless I had been. Even as a vampire, I had nearly been killed and did little to help in the fight. Milo almost died, and I was powerless to save him. Just turning wouldn't be enough. I had to be strong enough to protect myself and the people I cared about, so Olivia had agreed to start training me.

"Alice, if you don't get down from there, I won't work with you anymore," Olivia warned me, not for the first time. "Although, I don't suppose that's as much of a threat as it used to be."

We had been going over our usual exercises, which weren't that different from training for karate or kick boxing. It did involve some minor strength training, but most of it was about learning to use the strength I already had and mastering my own grace and stamina.

Tonight I had gotten her pinned with relative ease, and Olivia started complaining about being out of practice. She hadn't hunted a vampire in over fifty years.

"I was working off some anger tonight. That's all," I said. I didn't look back at her, but I felt her come up to my side. I had just gone to Jane's funeral yesterday, and this was my first time with Olivia since before my birthday.

"How are you doing with all of that?" Olivia leaned on the rail next to me.

I stood on the ledge with my entire upper body hanging over the edge, but she didn't say anything more about me getting down. A gust of wind came up, whipping her long black hair around us. I kept my hair pulled back in a ponytail when I trained, but Olivia insisted that I'd have to learn to work with the length of my hair.

"Where was she?" I asked, and Olivia didn't immediately answer, so I looked over at her. "Where was Jane when you saw her?"

"On Hennepin." She nodded down to the street below us. "A block or so that way."

"Did you see her?" I squinted, staring at the sidewalk. I was too far away to see much, but even if I was right up close, I doubt that there would be much to offer.

"Just enough to notice it was her." Olivia stepped back from the ledge and walked towards the door. She had found a new tactic to entice me off the ledge - information.

"How did you even know she was there?" I jumped down and hurried after her.

"Someone died a block away from my club," Olivia looked at me seriously. "It's my job to know when anybody dies, and take care of it."

"Did you take care of Jane?" I asked.

"The police were already there when I found out about it. There was nothing for me to see, nothing for me to do." She opened the door to the stairwell and started down them. "From what I've heard, she didn't have any bite marks on her. So I don't think it was a vampire."

"But you don't know?" I jogged down the steps after her.

"I can't say anything with certainty, except that the poor girl is dead," Olivia said bluntly and pushed open the door to her apartment.

The penthouse was a massive, luxurious loft. The building had a weird angle to it, more of a triangle than a square, and all the outer walls were floor-to-ceiling windows. Marble floors ran throughout. The steps opened in the center of her suite, going into her living room.

Plush, overstuffed furniture filled the living room. It all looked pretty too, but Olivia's main purpose in life was to lounge and be comfortable. She had a small kitchen off to the side, to feed the many humans she kept since she refused to drink bag blood. "If it's not fresh, it's not food" was her motto.

In the center, to the back of the stairwell, was a squared off area. It contained the elevator that could only go down to the basement. The only way into her place was through the vampire club.

The rest of the walled off area were three lush bedrooms, all of them without any windows. One was her bedroom, and the other two were for the occasional company she had stay with her.

"You really don't know anything?" I asked as Olivia went over and stretched out on one of her extravagant sofas. The only thing she ever wore was tight fitting leather, and when she stretched, it pulled back, revealing her flawless pale skin.

"I know lots of things, but nothing useful about your friend." She yawned and rolled over onto her stomach, so her back was to me, and I sat back in one of the chairs.

"But you hear everything in the club!"

"Nobody cares about one dead human." Olivia had turned her head from mine, so she spoke into a pillow. "No offense, honey. They're not saying anything about it."

"But it's more than one dead human. They think it's a serial killer," I said.

"A *human* serial killer."

"I don't know why that matters. Murder is murder."

I leaned back deeper in the chair. I hated hearing about how little vampires cared for life. Just because they lived forever didn't mean that everything else was incidental.

"I'm going to find out whoever did this to Jane, and I don't care if he killed other people or he's a vampire or the prince of Egypt. I'm gonna kill that bastard." It wasn't until I said it aloud that I realized that I meant it.

"That's why you're trying to pump me for information?" Olivia looked at me over her shoulder. "You think you're going to get revenge?" She raised a sardonic eyebrow and laughed.

"What? Why is that funny? I kicked your ass today," I said defensively.

"I'm old!" Olivia laughed again. "And I am out of practice. If you're serious about this, you're going to need someone new to train you. I'm not making the cut."

"Of course I'm serious about it." I stood up. "Someone killed my best friend!"

"Easy, sweetheart," Olivia said, not unkindly. "I know. You're a passionate girl. That's what I like about you."

"So what does that mean?"

"It means that you need to grieve properly, and then we'll talk." She rolled back over on her stomach, letting her hair fall around like a shawl, and that was the end of topic for her. Olivia liked me, but she had little tolerance for any conversation that didn't interest her.

"Whatever," I sighed. "I'm heading out then."

"Are you going down to the club?" Olivia perked up a little.

"I guess," I shrugged. "Milo and Bobby are down there, so I'll probably check it out for a minute."

"Can you send up a girl then?"

"What girl?" I asked wearily.

"Any girl." She waved vaguely at me and sunk deeper into the couch. "You know what I like."

"You know I'm not sending up a girl, right?" I said, pushing the elevator button so the doors would open.

I didn't like encouraging her use of humans as food, but she had a harem of girls that loved it when she bit them. After what that had done to Jane, I knew I shouldn't even tolerate the idea, but at least Olivia didn't kill the girls and treated them with some respect.

Olivia used to drink blood every day, sometimes several times a day, which is how a vampire gets drunk. The blood hits us hard, making us feel high and happy. But if we only eat when we need to, about once a week or so, the high doesn't last long, and we're functional.

Since she's been training me, Olivia's cut down a lot. Before that, she was pretty strung out and incoherent. Even now, the reason I beat her has nothing to do with her age. Drinking too much blood made her slow and lazy.

The elevator opened into a black hallway at the back of the club. I made my way through a labyrinth of black tunnels to make it to the main floor. The first few times I went up to Olivia's suite, I got horribly lost, but I finally had it down.

I pushed open a massive door, revealing the dance floor splashed in cool blue light. The DJ played a new song by Cobra Starship, and the crowd surged on the floor. A lot of them were vampires and donors, but not all of them. Some of them were just normal people who just came here to dance. Maybe that's all that would happen for them. But maybe, they'd end up as someone's snack tonight.

I ignored the thought. I couldn't save every person, and most of them didn't even need saving. Vampires generally tried not to kill people, because it made eating and living a lot easier if there weren't a pile of corpses lying about.

I was just starting to realize how revolting this lifestyle really was. But right now, I didn't need to worry about everybody in the club. I just needed to find my brother and Bobby.

They weren't that hard to spot, thanks to Bobby's newfound love of break dancing. In the corner by the bar, the crowd had dispersed a little so he could try out of some of his slick moves. They weren't terrible, but he wouldn't make it past round two on *So You Think You Can Dance*.

Ever supportive, Milo stood at the side, cheering him on. I walked over to them and watched Bobby twirl about for a minute, then tapped Milo on the shoulder.

"Isn't the first day of school tomorrow?" I asked. The fanciest thing about being a vampire was that I didn't have to shout to be heard over the music. I'm sure Bobby couldn't hear anything, but Milo nodded.

"What time is it?" Milo asked as he clapped when Bobby landed a hand jump thing.

"It's after three in the morning."

"Shit," Milo grimaced. "I didn't realize it was so late." He left his position at the sidelines to get Bobby's attention. "Bobby!" Reluctantly, Bobby stopped his dancing and got to his feet. The crowd applauded, but I'm not sure if it was over his performance or because he stopped. "We gotta get going."

"Alright!" Bobby shrugged and headed to the door, but Milo stopped him. Bobby was shirtless, wearing only a pair of black skinny jeans, so he could show off his tattooed torso.

"Where's your shirt?" Milo asked him.

"Uh… I don't know?" Bobby looked around, but everyone had gone back to doing their own thing, and his sweatshirt wasn't lying about. "Whatever. It's fine. Let's go."

"It's like twenty degrees outside!" Milo sounded irritated. "And you're covered in sweat! You'll get hypothermia if you go out like that!" He turned to me apologetically. "Sorry. We gotta go find his shirt. Or at least *a* shirt."

Milo and Bobby disappeared onto the dance floor to scour for his shirt, but my bet was on them coming up empty handed. Milo wore a thin tee shirt, so he didn't have anything to lend him. I looked around for anything Bobby could put on.

I bumped into a girl when I wasn't paying attention.

"Sorry," I said, glancing over at her. Then I realized who it was, and we both stopped.

Before I had turned, a pair of vampires had decided they wanted to eat me. Peter had taken care of the guy, but the girl – Violet – had gotten away. She had this whole Halloween get up when she was with him – too much makeup, fake fangs, and bright purple hair.

Since he died, she'd traded it all in for a normal, pretty look, going back to her natural blond hair and subtle makeup. I'd seen her around the club a few times, but I'd only ever talked to her once. She seemed too afraid of me, and after what Peter did to her friend, I didn't really blame her.

"Sorry," Violet said quickly, even though I was the one who had run into her.

"Hey!" I said as cheerily as I could and stopped her from scampering away.

Sure, she had tried to kill me, or at least attempt to facilitate my kidnapping, but she seemed like a lost kid. She had turned when she was only fourteen because she was love struck with some stupid boy, and that'd only been two years ago. If I were being perfectly honest with myself, I saw a lot of Jane in her.

"Hey, sorry." Violet talked to me to be polite, but her eyes scanned everywhere else. "I'll try and watch where I'm going next time."

"No, it was my bad," I apologized, and she gave me a funny look. "How are you doing?"

"Great." Her strange purple eyes eyed me up for a minute, then her face softened. "I heard about your friend. I'm sorry."

"You heard about her?" I asked and my heart sped. "What'd you hear?"

"Um, nothing, really," she said took a step back. "I just... I knew that she'd died. I saw her picture on the TV, and I met her once, when she was with you." Violet used the term "met" loosely. She'd nearly killed Jane that night, too.

Something in my gut twisted. Peter had killed her friend to save me. Would Violet stoop so low as to kill Jane to get back at me? My expression must've changed, because Violet blanched and her heart beat faster.

"I don't know anything about it! Honest!" Her fear made her look younger. "I just... I thought... I was trying to be nice."

"Yeah, no, I know," I shook my head, trying to shake away any hint of an accusation. "Yeah. Sorry. Thanks. I mean, for your condolences."

"Yeah," Violet nodded. Chewing her lip, she stared at me for a minute, then gestured vaguely to the left of her. "I'm gonna... go. Dance or whatever."

"Yeah, alright," I nodded and smiled at her. "Have fun."

The dance floor swallowed her, and I wondered why exactly I forced that conversation with her. Just because she was lost didn't mean I had to find her. It wasn't like I had been that helpful to Jane.

In fact, I never seemed to help anyone. I just made their lives worse, and I seemed to get everyone I cared about in near death situations. It was probably in Violet's best interest if she avoided me.

Milo and Bobby found me a minute later. Bobby was wearing a sexy black Member's Only Jacket that Milo had to buy off another vampire. Milo grumbled about it the entire way to the car, but Bobby just chattered on about his awesome dance moves.

With Peter gone, I had taken to driving his Audi, since I had finally gotten my license. The Audi didn't have a backseat, so we had been forced to take the Jetta tonight, but I drove, because as it turned out, I loved driving. I had spent all this time fighting it, and it was awesome.

In the car, I blasted the music to drown at the beginnings of Milo and Bobby's bickering.

But my mind wasn't on them. I pushed the car as fast it would go, despite Milo's protests from the backseat, and thought about what I had said to Olivia. I had been training for over two months. I wasn't the best, but I could definitely take out Jane's killer. I mean, he only preyed on weak, human girls. That was no match for me, right?

Now, all I had to do was figure out who it was.

- 6-

Jack slept sprawled out on his stomach across the bed, and I curled up next to him, resting my head on his back. We both slept soundly after another rough morning trying to get to sleep.

I'm not sure if it was still jetlag from Australia, but I had a terrible time falling asleep, and Jack forced himself to stay up with me.

Milo burst into the room without knocking. He'd just gotten home from his first day at of his new school, and he overflowed with excitement. Bobby was still at college and he had nobody else to talk to, so he woke us up. Or at least he tried to.

I was happy for Milo, but I'd only been asleep for a few hours when he rushed in. Jack managed to sit up and engage in conversation, but I curled up closer to Jack and learned things through osmosis.

The teachers appreciated Milo's genius, and the girls kept hitting on him. He debated about whether or not he wanted to be openly gay, or fly under the radar. Jack gave him some sage advice about just being himself, and people could make of him what they wanted.

Jack was awake after that, but he knew I slept better when he was around, so he grabbed the laptop and sat in bed next to me. I couldn't really sleep either, but I loved lying in bed next to him. Then, abruptly, he slammed the laptop shut and hopped out of bed.

"What's going on?" I asked, watching as he rushed into the walk-in closet. I sat up when he didn't answer, and he came out a few minutes later, pulling on a tee shirt. "Are you going somewhere?"

"Yeah," he nodded. He grabbed his wallet off the dresser and shoved it in his back pocket, and when he turned to look at me, he grinned like a fool. "I've got something awesome to do."

"What does that mean?"

"You'll see." He came over and kissed me quickly on the cheek. "I'll be back in a bit."

"Okay?" I asked, but he just laughed as he walked out of the room.

After he'd gone, I showered and got ready for the day. When I got done, I checked on Milo and Bobby across the hall, in Peter's old room. Peter had actually packed up his stuff because he left this time for good. I hated to admit it, but I felt a pang in my heart every time I saw his empty room.

Well, it wasn't empty completely. His four-post bed had been dismantled and sat propped up in the corner, with the mattress and bedspring shoved in the walk-in closet. His empty bookcases lined the walls, and all his furniture and other belongings were gone.

Peter had also left a copy of his book *A Brief History of Vampyres* behind on his bed, and I know he'd done it for me. But I couldn't keep it. I'd taken it before Jack could see, and shoved it in the box with the rest of Peter's odds and ends stuff, burying it below a shirt and some old records.

72

With Peter gone, the boys had turned the empty room into a playroom. Before Christmas, Jack and Bobby had discovered a massive sale on *Star Wars* Legos at the Toys R' Us, and they "had" to buy them all. That somehow translated into them bringing them all into Peter's old room to put them together.

So far, they had managed to build the Death Star and a walking AT-AT, set carefully on the bookcases, and they had moved onto a giant Millennium Falcon. Bobby sat cross-legged on the floor, carefully sorting through the Lego pieces, and Milo laid on his belly, a textbook splayed open in front of him.

The new Silversun Pickups CD played softly on the stereo, and the door to the balcony had been propped open, letting the cool winter breeze blow in. Bobby had flipped up the hood on his sweatshirt, but he didn't mind the cold that much anymore.

It still felt weird to me stepping into Peter's room, even though it wasn't his room anymore, and it didn't even really look like it. I breathed in deeply, still able to smell him faintly. I wrapped my arms around myself and shook my head to clear it of thoughts of him.

"What are you guys doing?" I asked.

"Stuff," Bobby said stiffly, adjusting his thick black glasses. He never wore them, but he needed them to see the small pieces of the Legos.

"Bobby had a rough day at school," Milo informed me without glancing up from his book. "He got some teacher that hates him. But he doesn't wanna talk about it."

"I see." I walked over to Milo and looked down at his textbook, and all the words were in a different language. "What are you studying?"

"French," Milo said. "How do you feel about going to France this summer?"

"Sure," I shrugged. I stepped away from him and looked around the room. It looked so barren and large without all of Peter's antiques cluttering it up.

I knew that Peter and I couldn't live together anymore, not if I wanted to make things work with Jack, but I didn't like the feel of empty space. But it wasn't just his absence that made the house seem empty. Mae had taken a good chunk of the warmth with her, and the house had the distinct feel of a bachelor pad.

Since Milo didn't seem to be in the mood to chat anymore, I went downstairs to check out the laundry situation. Under ordinary circumstances, Ezra would've been a rather clean, orderly guy, I'm sure, but he'd been all mopey without Mae. Milo was the only one who really picked up after himself, and I'd felt like I had to step up my game lately.

The laundry room was overflowing in a way that would've made Mae faint. Jack had once made a joke about how unreasonable it would be to wear a new outfit every day, but he had enough clothes where he could go months without washing it and still have clean stuff to wear. So, that's what happened.

I shoved as many clothes as I could into the two washing machines and turned them on. Pushing the hair off my forehead, I surveyed the room and I'd barely made a dent on the laundry.

Sighing, I turned to leave, since I couldn't do much more for the time being.

I paused in the doorway and looked down the hall, towards Ezra's den. The door stood partially open, and I could see the dim blue glow from the computer. He'd holed himself up in there since Mae had been gone.

Chewing my lip, I walked slowly down the hall to the den. I always felt I was invading his space, but I couldn't just let him sulk anymore. Mae had left months ago, and Ezra had to move on at some point.

"Hello?" I asked and pushed the door open wider. I'd expected to see Ezra sitting at the computer, but he lay on the sofa, his arm draped over his forehead.

"Did you need something?" Ezra lifted his arm from his eyes so he could look at me.

"No, I just…" I shrugged and leaned up against the doorframe. I wanted to make sure he was okay, but that sounded silly to say. Of course Ezra was okay. He was Ezra. "What are you doing?"

"I don't know," he admitted. He dropped his arm to the side and stared up at the ceiling for a moment, his deep brown eyes looking beyond the wood. "I suppose it is time that I get up."

"No, you don't have to," I said. "Nothing's going on."

"But you're worried about me." He sat up and looked around his den, which was unusually messy. Books and papers were strewn about, and a blanket lay rumpled on the floor. He'd been sleeping on the couch, preferring the distressed leather to the empty space of his bed.

"Is that a bad thing?" I asked.

"No," he shook his head. "But I've spent too much time in here." He rested his heavy gaze on me for the first time. "I'm being selfish and ridiculous. You have real things to mourn, and I've been sulking about like a whiny child."

"Come on, Ezra. You and Mae were together for over fifty years. I can't even fathom that."

"But she's alive and happy. Happier than I could make her." He breathed deeply and turned away from me. "At least I have that."

"She's not happier," I said. "She just... thinks she is, but she's not."

"A child was the one thing I could never give her, and it was the one thing she wanted more than anything else." He spoke so quietly, I barely heard him, and then he shook his head and looked back over at me. "But how are you holding up with everything that's been happening?"

"Great," I shrugged. "Everything is about as good as can be expected."

"Is it?" Ezra tilted his head, and his concern made me squirm. I lowered my eyes and fidgeted with the hem of my shirt.

"Hi, honey, I'm home!" Jack shouted from the other side of the house, and I smiled in relief. I didn't want to delve into how I really felt, not even with Ezra.

"Jack's back," I said, as if Ezra hadn't heard the same thing I had. "I'm gonna go." I edged back out the door, but I waited until he nodded before I sprinted down the hall.

"Good, you're here," Jack grinned when he saw me. He stood in the middle of the dining room, and his excitement crackled through me.

"Yeah. Why?" I asked, raising an eyebrow.

"I told you. I did something awesome." His eyes sparkled, and he grabbed my hand. "Come on. I wanna show you."

"What?" I repeated.

"Okay, remember how you're driving now?" Jack asked, pulling me along towards the garage.

"I can't really forget it."

"And with me, you, Ezra, Milo, and Bobby all driving our own cars, it doesn't really seem like we have enough vehicles?" He paused at the door leading to the garage. "And how I've been needing to buy a new car since I lost my Jeep?"

"You didn't lose your Jeep. You totaled it," I reminded him.

"Semantics." He waved it off. "So I've been looking for a car to replace mine, and today I found the perfect one."

With dramatic flair, he pushed open the door to the garage and stepped inside. Sitting next to the bright red Lamborghini was a small silver car. For a moment, I was dumbfounded. His new car looked old, like from the eighties. Don't get me wrong – it was in good shape, almost mint condition, I'd guess, but it was not at all what I'd expected. I'd thought Jack would want something as equally flashy as the Lamborghini.

"So?" He stared at me expectantly.

"It's nice." I forced a smile, trying to match his enthusiasm and failing.

77

"You don't get it." His face fell with surprise and disappointment. "I can't believe it."

"No, it's nice," I said again and walked closer so I could see it better. I had to be missing something since he was that excited about it.

"It's more than *nice!*" Jack insisted, still looking appalled. "This is a completely rebuilt 1982 Delorean!" He gestured to it as if that would make me understand, but something about the name clicked with me.

"Oh wait. Is that the car from *Back to the Future?*" I asked.

"Yes!" He dashed over to his new car. "But it's better. It's been modified, so it has keyless entry, an iPod interface, and lots of other stuff. But look!" He pulled on the handle and doors open, lifting up instead of out. "Gull doors!"

"So are you gonna take me for a ride?" I went over and peered inside, admiring the interior that looked brand new for being nearly 30-years-old.

"Yes, definitely," he smiled. "But first, I gotta talk to Ezra."

"Why?"

"Well, for one thing, I just pulled nearly a hundred grand out of our savings." Jack leaned into the car and flipped open the glove box. He grabbed a few papers, which I'm assuming had something to do with his transaction. "And I need to talk to him about getting this thing insured. I don't know if I need special like collector's insurance or something."

"You paid almost a hundred grand for this?" I gaped at him.

"It was totally worth it." He closed the doors to the car and walked back to the house. "And if you think that's bad, you should hear what Ezra paid for the Lamborghini."

"You guys are ridiculous."

"Ezra!" Jack shouted as he went inside. By the time we made it to the dining room, Ezra was already at the end of the hall. "Good. I need to talk you. I bought a car."

"Good," Ezra said, and if he was surprised, he didn't show it. "What kind?"

"A rebuilt 1982 DMC-12," Jack said, and Ezra smiled approvingly.

"Nice," he nodded. "What'd you pay?"

"Here." Jack handed him the papers he'd pulled from the glove box.

Ezra sat down at the dining room table as he read through them, and Jack sat next to him. I peered over Ezra's shoulders and saw that Jack had gotten some kind of warranty to go with it, and Ezra was apparently deciphering the terms of it.

"What are you guys doing?" Milo asked. He and Bobby came downstairs, and Milo stopped in the dining room to see what we were doing. Bobby ventured on, going into the kitchen to go through the fridge.

"Jack bought a car," I said.

"A Delorean," Jack smiled, and he puffed up every time he mentioned it.

"The car from *Back to the Future*?" Milo raised an eyebrow.

"Yeah." Jack's smile grew broader.

"Does it come with a flux capacitor?" Milo asked.

"No." Jack looked at him like he was an idiot.

"So it can't really travel time?" Milo asked.

"Well, no. Of course not," Jack said, sounding a little deflated. "It's a car."

"An old car." Milo crossed his arms over his chest.

"My cousin would've sold you his Gremlin for a lot less, I bet," Bobby said, coming back into the room with a Diet Cherry Coke.

"Whatever. It's awesome," Jack said defensively. "You'd know if you saw it."

"Can we see it?" Milo asked.

"Yeah." Jack pulled the keys out of his pocket and tossed them to Milo. "Go ahead. But don't break anything and don't drive it. You can just look."

"Yes, sir," Milo said, stepping towards the door. He turned to Bobby. "Wanna see it?"

"Sure. Why not?" Bobby shrugged.

"Bobby, don't even think about taking that pop in the car!" Jack called after them, and Bobby set his can of pop on the kitchen counter before following Milo out to the garage.

"It is a really cool car," I told Jack once they were gone.

"I know." He looped an arm around my waist and pulled me close to him, so I was leaning on his lap.

"This all sounds good," Ezra said finally. He tapped the papers on the table and looked at Jack. "It was maybe a tad overpriced, but everything is in order."

"So it's cool that I took the money?" Jack asked.

80

"You earned it. You can do with as you see fit," Ezra said mildly. "We need to get insurance started on it, and while I'm doing that, we should transfer the Audi into Alice's name, and the Jetta into Milo's."

"What?" I asked, feeling a little startled. "Those aren't our cars."

"Nobody else is driving them." Ezra pushed back his chair and stood. "They're not coming back, Alice. It makes more sense to have everything in your name, in case you get pulled over or in accident. You'd have enough questions to answer without dealing with car ownership."

"I guess," I said, but it still felt strange to me.

"Let me get some papers. I think I might actually have title papers," Ezra said and went down to the den. He stockpiled all sorts of legal papers. It made things easier when he had to transfer things, since most of the transfers were to different versions of himself.

"If you don't like the Audi, we can get you a different car," Jack said, misinterpreting my unease.

"No, the Audi's a great car." I shook my head. "And I shouldn't get a new car. You had to work for yours, and I should too."

"But you don't work," Jack looked at me quizzically.

"I don't know where they're at," Ezra sighed, coming back to the room a few minutes later. He had a Post-It note and a pen in his hand. Under his breath, he muttered, "Without Mae, I can't find anything in that damn den."

"I can help you look, if you want," I offered.

81

"No, I'll just get the information, and I'll call my lawyer tomorrow," Ezra said, sitting back down at the table.

"You need a lawyer to transfer a title?" I asked.

"No, my lawyer can get the papers I need." He scratched the back of his neck. "What do I need to get from him? Just titles and registration for you and Milo? And I need to call about insurance for the Delorean?"

"Yeah, I think so," Jack nodded.

"Sorry, I have to make notes." Ezra smiled sadly as he scribbled down on the paper. "I can't seem to remember anything anymore."

Ezra had astonishingly beautiful handwriting, and I leaned forward to watch as he wrote down Milo's name and the Jetta, and then Audi, followed by *Alice Townsend* instead of *Alice Bonham*.

"Um, it's Bonham," I said, correcting him. "Instead of Townsend."

"Oh yes. Sorry. I always forget." Ezra shook his head and crossed out Townsend and wrote my last name above it.

"Why don't we just leave it Townsend?" Jack suggested, looking up at me.

"Cause it won't match my driver's license," I said.

"I know but... why don't you change that?" Jack asked.

"Not this again," I rolled my eyes.

"Oh, come on, Alice. It's weird!"

"No, it's not!" I stood up, and Jack tried to hang onto my waist, but I pulled away from him. "You know what's weird? Taking the last name of your boyfriend and his entire family."

"It's your brother's last name too!" Jack pointed out. "And I just don't understand why you're so against it. It's not a bad last name."

"No, it's not." I crossed my arms over chest. "I don't have any problem with your last name. It's just not *my* name."

"Mae took Ezra's last name," Jack countered, as if that would validate his point someway.

"I don't really want to be involved with this," Ezra said, slowly standing up.

"Jack, we shouldn't really be talking about her." I hurried to use Mae as a shield to deflect the argument.

"It won't kill him to hear her name," Jack scoffed. "Lord knows you never stopped talking about Peter around me."

"Alright. I am going to the den." Ezra turned and walked out of the room, escaping the tension so quickly it made me envious.

"I hardly ever talk about Peter around you! I'm always biting my tongue!" I shouted, and realized just a moment too late that that statement made things a lot worse.

"Always?" Jack narrowed his eyes and stood up. "Sorry, Alice. I didn't mean to stop your Peter gushing. I didn't know it was so hard for you to not speak about him."

"That's not what I meant," I sighed. "I've been careful of your feelings is all, and I think you should show the same respect to Ezra, since you know how he feels."

"No. I don't know how he feels. He had a woman who loved him and wanted to spend the rest of her life with him, so she didn't see anything wrong with taking his last name."

"She left him, Jack! Their relationship isn't something we should strive for." I shook my head and stepped away from him.

"You're missing the point."

"You're missing the point," I said. "Why can't you let me have one thing that's mine?"

"What?" Jack was taken aback. "I don't understand. This is all yours."

"No. This is all yours." I gestured widely to the house. "Everything here belongs to you."

"Not any more than it belongs to you," he shook his head. "This is *ours*. This is our life."

"No, it's not, Jack! This is *your* life. Everything I've done has been for you, and I've changed everything to be with you. I gave up everything!"

"No, you…" His expression crumpled. "I thought you wanted this."

"I did. I do," I sighed and looked away from him. "I do. I just wanted something for me."

"You really feel that way?"

"What way?" I asked, not sure what part he was referring to.

"That you gave up everything." His blue eyes were so wounded, and I hated when he looked that way. "I was trying to give you everything."

"No, Jack, I know that." I rubbed my forehead, struggling to think of what I meant. "I don't regret being here, and I know that you only try to make me happy."

"But I'm not. Am I?" He leaned back, resting on the edge of the dining table behind him.

"Yes, you do. You make me so happy." I stepped over to him, meaning to reassure him. "But maybe that's not the only thing in life that matters."

A knock at the French doors made Matilda bark, and Leif stood outside in the snow, tapping at the door. Jack rolled his eyes and stood up straighter, but he didn't go anywhere. I waved Leif in, and he opened the door, letting an icy draft blow in.

"Is this a bad time?" Leif asked.

"Yes," Jack said too loudly, and I shot him a look.

"No, come on in," I told Leif, giving him a much softer look than one I gave Jack. "We're just talking."

"I didn't mean to interrupt. The snow's been really coming down today, but I can always find another place to sleep, if it's a problem." Leif had stepped inside the house, but he waited by the open door, ready for us to kick him to the streets.

"You know you're always welcome here," I said, but Leif looked at Jack, waiting for him to give his approval. When Jack didn't say anything, I hit him in the arm. "Isn't he, Jack?"

"Yes," Jack said.

"I really don't want to bother-" Leif started.

"No, you're fine," Jack said and waved him in. "You can crash on the couch in the living room if you want. The blankets and stuff are in the hall closet, and you can get cleaned up or whatever."

"Thank you," Leif said gratefully as he walked past us, down the hall.

"I see how it is," Jack smiled after Leif had disappeared down the hall.

"What?" I asked.

"You do too think this is *our* house. If this really felt like my house, and not yours too, you wouldn't have invited him in," Jack said, looking a bit too smug.

"Oh, come off it! It's supposed to snow like 12 inches by tomorrow. He doesn't need to sleep outside in this," I said.

"I wouldn't make him sleep outside, but I'm not gonna pretend that we're not in the middle of fighting just because he showed up."

"You're being rude," I lowered my voice, even though Leif could probably hear everything I said anyway.

"You're being rude," Jack countered.

"How am I being rude?"

"Your brother had no problem changing his name. He's more connected to me than you are."

"That's not rude! That's just... Ugh!" I groaned, completely irritated by this whole thing. "My name is Alice Bonham because I *am* Alice Bonham! Why is that so hard for you to understand?"

"Didn't you read *Romeo & Juliet*?" Jack asked. "A rose would still smell sweet and all that? You won't stop being you if you change your name."

"And I won't turn into something else if I do change it, so what does it matter? Why can't I just stay the same?" I asked.

"Your name is Alice Bonham," Leif said. I looked away from Jack to see Leif standing at the edge of the room, holding blankets and pillows. His skin looked pale, and his expression had hardened.

"Yeah, sorry. You didn't need to hear all that," I said, my cheeks reddening.

"You're from here?" Leif asked.

"That's another reason you should change your name," Jack interjected. "So people don't associate you with the old, human you."

"I'm not actually from here, so-" I stuck my tongue out at Jack, displaying the full magnitude of my maturity. "I was born in Idaho. We didn't move here until I was like five because my gramma lived here, but she passed away, so I don't have any other family to come looking for me."

"Milo is your real brother?" Leif asked, and even though he was looking at me, I had the impression that he was staring off at something else entirely. "Not like... not like vampires."

"No, he's my actual brother. We have the same Mom. But listen, are you alright?" I asked. Something about him suddenly looked off.

"Yes, I'm fine. I think I'm... I'm just tired." He forced a smile, but it only drew attention to how ill he looked.

"Are you sure you're okay?" Jack asked, and even he sounded concerned, so it had to be bad.

"I'm quite alright." Leif swallowed and went into the living room.

"Do you think he's alright?" I whispered to Jack after Leif'd gone. "I mean, can vampires get sick?"

"I don't know." Jack shook his head and looked as dumbfounded as I felt. When he met my eyes, he'd softened.

"I don't wanna fight about this anymore," I said. "I love you. Can we just leave it at that for now?"

"Yeah. I'm sorry." He stepped closer to me and looped his arm around my shoulders. "I don't understand this, but... I said I'd always do whatever I could to make you happy, so if this makes you happy..."

"It does." I leaned into him.

Leif had left by the time I got up the next day, but that was nothing new. He usually came and went without much notice.

The snow continued falling, blanketing the world. Jack went outside to clear it up, and even though we had a snow blower, it didn't really work on the stone patio. He spent the majority of the afternoon shoveling it up, but Matilda was outside "helping" him, so I suspected a lot more time was spent roughhousing than actual shoveling.

Since Jack had the manual labor covered, I went to straighten up the living room. I found Bobby sitting on the couch, his laptop open on his lap.

"Where's Milo?" I picked up the blanket balled up next to Bobby and began folding it.

"Um, school." Bobby scrambled to click things on the computer, and when I peeked over to see what he was looking at, he slammed the screen shut. "Milo joined the debate team or something. You can call him if you wanna know for sure."

"What were you just looking at?" I narrowed my eyes at him.

"Um, me? Nothing." He flicked his black bangs from his eyes and refused to look at me. "Just browsing. You know, surfing the interweb."

"You're being a spaz," I said. "What are you up to? Downloading porn?"

"Yeah, like I'd look at porn in the living room," he scoffed. I kept staring at him, so he sighed and opened the laptop. "I just didn't think you needed to see this."

"What?" I reached for his computer, tilting the screen towards me, and then I saw it.

- 7 -

The giant photo on the screen was color, but the overcast day, gray concrete, and dirty snow almost made it look black and white. I would've thought it was, if it wasn't for the dark reddish stains that spilled out in the center of the photo, and the black policeman's shoes standing next to it.

The headline over it read, "Minneapolis Officials Deny Serial Killer," and in smaller print below it, "After the third death in a string of similar murders, residents fear for their safety."

But I barely even read the words. My eyes were focused on the blood splashed over the sidewalk. I could see just enough of the buildings to make out that it was Hennepin Avenue, where Jane had been found. This was her crime scene.

"That's... this's Jane's blood?" I asked numbly and sat down on the couch next to Bobby.

"Sorry." Bobby moved to close the box, but I stopped him and took the laptop from him. "Are you sure wanna look at that?"

"No," I said but clicked on the link to read the full story.

The article didn't say much more than Jack had already told me. Three girls, aged eighteen and nineteen, had been left discarded around downtown Minneapolis in the early morning hours. Since the crime scenes yielded no evidence, they assumed the girls had been killed elsewhere and were posed to be found.

The most surreal part of it was reading about Jane in such matter of fact way, like she wasn't a flesh and blood person I'd known for ten years.

"Jane Kress, 18, is the latest suspected victim. Her body was discovered at 4:35 am on January 16. She suffered multiple stab wounds, like the other two victims.

Kress had been known to frequent the nightclubs in the area and had returned from a treatment center on January 14. It had been a planned 90-day stay, but Kress left after only 24 days. When asked for comment, both the center and her family declined to say what Kress had been treated for, or what led to her early departure."

I read the article through three times, and Bobby sat on the couch next to me, saying nothing. I leaned back on the couch, staring at the screen as if I expected something new to happen. But nothing did. It didn't tell me anything more about why Jane was dead.

"Why were you looking at this?" I asked.

"They were talking about it in class today." Bobby sounded apologetic and pulled at the ends of his sleeves, making them swallow his hands. "I didn't know very much about what happened, or her for that matter, so I just… I'm sorry. I shouldn't have."

"No, it's okay." I shook my head. "I'm not mad."

"Are you sure?"

"Yeah. Where did you find this?" I asked.

"I just Googled it," Bobby shrugged. "Why?"

"Do you think there's more information?" I was already typing Google in, preparing to do a search for everything I could find on Jane's murder.

"Yeah, there's tons of information." He moved closer so he could look at the screen with me. "A lot of the major news networks have picked up the stories, especially since Jane got murdered."

"Why?" I glanced over at him as I sifted through the endless list Google gave me, all mentioning Jane's name.

"Cause she's rich and beautiful. The other two girls were poor, and one of them was allegedly a hooker," Bobby said. "But what are you trying to find out?"

"I want to find Jane's killer." I paused as Bobby looked expectantly at me. "I'm going to kill him."

"That's a little sexist, don't you think?"

"How is revenge murder sexist?" I shot him a look.

"You automatically assumed her murderer is a guy," he said. "It could be a girl." I thought of Violet again, but I pushed her from my mind.

"Serial killers aren't usually women, but alright, whatever," I shrugged. "I'm going to kill whoever killed Jane."

"Do you think a human killed her?" Bobby asked.

I was pleasantly surprised that he hadn't tried talking me out of it. He didn't even question it, as if going after a serial killer was the most logical thing in the world. It was stuff like that that made me dig Bobby.

"I don't know what to think." I clicked a link and leaned into the screen, devouring as much information about the whole thing as

I could. "I mean, at first, I thought it was a vampire. For sure. But now... all these articles are saying there wasn't a mark on the girls."

"That doesn't mean anything," Bobby said, and I looked over at him.

"What do you mean?"

"There's always one detail the police hold back," he explained. "That's how they can verify people's claims when they say they killed her or they saw it happen or whatever. There's always one thing they keep out of the press that only the killer would know."

"And that one thing could be bite marks?" I asked, and my heart thudded in my chest.

"Right," Bobby nodded. "And I've always wondered what kind of relationship vampires had with city officials anyway."

"What kind of relationship?" I wrinkled my nose.

"Well, remember in the fall, when the lycan killed that guy in the park and Ezra's car was right there?" Bobby asked. "Ezra got the Lexus out of impound without any problems. He was never questioned in the homicide, and I'm pretty sure that guy's murder was written up as mugging related."

"That could never pass for a mugging," I said incredulously. "He had his throat ripped out."

"Exactly," he nodded. "And *V* is open until seven in the morning. How could they possibly get licensing for that? And they don't card anyone that goes in there, ever. It's easier to get into a vampire club than it is any other club in the city."

"You think that the city officials are on a vampire payroll or something?" I raised an eyebrow.

"I don't know," he shrugged. "Probably not a payroll, but some of them have to be involved with the vampires in some way to cover this all up."

"And if they are, and these murders are vampire related, they'd probably cover that up too," I said.

"You guys try really hard not to kill humans, and I'm grateful for that, but sometimes, some people have to die," Bobby said. "And you never hear of people dying with all the blood drained from their body."

"Oh my gosh." I exhaled and leaned back. "They had to have covered up vampire deaths before. And if Jane and these other girls were killed by vampires, they would've covered them up too, except they were out in the open. People saw the body before they could fix it."

"But whoever is doing this wants to get caught." Bobby sounded excited, not about the death, but about solving a crime. He sat on his knees and faced me. "I don't think it's the normal serial killer like Hannibal Lecter doing it for attention. Maybe he's trying to expose vampires."

"You said 'he' too," I pointed out.

"Sorry, he or she," he corrected himself.

"But why would anybody want to expose vampires?" I asked.

"I don't know." He shook his head. "But why else would he leave the bodies for everyone to find?"

"I don't know," I sighed and looked back at the screen. "But this is based on a lot of conjecture. It's more likely that it's just some twisted human."

"They found Jane a block from V. You think that's coincidence?" He tilted his head skeptically.

"Yeah, and that happens to be within a few blocks of like 10 other clubs. Maybe it's an angry bartender sick of getting stiffed on tips."

"You really think that?" Bobby asked.

"I don't know what to think." I rested my head back on the couch and stared up on the ceiling.

"The patio is officially cleared off!" Jack announced and walked into the living room. His jeans and hoodie were covered in packed snow, and some of it fell off and dripped onto the floor.

"Good job." I wanted to smile up at him, but I didn't feel like smiling. "You're dripping snow all over."

"Yeah, I'm gonna go change and hop in the shower." Jack brushed chunks of melting snow from his hair. "I just thought I'd let you know." He stood there for a minute, eyeing up Bobby and me. "Is something wrong? It seems pretty somber in here."

"Nah, me and Bobby were just talking. Everything's fine." This time I did force a smile.

"Alright." Jack looked hesitant, but he shrugged and decided to believe me. "I'll be upstairs if you need me."

I didn't have any real reason not to tell him that Bobby and I were talking about Jane, but I didn't really want him to know. It'd make him worry or stop me.

I didn't have the energy for arguing about whether or not I should do what I'm doing, or feel what I'm feeling. I knew what I had to do and I wouldn't let anyone stand in my way.

"We need somebody in the know," Bobby said, picking up on where our conversation left off before Jack came in. "That's how we'll find out what really happened to Jane."

"Well, yeah, duh," I said. "That'd be nice if we-" I hadn't even finished my sentence when it occurred to me. "We do know somebody."

"Who?" Bobby asked.

Without telling him, I shut his laptop and got off the couch. Bobby followed me, and I think he figured it out when we turned down the hall and walked toward the den. We knew Ezra.

"You have got to stop moping," I said. I pushed open the door and flicked on the lights without waiting for Ezra to respond.

Ezra stood in front of the large windows that faced the frozen lake behind the house. He had his back to us, and he didn't turn around. The speakers on his computer played out the same classical music it had over the past few months.

"I don't know how you can listen to this all the time," I said, walking around the desk. I clicked off the computer, noting the name of the composer Joseph Haydn before closing Ezra's iTunes. "I'd get sick of listening to the same piece over and over."

"I saw him perform once." Ezra said as he turned around to face me. "Back when I was still under Willem, my maker. We saw him in London towards the end of the 18th century, I believe. It was quite moving. I don't think you understand what it was to see a concert like that, when music was so unavailable."

"This isn't gonna turn into 'the internet is magic' speech again, is it?" Bobby asked. He'd gone over to Ezra's bookshelf and picked up something that looked like an antique slinky.

"Of course not. I wouldn't want to bore you," Ezra said with exaggerated indifference and lowered his eyes, so I shot a glare at Bobby. He shrugged sheepishly in return and sat down on the sofa.

"You need to stop sitting in the dark, listening to music," I said, leaning up against his desk.

"So you came in for a pep talk?" Ezra raised an eyebrow and sat down in the office chair next to me.

"Well… no, but that doesn't mean you don't need one," I said.

"What can I do for you?" Ezra leaned back in the chair, ignoring my advice, much the same way he did every day prior.

"What do you know about the cops?" I asked.

His expression changed and he shifted his eyes between Bobby and me. For a change, Bobby kept his mouth shut and crossed his legs so he could play with his shoelace.

"I'm afraid you're going to have be more specific," Ezra said, resting his gaze back on me.

"How come you weren't questioned in November when the lycan attacked?" I asked pointblank, and his dark eyes never left mine.

"I've lived here for a very long time, and it suits me well to have an understanding with the people in power," Ezra answered evenly. "But if you're looking to get out of a speeding ticket, I won't get involved with that."

"No. It's not that." I chewed my lip and looked to Bobby for help.

"Ah," Ezra said knowingly and swiveled the chair side-to-side. "This is about Jane."

"Yes," I nodded.

"Nothing you find will bring her back or bring you any comfort." He looked out the darkness behind the house, the frozen lake looking black in the night. "Death, unfortunately, doesn't have a cure, not even for the pain of those left behind."

"Maybe not," I said, but I wasn't sure that I believed that. "But someone is out there killing girls, and I'd rest a lot easier if I knew who it was."

"And you think that the police know who it is but haven't bothered to catch him?" Ezra asked when he looked back at me.

"No." I sighed and shook my head. "I don't know. But I think they know something."

"Maybe they do," Ezra allowed. "What would you do with that information that they aren't already doing? You're presuming that they're hiding something for a reason. What would they hope to gain from this?"

"I don't know," I sighed, growing frustrated. All of this felt so logical in the living room with Bobby, but Ezra had a way of punching through everything.

"Just because we don't understand why they'd cover up something doesn't mean they aren't," Bobby said, and we both turned to look at him.

"Now you just sound paranoid," I said.

"Just because you're paranoid doesn't mean they're not after you," Bobby said with an expression so serious that I couldn't help but laugh.

Milo came home a few minutes later, breaking up any chance I had of convincing Ezra that I needed to know what the police were up to. I'm not sure that I did actually need to, and I hated that he had a point.

What could I do that the cops already weren't? It wasn't like I had any experience with solving crimes or forensic equipment. My knowledge was *Law & Order* reruns on TNT, and I doubted that would help me catch a serial killer.

As soon as Milo came in, he started making supper for Bobby. He still loved to cook, and it was a shame that hardly anybody around him could eat it anymore. When Milo asked what we'd been up to, Bobby made a point of not telling him about Jane. Apparently, we'd both decided that it'd be better if our respective boyfriends didn't know what we were doing.

Jack had to go away for work the next day, so I spent the evening curled up with him. He'd been handling most of the business affairs by himself lately, since Ezra didn't feel like doing much of anything, and I was really proud of Jack for stepping up. I just hated that he had to be away so much.

We went to bed early since he had an eight a.m. flight, and I still didn't understand how he learned to handle himself so well in the daytime. I'd gotten much better about being in the sun, but it would never be anything I'd enjoy.

I woke up with him to see him off, and Matilda whimpered as soon as he was out the door. I tried to reassure her by telling her that he'd be back in a few days, but I'm not sure that she understood me. Or if she did, it still hurt too much to be away from him. I agreed with her on that point.

I crawled back into bed and began crying. I hated the empty space left behind when Jack went away. I felt lonelier than I had in a while, and everything felt off-kilter. Not just because Jack was gone, but everything with Ezra and Mae and Jane. Milo was busier with school, Jack was busy with work, and I was just here... doing nothing.

"Alice?" Bobby knocked on my bedroom door, and I hurried to wipe away the tears before he could see them. He opened the door without waiting for me to respond. "Are you awake?"

"Yeah. What do you need?" I sat up in bed and rubbed at my eyes, covering up my sadness by looking sleepy.

"Milo just went to school, and I saw that Jack left for work," Bobby said, walking into the bedroom.

"So? Shouldn't you be at school?" I asked, looking over at him once I felt certain my tears were gone.

"Yeah, but I decided to skip." He bit his lip and shoved his hands in the pockets of his skinny jeans. "I've got an idea for a better way to spend the day."

"Yeah? What's that?"

"Let's go find Jane's killer."

"Like now? Like right now? How?" I asked as I pushed off the covers. I'm pretty sure Bobby didn't have a plan, but it already sounded better than anything else I would probably do today.

"Milo and Jack are gone, so it seems like the best time," Bobby shrugged. "And I thought we could just go downtown, check out the crime scenes. I mean, I know stuff's gone, but I thought we might find something. I wrote down all the addresses." He held his hand out to me, and he'd written a couple locations on the back of it.

"Alright. Let me get dressed."

Bobby smiled and went outside to wait for me. I'm not sure why exactly, but as I pulled on my jeans, I felt better than I had since I'd gotten back from Australia. I was actually doing something. And even if it was a long shot, it was something that actually mattered. Or it would, if we could catch the killer before another girl got hurt.

- 8 -

We stood on Eighth Street, with the buildings blocking out the morning sun. I'd donned a jacket, a hat, and giant sunglasses, so the sun wouldn't be much of an issue for me anyway. As we walked away from the second crime scene, I felt queasy.

This time of the day, downtown was bustling, and I wasn't used it. I'd gotten accustomed to the quiet of the night. We brushed past people, some of them bumping into me. Being in crowds didn't bother me anymore, and the open air helped alleviate the scent of their blood. Lately, my bloodlust hadn't been bad at all, and Ezra commended my ability to get it under control so quickly.

"I don't think this is gonna work," I told Bobby as we waited at a crosswalk for the light to turn green.

"I know we didn't see much back there, but we still might find something," Bobby said. "Anyway, it's better than doing nothing."

Other than a piece of battered police tape stuck to the side of a pole, there hadn't been anything at the last scene. The one before had even less evidence than that. I'm not even sure what we were looking for, but we found nothing.

The closer we got to the spot where Jane had been found, the sicker I felt. My mouth and throat felt dry, and it was hard to swallow. The jacket and hat were making me too hot, and cold sweat broke out all over my skin.

"I don't know." I shook my head and stayed a step behind Bobby.

"It won't hurt to look."

He slipped on a patch of ice, and my arm shot out instinctively. I caught him, holding him by his arm for a second before he got his footing again. A man passing by gave me an odd look. I shoved my hands in my pocket and tried to look inconspicuous as Bobby straightened out his jacket.

"Thanks," he said.

"No problem," I mumbled and took his elbow to hurry him along. A few other people kept glancing over at us, and I didn't like it.

If I hadn't felt so nervous, I might've taken a moment to be proud that I moved quick enough to elicit weird stares. My reflexes were getting much quicker, and I didn't slip on the ice anymore, not even when I hurried across it. I'd begun to feel really comfortable in my new skin.

"Is there a reason we're jogging?" Bobby asked, giving me a sidelong glance.

"We're not jogging." I was going faster than I meant to, and I slowed down.

When we turned the corner onto Hennepin Avenue, I let go of Bobby's arm, but I wished I'd hung onto him. I shoved my hands deep in my pockets and slowed down even more, so we were barely moving. We were getting close to V, and past that, I could see the empty space on the concrete where Jane had been found.

"Are you okay?" Bobby asked. "You look pale."

"Yeah," I lied, but I stopped walking. We were in the middle of the sidewalk, so people had to part around us, but I didn't care. "Why are you doing this?"

"What?"

"This. Helping me. Trying to solve this or whatever."

"I'm from St. Joseph, Minnesota," Bobby said, and I shrugged, not seeing any significance. "My mom was pregnant with me when Jacob Wetterling went missing. I have a brother nine years older than me, and he knew the Wetterling kids."

I didn't know a ton about the case, but I'd heard enough over the years to get the gist of it. Jacob had been eleven-years-old when he was abducted near his home in St. Joseph. Twenty years later, the police weren't any closer to finding out what happened to him or who took him.

"I grew up with a crazy over protective mother, always talking about him." Bobby squinted up at the sun that peaked over the top of the buildings. "It's like a mystery hanging over everything, and I never even met him. But it still bothers me that I don't know what happened to him."

"You're looking for Jane's killer because you can't find Jacob Wetterling?" I asked.

"My mom always talked about how she didn't know how his mother went on, how she could survive without knowing what happened to her son," he said. "And Jane's not missing, and she

105

wasn't your kid, but I know you need to know what happened. I wanna know, and she wasn't my best friend."

"I don't know if she was really even my best friend anymore." I exhaled and stared down the street, to where her body had been found.

"Well, since I'm now your de facto best friend, I have to help you with this."

"How are you my best friend?" I raised an eyebrow.

"You can't count your boyfriend or your brother, or your boyfriend's brothers, so it has to be me." Bobby grinned at me. "I'm your new best friend."

"What about Leif? Or Olivia?" I asked.

"Leif's not your friend." He shook his head and furrowed his brow. "I'm not sure what he is, but he's not your friend. And Olivia's your trainer. She's like a boss. Doesn't count."

"There sure are a lot of stipulations that constitute who can or can't be a best friend."

"I didn't make the rules," he shrugged. "But as your best friend, it's my civic duty to help you with this."

"And you think looking at this will help?" I asked.

"I do," Bobby nodded. "Come on."

"Alright." I took a deep breath and walked with him, moving in closer to him. "So, how does your crazy protective mom feel about you living here? Do you ever even go home?

"Um… she doesn't feel anything about it," Bobby said. "She died of cancer when I was 12. And I don't go home very much. My brother lives in Oregon now."

"Oh. I'm sorry," I said, feeling stupid that I didn't know that.

"It's okay." He shrugged. "I mean, it's not. But it was a long time ago. So…"

We reached the spot, and we both just stopped. People were already making big arcs around the place where Jane had been dumped, so they didn't mind that we just stood there. A fresh bit of police tape flapped in the wind, but the rest had been cut down.

I expected to feel worse when I got here, considering the built up nausea I had walking up to it. Once here, seeing it up close, I only felt that strange blankness inside me. Like my emotions just shut off completely.

Six inches of snow had been dumped on us the day before, and the ensuing cleanup had scooped most traces that would be left. But I could still see faint stains where her blood had been, especially in the cracks.

I crouched down, and I could still smell her. Very faintly, underneath the scent of snow, salt, exhaust, and all the people around. If I hadn't known Jane, I probably wouldn't be able to smell her at all. I breathed in deep, as if I would learn something new.

I reached out to touch the darkest part of the stain. As soon as I touched it, an electric shock shot through my fingertips, and I yanked my hand back.

"Are you okay?" Bobby asked.

"Yeah, I'm fine." I shook it off and stood back up. "Do you see that?"

"What?"

"Her blood." I pointed to it. I hadn't seen any at the other crime scenes, and I wasn't sure if it was because I was tuned into Jane.

"Yeah," he nodded. "It's faint. But I see it."

"Did you see any at the other spots?"

"No." His forehead crinkled as he thought about it. "No, I didn't see anything."

"That doesn't really mean anything, I guess," I said. "They did happen a long time ago. The first one was before Christmas."

I looked over at the building V was in. It looked so ordinary, like all the other buildings around it. Nobody would ever guess it housed hundreds of vampires every night in its basement.

"But I don't remember seeing that much blood in the other crime scene photos," Bobby said. "Maybe they had less to clean up."

"Did you see real crime scene pictures? Or just the ones they let them post in the paper and stuff?" I asked. "I mean, they have to keep out the truly gruesome ones."

"You can find anything on the internet." He waved off my doubt. "I've seen some brutal ones."

"You're a twisted guy, you know that?"

"It was research!" Bobby looked defensive for a moment before moving on. "Anyway, the point is, maybe Jane had a little more overkill, so there was more blood."

"I don't wanna think about that," I grimaced.

"Sorry. But I'm just saying that when things have overkill, it usually means its personal," Bobby said.

"Lots of people were pissed at Jane," I sighed. He had a point, but I felt too agitated to think. I kept my eyes on the club, but I could see her blood stains out of the corner of my eye. "Look, can we walk and talk?"

"Uh, yeah, sure thing."

"The sun is bothering me," I lied.

The sun had started shining over the buildings, but it hadn't bothered me yet. I walked across the street, more towards *V*, so I'd be in the shadows again.

"So, what do you think?" Bobby hurried to keep up with me. He slipped on snow again, and I caught him, but this time I made sure to do it more slowly, like a human would.

"I don't know what to think," I admitted.

We reached the alley by *V*, and I glanced at it out of habit. But I saw something that made my heart skip a beat, and I stopped.

"What?" Bobby asked.

"Oh no. Please tell me it's not another one," I whispered under my breath.

In a snow pile pushed up to the building, I could see long blond hair. A long coat lay next to it, covering the shape of a body. The entrance to *V* was kinda hidden in the alley, so it wouldn't be as out in the open as the others had been, but it appeared to be a body discarded near the door.

"What?" Bobby repeated.

"Stay behind me," I commanded.

I held my arm up in front of him, and we walked slowly down the alley. By the time we reached the snow bank, my heart hammered so loud in my ears, I could barely hear myself think.

My hand would've been trembling, but I stopped shaking. In the past month or so, I'd become incapable of it. Inside, my muscles felt rubbery, even though I knew they'd react like marble if I needed them to.

I reached forward and peeled back the jacket. I expected a corpse, but what I found scared the hell out of me. Bobby screamed behind me

A vampire jumped up, moving with the speed only we could master, and she nearly lunged at me before she saw who it was. Violet stared at me, her weird purple eyes wide and shocked. Her skin looked bluish from where it had pressed against the snow bank, and her clothes were dirty and wet.

"Why are you always bothering me?" Violet snapped. "Are you like stalking me or something?"

"No, I'm not stalking you," I said. "I just saw you and I thought-" I didn't want to admit what I'd thought, so I let it hang in the air.

"You know each other?" Bobby asked, once he got over the scare.

"Not really." Violet tucked a strand of blond hair behind her ears and crossed her arms.

"What are you doing out here?" I asked.

"It's not really any of your business, is it?" She glared at me for a moment but almost instantly lost her nerve. She turned away and pulled on her long jacket. "But I guess I better be on my way."

"Do you even have anywhere to go?" I asked, and Violet swallowed hard. "Why were you sleeping outside, during the day?"

"I didn't have anywhere to go, okay?" Her intense eyes met mine, and her lip quivered a bit. "I usually find somebody to take me home so I can crash with them, but the clubs have been dry lately. That damn serial killer is keeping people off the streets."

"Yeah, he's making it rough on all of us," I muttered dryly.

"I already apologized about your friend," Violet said, but she softened a little. I think she felt guilty about everything that had transpired between us before, and that counted for something.

"Why do you have to find people to crash with? Why don't you have your own place?" I asked.

"I'm sixteen and I look sixteen!" She gestured to herself, and she had a point. Sometimes, she even looked younger than that. Her eyes had a strange innocence to them when she let down her guard. "I don't have my social security card, so I can't get a job, but even if I could, working part-time at Starbucks won't pay the bills. Even when I do have money, nobody will rent me an apartment or a hotel room. I don't even have a frickin driver's license. What else am I supposed to do?"

I'd never thought about what it would be like for everyone else to be a vampire. I'd come into a rich family who take care of everything, from money to housing and phony social security cards. I couldn't imagine how anyone else survived without them, especially someone that looked so young, like Violet.

"Now, if you'll excuse me, I've gotta find somewhere new to sleep." She started to walk past me.

"Wait," I said, stopping her.

"What?" Violet asked, giving me an impatient look.

I didn't want to leave Violet on the streets, but I couldn't take her home. We didn't really have the room for it, and even if we did, I didn't trust her *that* much. Fortunately, I knew of someone that would know exactly what to do with wayward teenage vampires.

"Come on. I know a place you can stay," I said.

"Really?" Violet asked.

"Yeah, really?" Bobby raised a skeptical eyebrow, probably afraid I would suggest our house.

"Yeah." I nodded towards the entrance to *V*, and Violet scoffed.

"It's closed. They close at 7 am and kick everyone out," Violet said. "Trust me. I've tried staying in there."

"Yeah, well, you don't know the owner like I do."

I walked over to the door, and even though they were dubious, both Violet and Bobby followed me. I pulled the keys out of my pocket. I often came over before Olivia got up, and she got sick of me calling and making her come down to let me in.

The door opened with a heavy push, and I held it so Violet and Bobby could walk past. The dim red light that normally lit the hallway was off, and I grabbed Bobby's hand to help him through. We had to go down a steep staircase in total darkness, and I knew

Bobby would break his neck, so I gave him a piggyback. It was the only way I could ensure he wouldn't get hurt.

When we got down to the tunnel in the basement, I set him down and grabbed his hand to lead him through. To go to the club, we'd turn off to our right, but I didn't want to go to the club, so I kept walking. Violet got confused and asked if I knew where I was going, but I'd done this a hundred times before.

Eventually, after weaving through the basement labyrinth, we reached the elevator in the center. The elevator was lit by fluorescent bulbs, making both Violet and I squint, but Bobby was relieved to be able to see again.

"So, are your eyes really purple?" Bobby asked as we rode up to Olivia's suite. "Or is that a vampire thing?"

"No, it's a me thing," Violet sighed. "One in like a million people have violet eyes. My name was going to be Mischa, but when my mom saw my eyes, she changed it."

"Oh," he nodded.

"Elizabeth Taylor has violet eyes, I guess," Violet said.

The elevator ride to the top of the building was rather long, and the awkward silence settled over us. Bobby started humming along with "The Girl From Ipanema" music that played through the speakers, and Violet stared up at the ceiling.

When the doors opened, I stepped out into Olivia's luxurious penthouse. Bobby had been up here with me a few times before, but this was obviously all new to Violet. She whistled loudly and stepped over to the window to admire the view.

"This is a really nice place," Violet commented, sounding awed.

"It's nicer when it's clean," I said.

Olivia had a maid come up and clean twice a week, and today was clearly not her day. Pillows were all over, and one of them had been torn open, so white puffballs of stuffing littered the furniture. A few wine bottles were tossed about, meaning the party had been mostly the human persuasion, but that was just the way Olivia liked it.

Two of her party guests were still passed out, sprawled out on her overstuffed furniture. One of them was a very pretty girl wearing only a black bra and leggings with blood dried on her neck. The other was a vampire with very high cheek bones. He reminded me of Daniel Johns from Silverchair when he'd been anorexic.

"Olivia!" I said loudly, kicking an empty wine bottle.

The vampire lifted his head a bit, squinting in the light. All the windows were tinted to keep out UV rays, but they didn't have any shades, and the sun hit the building straight on. I don't know why the vampire hadn't gone back to one of the rooms to sleep, but I didn't really care either.

"Olivia owns the club?" Violet asked, sounding shocked.

She knew Olivia, as did most people, but Olivia kept her status under wraps. She didn't want anybody to know what power she still held. She liked staying under the radar.

"Yep." I walked over to Olivia's bedroom door and knocked it. "Olivia, wake up."

"She doesn't like me very much," Violet said.

"You're hot. She likes you," Bobby said, sitting down on the couch. He picked up a bottle of wine by his feet and swooshed it around. It still had some in, so he took a swig.

"Bobby, it's nine in the morning! Do you really need to drink?" I asked.

"It's red wine and I had one drink," he scoffed. "It's not like I'm blitzed."

"Who the hell are you people and why are you here?" the Daniel Johns vampire asked.

"We're not here. It's just a dream. Go back to sleep," Bobby said.

"Olivia!" I pounded on her door again, and when she didn't get up, I pushed it open. "Olivia!"

"What?" Olivia grumbled, her face buried in a pillow.

She lay in a massive bed, curled up in silk sheets. A beautiful, topless girl lay in bed next to her. I'd seen her a few times before, so she was a semi-regular of Olivia's, but I never learned her name. I didn't want to. It made it easier to let Olivia feed on people if I didn't actually think of them as people.

"I need you to come out here for a minute," I said. I stood in the doorway, because if I walked away, she'd just fall back to sleep.

As Olivia got up, she mumbled something under her breath and pulled on a satin housecoat. It was so weird seeing her wear things that weren't leather, but she did exclusively wear black. Her long hair shimmered down her back, completely smooth and silky, even though she'd just woken up.

"It's too bright out there." Olivia paused in the doorway and refused to step out further. "What do you need from me? I just went to bed."

"I brought you a present." I stepped back and gestured to Violet, who stood to the side.

"Hi." Violet forced a smile and wiggled her fingers meekly.

"Didn't that girl try to kill you?" Olivia arched her eyebrow at me.

"I say let bygones be bygones," I shrugged. "But she doesn't have a place to stay. So she's gonna stay with you for a while."

"Fine, fine." Olivia yawned and waved her hand at me. "The second bedroom is open." She pointed at the room next to hers. "She can stay there. Just be quiet when I'm sleeping."

"Thank you," Violet said, but Olivia didn't acknowledge her.

"Thanks," I echoed, and Olivia nodded.

"Next time wait until later in the day." She started shutting the door, then stopped. "Are you coming over tonight to train?"

"Sure."

"Alright. See you tonight then." Olivia yawned again and shut the door.

"There you go," I told Violet and stepped away from the room. Olivia's sleepiness was contagious, and I yawned myself.

"Thanks." Violet looked unsure about everything, but I didn't really want to reassure her. She'd be fine here, and I'd done my part. Now the lack of sleep and stress of the day started to hit me.

"No problem," I said and walked over to the elevator.

Violet just stood off to the side, almost as if she was afraid to move. When the elevator doors opened, I stepped inside, and I had to hold them open for Bobby.

"Why are you helping me?" Violet asked as Bobby stepped in.

"I don't know," I said honestly, and the doors slid shut.

"I thought of something," Bobby said. "After we met Violet, but I didn't say something when she was around."

"What's that?" I leaned back against the wall and rubbed the bridge of my nose as the elevator went down.

"You know how Jane's dumpsite had more blood than the others?" Bobby asked. "Maybe it's not because the killer was more aggressive. Maybe the first two victims were drained of their blood."

"You mean by a vampire?" I asked, looking over at him.

"Yeah," he nodded.

"But then why wouldn't Jane be drained too?" I asked. "If it's a vampire, why not drink her blood? And then why kill her at all?"

"I don't know," he shrugged. "Maybe they meant to kill her and drain her, but they couldn't."

"Why wouldn't they be able to? It's not like we get full easy or something."

"After you bit me, Milo wouldn't bite me," Bobby said. "My blood was tainted, and it made him sick when he could even smell you on him. So maybe if Jane was bitten by someone else, they wouldn't bite her. But she was all part of their murder scheme, so they went ahead and killed her anyway."

117

"She just got out of rehab, though. And I talked to her. She'd been doing good. I don't think she got out and just went straight back into it," I shook my head.

"She's a junkie," Bobby said, as we reached the ground floor. "You can never be sure. And you don't know who the last vampire was that bit her."

"Actually," I said as the doors slid open, "as far as I know, I was the last to bite her."

- 9 -

Milo had taken to napping when he got home from school, since he had to be up all day, and he was getting home later and later. Last night was the debate team practice, and tonight it was something about tutoring a girl in calculus. He'd also started talking a lot in French, but since I'd barely passed the class the two years I'd taken it, he only ended up confusing me.

Jack was still gone with work, and the *Gossip Girl* marathon on the CW seemed like a good way to spend the evening. I sprawled out on the couch, still in my pajamas, but I'd only been awake for an hour or two, so it didn't seem that bad.

Ezra walked into the room, carrying two thick books in his hands. He looked better than he had lately, meaning his hair had been brushed and his shirt looked pressed. He'd never gone through a sweat-pants-and-no-shaving-or-bathing phase, thank god, and he always managed to look good.

When he came over to the sofa, he glanced back at the TV and raised an eyebrow.

"What is this?" Ezra asked.

"That's Chuck Bass." I pointed at the screen to Ed Westwick.

"He's wearing a bowtie. Is that a modern trend again?"

119

"Hell if I know," I shrugged. "He's Chuck Bass. He does what he wants."

"Well, that's enough of that." Ezra grabbed the remote from off the couch next to me and clicked off the TV.

"What'd you do that for?" I asked, with feigned anger. "I was just about to find out if his womanizing ways would catch up with him."

"Let's just assume they will. You have reading to do." With that, Ezra dropped the books on my stomach, and I made an *oof* sound as they pushed all the air out of my lungs.

"What the hell." I lifted up the books and rubbed at my stomach, even though the pain had already disappeared. "What'd you do that for?"

"Because you were right. I need to stop moping about, and so do you."

"I'm not moping about." I sat up and looked down at the books. "*A History of Modern Europe: From the Renaissance to the Present* and *Gray's Anatomy: The Anatomical Basis of Clinical Practice.* I'm assuming this isn't about the TV show, since its several thousand pages long."

"No, it's not," Ezra said, and I looked up at him. "You do absolutely nothing."

"I don't do 'nothing,'" I shook my head. "I mean, I don't do much, but it's not cause I'm not trying. I've been cleaning the house, and I even feed Bobby sometimes."

"You do realize Bobby isn't a pet, don't you?" He crossed his arms over his chest, as if he really wasn't convinced that I knew the difference.

"Yes, I do." I rolled my eyes. "But the point is that I'm trying. I've been training with Olivia, and I have to go over to her place later tonight."

"Training with Olivia is good, but it's not enough," he said. "Having a mastery of your body and strength means nothing if you're incompetent. You need a good education behind it, and since you dropped out of high school, I'll have to see to it that you get one."

"Look, I'm not against learning things. I just..." I stared down at the textbooks, running my hands over the glossy covers. "I don't know that I understand the point of anything. I already *have* everything. What more is there?"

"Yes, life is terribly rough for you," Ezra said dryly.

"No, I didn't mean that." I sighed. "I thought all I wanted was to be with Jack, and then my life would be complete. We could live happily ever after. And I do love Jack, and I want to be with him. But now that I have this, and I'm realizing exactly how long happily ever after goes on for, and... I don't know what to do."

"You need a purpose," Ezra said knowingly, and I looked up at him

"Yeah, I do," I nodded. "How do you do it? When you have forever, how do you... fill it? Endless games of solitaire?"

"Your concept of time will change." He sat down on the sofa next to me. "Eventually, it moves faster, and it tends to blur together, so years feel like weeks."

"And that's how you make it through?"

"Sometimes." His mahogany eyes went far away for a moment, but he took a deep breath and it vanished. "But you have to learn to enjoy the moments you're in, to treasure the things around you. It's the fleetingness of life that gives it its value, and even though we're here forever, nothing else is."

"So you're saying that I should relish the things that will die?" I asked. "That death equates happiness?"

"Not exactly." He leaned back and exhaled. "The problem with giving someone the choice to become a vampire is that it isn't really a choice. You don't really understand what you're agreeing to. You can't possibly fathom what eternity feels like."

"I'm not seeing much in the way of advice in that sentiment."

"Loving another person, even several people, will make your life fuller." Ezra looked at me, resting his deep eyes on mine. "But it will not make it complete. *You* have to do that. You must decide what you live for."

"So… you brought me text books?" I held them up, and he gave a bemused chuckle.

"No, I gave you text books because I want you to have all the tools you need to do whatever it is you decide to do, and knowledge truly is the most powerful tool."

"What are you doing?" Milo yawned and walked into the living room.

"Oh my gosh, you're like the Pavlov's dog of geeks," I laughed. "I say the word text books, and you come running."

"Are you going to school?" Milo's eyes widened with excitement.

"Well, Ezra's tutoring me, I guess, if that counts," I said.

"Oh that's fantastic!" Milo clapped his hands together and rushed over to the couch. "Let me see!" He snatched the books from my hands, not that I really put up a fight.

"Read the first three chapters in both books," Ezra told me as Milo flipped through the books and gushed over it. "We'll talk about them tomorrow."

"Tomorrow?" I asked. "I have to train with Olivia tonight. I won't have time."

"Make time." Ezra used that tone he did when he meant business. It wasn't loud or gruff, but it was firm enough where I knew not to argue with it.

"Oh come on, Alice, it'll be fun!" Milo said with far too much glee. "This'll be so good for you. And you don't even have to get up early. It's way better than what I'm doing."

"Good luck." Ezra stood up and smiled down at me.

"Hey, wait. Why did you pick these books?" I asked. "I mean, the history I kinda understand. But why an anatomy text?"

"You said you wanted to be a doctor." Ezra shrugged. "I thought it might pique your interest."

He left me alone with Milo, who immediately launched into the history book. Shock of all shocks, Milo happened to be a history buff. He especially liked the really old stuff, like about Mesopotamia and early civilization, but all history fascinated him.

"If we don't learn from our mistakes, we'll be doomed to repeat them," Milo said when he noticed my interest waning. "You need to know what other people did so you don't do it."

"That's really good advice, but it's not like I plan on ever leading a revolution or anything," I said.

"You might," Milo smiled. "We're gonna be around for a long time. Who knows what you'll end up doing."

I studied with Milo for two more hours, but thankfully, Bobby came home and rescued me. He'd been working on some dramatic arts piece, and it ended up running late.

At first, I was relieved to see Bobby. I tried to engage him in real conversation, since Milo's incessant talk of history turned my mind to mush. But almost immediately after Bobby got home, they started making out.

It was just as well, since I had to get ready to go over to Olivia's. I showered and dressed, and when I left, Milo and Bobby were still in the living room, whispering sweet nothings to each other.

As I sped downtown in the Audi, I thought about how weird it was that I'd been so nervous about driving. I *loved* driving. Speeding through the lanes of traffic on I-35 with Metric blasting out the car stereo had to be in my top five favorite activities.

My joy over the car ride stopped when I caught sight of a billboard. It showed a gorgeous guy in black and white, his shirt open to reveal the perfect muscles of his abs. He looked bored in that off-handedly sexy way all models seemed to. The ad mostly featured his torso, with only the waistband of his pants showing above the bottom of the billboard, so naturally, it was advertising jeans.

That's not what made me sneer or stop singing along with the radio. The guy in the ad — that was Jonathan, Jane's "ex-boyfriend," for lack of a better term. The last time I'd seen him, he'd been gnawing out her throat, and that seemed like a marvelous idea to her.

I pressed on the pedal harder so I could speed past it. I didn't want to think about Jane anymore. At least not anymore tonight. I needed a day off from the constant guilt.

When I arrived at *V*, I took the tunnel behind it so I wouldn't have to deal with the crowd, but I peeked out onto the dance floor. Even though it was after midnight, the club looked to be down about a third of its normal capacity. That's still a lot of people, but Violet hadn't been kidding. The serial killer scare really had people locking their doors at night.

That didn't stop Olivia from finding guests. Even though she'd said she'd been cutting down on her blood intake, and for a while, she really seemed to be, the party was in full swing in the penthouse when I got off the elevator.

Music with high bass and vocals that sounded like Maynard James Keenan pulsated through the room. The lights were dim, and the fifty or so people strewn about the place all seemed incredibly messed up. Humans and vampires alike were blitzed out in their own ways.

I stood by the elevator for a minute. Watching two girls do a sinewy dance for a vampire, I considered leaving. In fact, I should leave. Olivia couldn't train me in this condition, and I hated this shit. I didn't live this lifestyle, and I didn't approve of it in others. Getting

125

drunk off human blood and using living beings to do it didn't sit well with me.

I turned to head out when Olivia spotted me. She'd been on the far side of the room, lounging on a faux bearskin rug. Before I made my escape, she called my name and scrambled to her feet, nearly tripping over someone in her race to stop me.

"Alice! I've been waiting for you!" She ran to greet me, and she didn't seem drunk at all. If she had been, I would've left right then and there.

"Yeah, I can tell." I scanned the room, looking as disapproving as possible.

"I would've called you, but you know how I feel about cell phones." Olivia waved her fingers dismissively. "I've found someone for you train with."

"Can I come back tomorrow to meet them?" I asked.

The room filled with the fresh scent of blood, and out of the corner of my eye, I saw a vampire bite into a guy's neck.

"You're already here." Olivia put her hand on my arm. I could pull away, but I sighed and decided against it. "Shall we go to the roof?"

I followed Olivia up the stairwell to the roof, and she whistled *Ode to Joy*. Olivia pushed the door open to the roof, and the blast of icy winter air filled the stairwell. When we reached the roof, I saw Violet at the edge of the roof, admiring the view.

"What the hell is she doing here?" I froze.

"She's going to train with you," Olivia smiled.

"She can't..." I wanted to pull Olivia aside but Violet had already seen us. "This is highly inappropriate, Olivia."

"Nonsense." Olivia brushed off my concern. "Violet and I were talking, and she's had to master a lot living on the streets. We had a practice fight today, and she's good. She'll give you a taste of what fighting a real vampire would be like."

"But Olivia-" I started but she cut me off.

"You needed more help than I could give," she said simply.

"I know that I wanted to train, but I don't 'need' help." I watched Violet walk around the edge of the roof and pick up a long metal pipe, a part broken off an old antenna.

"Oh, but sweetheart, you do," Olivia touched my arm. "You've got that draw to you, and I've seen it in a few vampires before. It always gets you in trouble."

"Draw? What the hell does that mean?" I asked.

"It's something in your blood. I don't know why it happens, but I understand little of why things happen." She looked at the cityscape. "You're like a beacon of light, and other vampires are moths. Not all of them are affected as strongly as others, but we all feel it, to some extent."

"What are you talking about?" I demanded.

"You sound ready for a fight," Violet smirked and flipped the pipe over her shoulders, moving like a ninja with a bo stick.

"No, I'm not," I shook my head. "I just wanna know what she's talking about."

"Train with her." Olivia gave me a serious look. "She's better than I am."

"Are you ready?" Violet asked, even though I clearly wasn't.

Olivia backed towards the stairs, and I took a step after her. When I did that, Violet appeared next to me, flicking the pipe in front of me so fast, it nearly hit me in the gut.

"What hell are you doing?" I asked.

"I wanna see what you can do." She shrugged and flipped the pipe again. I bent backwards, as if doing the limbo, and nearly missed it striking me in the chin. "Nice reflexes."

I heard the door swing shut, and I looked back to see that Olivia had gone downstairs. I broke my attention from Violet for a second, and the bo struck me hard across the head.

"Pay attention," she commanded.

Once the blinding pain in my skull stopped, along with the tingling as the fresh gash healed, I growled and dove at her. I didn't want to be training. I wanted to know what the hell Olivia meant, and I didn't even really trust Violet. I tended to hate people that hit me in the head without warning.

When I lunged at her, she easily moved out of the way. I'd seen vampires move faster than her, like the lycan Stellan who's speed was something that bordered on teleportation. But Violet had a quick grace that made me blink my eyes to be sure she was really gone.

Then she was behind me, nearly striking me in the back, so I leapt into the air, doing a back flip before landing on the roof. I'd actually never done that before, at least not reflexively. I wanted to take a second to admire how bad ass that was, but Violet charged at me again.

"It's not fair that you have a weapon!" I shouted as she swung the rod out, trying to swipe out my legs, but I jumped up over it. She moved to stab at the air, so she'd hit me if I jumped again, and I dropped to the ground, lying flat on my belly.

"Who said life was fair?" Violet shot back, and I narrowly rolled out of the way. She drove the pipe into the roof, and if I hadn't moved, she would've impaled me through the stomach. I leapt up to my feet and knew I had to launch a counter attack, or this would just keep going.

I ran to the edge, and she threw the pipe like a spear, aiming it so it would hit the center of my back. I ran forward and jumped up, landing with my feet on the railing at the edge of the building. I pushed off and leapt backwards, feeling the pipe as it grazed the back of my calf before soaring off the building.

I flipped backwards and stretched my feet out in front of me. Violet moved, so instead of my feet colliding with her head the way I'd hoped, I merely kicked her in the chest. I landed on her, but I didn't even pin her down. She had me flipped over onto my back, one of her hands gripping my shoulders.

Raising my feet up, I pressed them into her stomach so I could push her off me. She moved her hand back in swift movement, grabbing something from the back of her jeans. I started to kick her off, then I felt a sharp pain in my chest as she poked something in it.

I looked down and the saw the pointed edge of a titanium stake pressed above my heart, hard enough to stain my shirt with blood.

- 10 -

"What the hell do you want?" I asked, my breath coming out in rasps. Terrified adrenaline pulsed through me, but I wasn't sure that I could get her off me before she drove the stake through my heart.

"I wanna make sure you don't get caught off guard like this again." Her violet eyes held mine, looking at me solemnly, then she got off me.

"What the fuck was that?" I jumped up, holding my hand over my heart. I had no serious injury, and the small wound would heal within minutes, but for a second there, I'd been certain she was gonna kill me.

"You've got good reflexes, and I think you have some real strength under there," Violet said, ignoring my confusion and rage. She brushed the dirt off her clothes and smoothed out her shirt. "But you need to think more, be less impulsive. You need to plan out your attack. Have you ever played chess?"

"Once and I suck at it," I said. "But you nearly killed me!"

"I didn't come anywhere close to killing you." She rolled her eyes. "If I really wanted to kill you, you'd be dead."

"So what were you doing then? That's not training! That's like... attempted murder." I fumbled for a biting comeback, but it didn't faze her at all.

"I want you to remember that. What it felt like believing you would die. If you really feel it, really own how horrifying it is, you'll make sure that you never feel that way again." Violet pointed at me using the stake, and that didn't really make me feel any better.

"I already don't want to die. I've been in shit before. I know what it's like to fight your life," I said. "You didn't need to do that."

"Maybe, maybe not." She wagged her head.

"How did you learn how to fight like that?" I asked. "You weren't that good the last time I saw you."

"No, I was, but Lucien wasn't, and I let him call the shots," she shrugged. "That was stupid. But living on the streets, alone, a lot of vampires will mess with you. You have to learn to fight back, or they'll kill you."

"I'm sorry to hear that," I said quietly.

"It doesn't matter." She shook her head as she walked back towards the stairwell. "Come back tomorrow. We can practice more then."

"Wait. Do you know what Olivia meant by what she said? That I have a 'draw?'" I asked.

"Who knows what Olivia means," she replied and went inside.

I rubbed at my chest, and my heart still pounded heavily underneath. I looked around, but I couldn't admire the skyline the way I normally did. I thought about how terrified I had been in that split second when I really believed Violet meant to kill me. I wondered if Jane felt like that. If she knew she was going to do die.

I climbed up on the edge, standing on the wall so my shins pressed against the railing. I could see the spot where Jane had been found, and I wondered if I would live if I jumped. My bones are hard to break, but it's not impossible.

Swallowing hard, I stared down for a minute. It was so hard to fathom life and death anymore. The idea of both had become such foreign concepts to me. In order to live forever, I'd be constantly surrounded by death. I'm not sure I could ever get used to that.

When I walked through the penthouse, I didn't look for Olivia to say goodbye. I just wanted to get out of there. I raced home to a quiet house, disappointed to find everyone in bed. Matilda was the only thing awake, and I stood outside with her, watching her play.

My body still rang with adrenaline. I didn't want to sleep, but I couldn't think of anything better to do. I made Matilda sleep with me since I didn't want to be alone. She usually slept by the door when Jack was gone, as if she could summon him that way.

Eventually, I managed to fall asleep, but it was fitful. Nightmares plagued me, and I kept having that same feeling I had when I'd been Australia. That panicked paralysis, and I'd wake up and kick my legs just to prove I could move.

Jack came into the room late that afternoon, sneaking as quietly as he could. Matilda whimpered with happiness, and he tried to shush her, so I pretended to be asleep. He climbed in bed and laid next me, his chest pressed to my back. When he wrapped his arm around me, I snuggled deeper into him.

"I missed you," I said, holding his arm to me.

"I missed you, too."

He kissed the back of my neck and hugged me tightly. He held me for a minute and then propped himself up on his elbow. I rolled onto my back so I could look up at him, and his blue eyes were etched with worry.

"Is something wrong?" Jack asked.

When I looked into his eyes, his feelings hit me even more intensely. His love and concern wrapped around me, enfolding me like a blanket and pushing away whatever I'd been feeling before.

"I'm just glad you're home." I reached up and touched his face, soft skin heating up against my touch.

He leaned down and his lips met mine. I kissed him deeply, parting his lips hungrily, and pulling him to me. The more I kissed him, the more he washed over me, and I needed him.

I needed to love him and feel how much he loved me. I had to erase all the horrible things I'd been feeling, and Jack was the only one that could really make me feel good.

I buried my fingers in his hair, and he moaned against my mouth. He was surprised by my reaction, but it didn't excite him any less. His hands roamed over my body, getting stronger and more forceful as they moved over my smoldering skin.

I stopped kissing him, and without thinking, I put my mouth on his neck and bit him. He gasped with surprise, but it quickly turned into a breathy moan. He'd bitten me several times, but this was the first time I'd bit him.

His blood hit my tongue, and the heat jolted through me, searing my veins. He tasted sweeter than honey and stronger than alcohol. He burned down my throat, with a pleasurable flame. I buried my fingers deeper in his flesh, digging them in so hard, it had to hurt, but I couldn't stop. I only gripped him tighter and swallowed him down.

His love felt amazing. It was like I could read his soul, and his kindness and sincerity always stunned me. I couldn't believe that anything could be as simply good as he was, and it pushed away any negative feelings I had. I could only feel him radiating through me.

My whole body pulsed in time with his heartbeat. I could feel him in every inch of my body, pouring through me. Pleasure ripped through me, and my heart felt it might explode.

Something changed. Something dark flickered through him, and I could taste it. Biting him still made him feel wonderful, and he groaned with pleasure, but something was off.

Almost too late, I realized it was death. I'd been drinking him for too long. His life was fading, to a dangerous level, and if I didn't stop, I could kill him.

Even with that thought, it was a fight to unlatch myself from his throat. I tasted it again, that darkness ebbing in and leaving bitter fear lingering on my tongue.

I jerked back, swallowing down what blood clung to my mouth, and Jack collapsed on the bed. He gasped for breath, and I'm not sure if it was because he was having trouble breathing now, or if he'd forgotten to breathe when I bit him.

Whenever Jack stopped biting me, I felt his painful cold separation, but when I stopped biting him, I felt nothing of the sort. I felt fuller than I ever had before, but in a really wonderful way. Like I was complete, whole for the very first time.

His blood made me woozy, and the whole world seemed to glow. The colors were so bright, they were almost painful to look at it. My vision had a hazy, blurred quality around the edge, and I struggled to sit up. Faintly, underneath that, I could feel weakness emanating from Jack.

"Jack." I reached out for him, touching his face, and his skin felt cold. "Jack. Are you alright?"

I listened, and I couldn't hear his heartbeat. I couldn't hear anything or feel anything from him. For the most horrifying moment of my life, I thought I'd killed him.

Then Jack exhaled deeply, and his heart thudded.

"Oh, my god, Jack!" I gasped, and his eyes fluttered open. "I thought you were dead."

"Not dead." He smiled crookedly. "Just… you took a lot out of me."

"I'm sorry." My cheeks flushed with shame, or at least flushed more than they already were.

"Don't be. I loved it." He let out a contented sigh. "You're so beautiful. You're glowing."

"That's the blood loss talking," I shook my head. "Do you want me to get you something to drink?"

"No. Not yet. I want to feel this. I can still feel you in my veins, and I don't want to lose that yet." He reached up, resting his palm against my cheek, and I leaned into it. "I love you."

"I love you, too." I kissed his palm and lay down with him, resting my head on his chest and wrapping my arm around him.

"Not that I'm complaining, but what made you decide to do that?" He ran his fingers through my hair, slow and weary.

"I don't know. I just… I needed to. I needed you." I snuggled up closer to him. "I don't know what I'd do without you."

"Me neither." He kissed the top of my head. "And let's hope we never have to find out."

"We better not." I pressed myself tighter to him, suppressing the chill that ran down my spine.

"Don't worry, Alice," he murmured into my hair as he drifted off to sleep. "We'll be together forever." I fell asleep in his arms and almost convinced myself that I believed him.

When he awoke later in the evening, I found him crabbier than I'd ever seen him before. With Jack, that didn't mean the same as it would if it were me, but he snapped at me without just cause and yelled at Matilda. I've *never* heard him raise his voice in anger to the dog, but being drained of blood did not sit well with him.

He went down to the kitchen, wearing only the pair of boxers he'd slept in. I admired the view but couldn't act on it. He devoured two bags of blood within three minutes, and Matilda and I waited on the other side of the room until we were certain he'd gotten his temper back under wraps.

"Sorry," Jack said, crumpling up an empty blood bag and tossing it in the garbage. "I didn't mean to be so… you know."

"It's okay. I didn't mean to drink so much of your blood," I said.

"It's okay," he shrugged. "It felt *really* good, and it's not like I haven't taken my share of your blood." He opened the fridge and pulled out another bag. "I can't believe how thirsty I am."

"Sorry," I said and hopped on the counter. He shook his head because he was too busy gulping down the blood to answer me.

Ezra must've heard us in the kitchen and came in to talk us. He eyed up Jack's underwear only attire with a raised eyebrow, but he didn't say anything about it.

"How did everything go?" Ezra asked Jack.

"Good. The transfer went off without a hitch." Jack squeezed the bag, making sure he got the last few drops from it. When he was satisfied, he threw it away and rolled his shoulders. "I wish I didn't have go there every few weeks to do it in person. It's the future. Technology ought to have caught up to us by now."

"It's good for you to work and get out of the house," Ezra said. "I've been spending too much time here, and I'll be joining you again next time."

"You sure you don't wanna just go in my place? I feel like I've spent more time away than I have at home in the past few months," Jack said.

"If that's what you want," Ezra shrugged.

"I barely remember what my girl looks like anymore," Jack grinned and walked over to me. He leaned on the counter next to me, looping one arm around my back. "You sure are pretty."

Ezra's phone rang in his pocket, and it was always surprised me that it was the Bee Gees. He'd apparently gone through some horrible disco phase in the seventies, and Peter had said he'd been terrified that Ezra would never come out of it.

"Aren't you gonna get that?" I asked.

"No."

"Is there any reason why not?" Jack asked, giving him the same odd look I was.

Ezra sighed heavily before answering. "It's Mae. I doubt I have anything to say to her."

"How do you know it's Mae? Are you like phone psychic?" I asked, getting excited. I hated seeing Mae and Ezra apart, and if she was calling him, maybe it was a step closer to them getting back together.

"She's been calling all day, and I've been avoiding it all day." He ran a hand through his hair and shook his head. "We've got nothing to talk about. I have no reason to answer her calls."

"Ezra! You love her. I think that's plenty of reason," I said.

"She made her choice." Ezra's voice resonated through everything when he got firm. He made it so hard to contradict him.

"I don't think she had a choice," Jack said, surprising me by coming to Mae's aide. He'd been pretty angry with her since he found she's the reason why he became a vampire. "At least she knows that you're alive and you'll be fine without her. But if she had picked you, the kid'd be dead."

"Maybe so." Ezra lowered his eyes, growing contemplative. "But I'm not ready to make amends."

"Have you even listened to the messages?" Jack asked.

"No." He breathed deeply. "I don't want to hear her voice." He shook his head and looked up at us. "And quite frankly, I don't want to have this conversation either. I've made my decision."

"I don't know why all your decisions get to be final." I crossed my arms over my chest.

"I'm older and wiser." The edge of his mouth curled into a hint of smile. "On the subject of which, how are your studies coming?"

"Great," I lied. I'd gotten through the three chapters in history with Milo, but I'd barely cracked open the anatomy book.

"I expect you'll be ready to go over them later," Ezra said. "Also, I left a copy of *To Kill a Mockingbird* in the living room for you to read."

"What? Why?" I wrinkled my nose. "I read that in like tenth grade."

"Read it again."

The subject was apparently closed because Ezra turned and walked over the kitchen, back to his den to do whatever he did to pass the time without Mae. I sighed loudly and leaned back, resting my shoulder against Jack's.

"Your studies?" Jack raised an eyebrow. "What's going on?"

"Ezra thinks that since I'm not going to school or working, I should be doing something so I don't end up a total dimwit." I picked at a few stray Matilda hairs that stuck to my jeans. "He's not wrong, but that doesn't mean I like it."

"So what are you studying for?" Jack asked, his interest piqued.

"I don't know. Right now, just history and anatomy and *To Kill a Mockingbird*, apparently." I gestured toward the living room and

140

grimaced. "You think a book with a character named Boo Radley would be more fun."

"It's not supposed to be fun. It's about the ability of good and evil to coexist in mankind, and the effect the knowledge of that has on innocence," he said. I gave him an odd look, and he smiled. "You forget that I'm an English major."

"Sometimes," I admitted. "So, how come you're working for Ezra and not teaching or whatever it is you planned on doing with your degree."

"There's no money in teaching." He laughed and kissed my temple, then went back over to the fridge. "Sorry. I'm still really thirsty."

"Sorry," I apologized again. My own belly felt full almost to the point of being distended, so I knew I'd drunken way too much. I'm not even sure how Jack was walking around.

"I don't actually have a degree, for one thing." Jack opened the fridge and pulled out another bag. He shut the door and turned back to me, leaning on the stainless steel. "And I don't think I really wanted to be a teacher. I don't know what I wanted. I just liked English."

"What did you wanna be when you were a kid?" I scooted back on the counter, crossing my legs underneath me.

"Batman." He laughed and opened the bag. "Or Luke Skywalker."

"Very realistic goals."

"No. I think I wanted to be a writer. Or a musician. You know something stereotypical like that." He shrugged and stared down at the bag, as if deciding if he wanted to drink or not. "I wanted to be a librarian for a while. I loved reading when I was in high school. I used to lock myself in my room and read and make all these bad mix tapes for this really, really hot cheerleader that didn't know I was alive. I was all very Duckie from *Pretty in Pink*."

"Really?" I laughed. "I always pictured you more as Andrew McCarthy."

"Well, you pictured very wrong," he smiled. "I had this bad Robert Smith hair, like a horrible black mess, and when I was 'dressing up,' I'd add black eye liner.

"I read constantly, mostly comic books and stuff," Jack went on. "Alan Moore came out with some really amazing stuff when I was in like ninth and tenth grade. I remember when I got my hands on the first issue of *The Watchmen,* and I thought, 'I want to do this.' I wanted to be a part of that."

He paused, taking a sip from the bag. He leaned more against the fridge and crossed his left foot over his ankle.

"I could never draw that well," he said. "But I worked with this buddy who could draw. We made all these really dark comics and did a whole series based on Edgar Allen Poe's *Masque of the Red Death*. One night, I broke into the principal's office and Xeroxed a bunch, and we sold them for a buck piece. Yeah, I thought I was pretty hot shit then."

"What happened to all that?" I asked.

"I got detention for breaking into the office," Jack smirked. "And my buddy got fired, and my girlfriend started taking up more of my time." He shrugged. "I don't know. Life happened, I guess. And I realized that I'd probably never make it writing comic books."

"So you just gave up on your dream?" I asked.

"I don't know if I would say that." He rested his head back on the door and smiled, but it looked sad around the edges. "I don't think it was every really my dream."

"What is your dream then?" I pressed.

"I don't know." He looked more seriously at me. "What's with all the questions?"

"I don't know. I'm having an existential crisis."

"I see." He downed the rest of the bag in one quick drink. It hit him harder than the rest had, and he shook his head to clear it of the haze. "What about you?"

"What?"

"What did you wanna be when you grew up?" He set the bag on the counter and walked over to me, but his steps were slow and deliberate.

"I don't know." I furrowed my brow, thinking. "In high school, we did all these aptitude tests, and by the time my senior year started, the teachers had all drilled it into my head that I needed to pick a college, pick a major, and decide right now what I wanted to do with the rest of my life."

"What did you decide?" Jack stood in front of me, putting one arm on either side of me, but that was mostly to support himself.

"I didn't decide anything. The pressure overwhelmed me, and I just froze." I shrugged. "When I was younger, what I wanted to be when I grew up changed weekly. I wanted to be a vet, a director, a puppeteer, a ninja, a fireman, a pianist." I shook my head. "I never really felt at home with any one idea."

"Luckily for you, you have forever." He grinned, but it was lopsided. "Now you can try every one of them. You can do and be anything you want."

"It'd be easier if I could only do or be one thing," I sighed.

"Yeah, but what good is easy?" He kissed my forehead, and with half-closed eyes, he smiled down at me. "As a great man once said, 'We learn so little from peace.'"

"Who said that? Dylan Thomas?" I asked.

"No. The guy who wrote *Fight Club*."

"Now you're an advocate for hardship? I thought you were the guy that took the easiest way out of everything," I teased.

"Maybe." He met my eyes, looking at me in a way that felt like he was looking straight through me. "But you're the hardest thing I've ever done, and you're also the best. So… I think that's the moral of the story here. Anything worth having is worth fighting for."

"Thank you. I think." I leaned up and kissed him softly, but he stumbled back before it got too deep.

"I'm so sorry." He shook his head and opened his eyes too wide, like he looked really startled. "But I think I'm gonna have to lie down."

"No, if you have to rest, go rest." I put my hand on his chest. "I'm sorry for draining you so completely."

I heard a screech in the garage, followed almost immediately by the sound of a car door slamming shut. Milo burst into the house a moment later, throwing open the door and stomping into the kitchen.

"Where the hell is Ezra?" Milo demanded.

"Dude, did you hit my car?" Jack asked, sounding as angry as a bleary, drunk person could sound.

"Why would I hit your car?" Milo asked, incredulous.

"You like… screeched into the garage. You drive like a maniac!" Jack pointed at him, but I'm not sure why. "You better not have hit my car."

"What's wrong with him?" Milo asked me.

"He drank too much blood," I shrugged. "Never mind him. Why are you looking for Ezra?"

"My car's a frickin Delorean. It's a time machine!" Jack lost his footing and started falling to the floor, and I had to grab his arms to catch him. I pulled him back up, and he leaned over on the counter, resting his head on the granite countertop. "I don't think I've ever drank that much blood before."

"I've been getting calls from Mae all day, but I was in class so I had my phone off." Milo pulled his phone out of his pocket and held it up to show me, as if to prove Mae called. "She left me six messages, and all she'd say is that it's very, very important she talk to me and that she'd been unable to get a hold of Ezra."

"So just call her back," I said.

"I've been trying! But you know how hard to is for them to get service in Australia!" Milo glowered down at the phone then jammed it back in his pocket. "And something's wrong and I don't know what it is!"

"I'm sure everything'll be fine." I said that, but I didn't believe it.

Mae wouldn't reach out to Ezra unless she had to. I should've realized that when he said she'd been calling him. Especially after the way Daisy attacked Bobby, and how Peter said she'd been acting.

"Ezra!" Milo shouted and walked into the dining room.

"Jack, stay put." I patted Jack on the back and hopped off the counter. He mumbled something, but I think he was mostly passed out anyway. I chased after Milo, following him to where he met Ezra in the living room.

"Why haven't you been answering the phone?" Milo yelled at Ezra.

"My phone calls are none of your concern," Ezra said, unfazed by Milo's apparent rage.

"Mae has been calling you, and she's in trouble," Milo glared up at him.

"Maybe you should try calling her back," I suggested. "Or at least check her messages."

From the other room, we heard a bang. I glanced back, and although I couldn't see him, I guessed that Jack had fallen off the counter onto the floor. The excess blood had hit him bad.

"Shouldn't you go check on your boyfriend?" Ezra asked, his tone barely revealing the ice underneath.

"I'm okay!" Jack yelled from the kitchen.

"He's okay." I pointed back in his direction, and Ezra rolled his eyes.

"Ezra, don't change the subject," Milo said. I had to admit it, I admired my little brother for talking to Ezra like that. Standing up to him took courage. "I know you're mad at Mae-"

"I'm not mad at her," Ezra cut him off. "I merely have nothing to say to her."

"Whatever," Milo sighed. "You loved her. You *still* love her, and even if you don't, you cared about her for so long that you can't shut it off. She is in serious trouble. How could you not at least hear her out? Don't you owe her that?"

"Of course I would help her if I could." Ezra swallowed hard, and for one of the few times since I'd met him, the pain in his voice was audible. It made his deep baritone tighten. "I just don't believe I can."

"If you'd answer the damn phone, you'd know for sure!" Milo shot back.

"Milo, yelling at him doesn't make this better," I said.

"I'm not yelling!" Milo yelled, then took a deep breath. "Sorry. I'm frustrated. I don't like knowing that something could be wrong, and I could help but... I can't."

My phone began to ring, and we all froze. For a second, we stared at each other, and then I scrambled to pull it out of my pocket. Before I answered, I checked the caller ID.

"Is it Mae?" Milo asked breathlessly.

"No. It's not Mae." I swallowed hard. "It's Peter."

"Hello?" I answered the phone after my initial shock.

"Alice?" Peter breathed a sigh of relief. "Thank god you answered."

"What's going on?" I asked. "Is something wrong? Where's Mae?"

"She's off dealing with the little problem," he said. "We... Ah, hell, Alice, we're in a major shit storm, and we've gotta get out of here. Now."

"Why? What happened? Are you guys okay?" I asked.

"Yeah, we're alright. Mae and that... child are fine, or as fine as can be after..." He cursed under his breath, "Mae got it in her head that Daisy was ready for a trip to the city. There was some carnival thing going on, and she thought it was a lovely way to spend the evening."

"What did she do?" My stomach dropped, and I stepped back so I could sit back on the couch.

"Daisy went berserk." Peter laughed hollowly. "She attacked several people in town. I tried to contain the situation and convince them it'd been an animal. I'm not sure what they believed, but we managed to get out of there alive. Daisy is unscathed, which is the important part, right?"

"Did she kill anyone?" I asked, and Ezra closed his eyes, shielding himself from it.

"No. Well, not that I know of," Peter corrected himself. "The way she went after some of them, it's entirely possible that they died after we left. She's not… safe. I don't know what to do. We chartered a plane, and we should be leaving on it soon. But I don't know where we'll go or what we'll do."

"What does Mae think you should do?" I asked.

"Lord knows what Mae thinks about anything anymore," Peter said. "I told her it was a mistake to bring Daisy out in public, but Mae has been in such denial about this whole thing. I think she's starting to realize it's a mistake, but she can't do anything now."

"Are you coming home?" I asked.

"I don't know if that's the right thing to do," he said at length. "I'm not even sure that Ezra or Jack would let us come home. And we can't live in a city with people everywhere."

"Do you want to talk to Ezra?" I asked and looked up at Ezra to make sure it would be okay.

"He's around?" Peter sounded surprised.

"Yeah. He's right here. You should talk to him." I stood up and held the phone out to Ezra, not waiting to hear Peter's response to it.

"Hello?" Ezra took the phone from me.

Milo stood next to me and watched anxiously as Ezra said very little on his end of the conversation. Other than a few murmured "mmm hmms," he offered nothing of value.

"What's going on?" Milo whispered.

150

"Daisy attacked some people at a carnival," I told him, but I kept my eyes locked on Ezra.

"Alright." Ezra hung up and turned back to us. Without saying anything, he walked over and handed the phone to me.

"Well?" I said.

"They're getting on a plane. They'll be here in a day or so." Ezra looked over at the window and shook his head. "I'm not sure what will happen when they get here but... it is what it is."

"What the hell does that mean?" Milo asked.

"They're desperate. I couldn't tell them no." Ezra tried to convince himself. Both Milo and I wouldn't say no to them either. "But they can't stay here. Not for more than a few days. Or maybe at all. The child can't be around people." He stared off at nothing, and he sounded completely lost. "I have no idea what will become of them."

After a moment of confused silence hanging over us all, Ezra turned and walked back down to his den. I tried to stop him, but he shook his head and said he had some thinking to do. I'm sure he did, but I didn't know if even he could come up with a plan to fix this.

This was exactly why he'd been so against Mae turning Daisy in the first place. He knew nothing good could come of it, and he couldn't clean it up.

"This is so messed up." Milo leaned back against the couch and let out a deep breath. "Did Peter say how bad things were?"

"He didn't go into graphic detail but things were definitely not good. Some people might be dead."

"And now she's coming here?" Milo looked up at me.

"And now she's coming here," I repeated.

"I want to help Mae, and I don't necessarily want Peter to die." He stood up straighter and crossed his arms over his chest. "But what are we supposed to do? Daisy is dangerous, *really* dangerous. And even if she wasn't, her poster is plastered all over town. Mae kidnapped her, remember?"

"I know," I nodded. "She can't live here, not in the city."

"Where else can she stay?" Milo asked.

"I don't know…" I trailed off, thinking. "But Olivia is the oldest vampire I've ever met. She might know something about child vampires."

"You've only met like five vampires. That doesn't really mean anything," Milo said.

"I've met way more than that," I scoffed. "And she's still like six-hundred-years-old or something. She has to know something about them."

Jack groaned from the other room, and I remembered that I'd heard him fall while Milo'd been arguing with Ezra.

"I gotta go take care of Jack, then I'm going to Olivia's," I said. "You can come with me if you want."

I went into the kitchen and found Jack passed out between the island and the counter. When I pulled him up, he barely even stirred, so I carried him up to our room and dropped him off. I'd never seen Jack this knocked out before, but I'd never seen him drained either.

Watching Jack sleeping on the bed, looking peaceful and vulnerable, I had this weird sensation. He'd never been the weaker one before. But lately, things had been shifting.

I'd become stronger as a vampire, and thanks to my training with Olivia, I'd become a better fighter than him. We'd done some play fighting the other day, and I'd tackled him without really trying. I was growing more powerful than Jack, and it felt… disorienting.

"Are you gonna just stare at Jack or are we gonna go?" Milo asked, poking his head into the bedroom.

"Hold on. I gotta change real quick." I hurried into the closet to throw some clothes on, and Milo stood impatiently by the door, texting on his phone. "Who are you talking to that's so important?"

"Bobby. I'm telling him not to come over after class."

"Why not?" I started walking towards the stairs, and Milo followed, still typing away on his phone.

"Because it's not safe here anymore," Milo said. "You saw what happened in Australia. He can't be around Daisy anymore. I won't risk it."

"Yeah, but she's not here *now*." I glanced back at him as went down the stairs.

"That's exactly what he said. I think you two spend too much time together."

"He's the only human friend I've got," I shrugged.

"I'm pretty sure he's the only friend you've got," Milo sighed.

Just as we reached the kitchen, Bobby walked in from the garage. Apparently, he planned on ignoring Milo's texts of warnings.

"Turn around," Milo said.

"Look, she's not here now. I'm not going anywhere," Bobby insisted.

"Well, we are." I brushed past him towards the garage. "We're going to Olivia's if you wanna come with."

I quickly regretted inviting Milo and Bobby to tag along. The car ride downtown consisted of the two of them arguing about whether or not it would be safe to visit the house. Bobby pointed out that he hadn't signed up for a dorm this semester, so he didn't have anywhere else to stay.

Milo relented and said Bobby could stay for tonight, and they'd figure something else out in the morning. But that only happened after ten minutes of constant bickering.

While I understood the beauty of the glass walls of the penthouse suite at night, during the afternoon, it made no sense to me. The sun had started to set, so it was level with the windows. Even though they were tinted, the bright pink rays stung my eyes and skin.

Her place looked clean, but Milo brushed off her sofa before sitting down, as if he thought he might catch something from it. Bobby had been here with me a lot more often than Milo had, so he was more comfortable with the surroundings and flopped down on the overstuffed sofa.

I'd tried convincing Milo to come here and train with me, but he wasn't into it. He didn't really care for Olivia, mostly because he thought she was a drunk, and he didn't like fighting either. He wanted to live a normal life, the same kind of life he would've had if he hadn't turned, and in his normal life, he wouldn't have done combat training. That was his stance.

Before I could knock on her bedroom door, she opened it. It scared me so much I gasped. She smiled tiredly at me, wrapping her silken robe more around herself. She wore her long black hair braided down her back, swinging like a rope as she walked out.

"What are you doing awake?" I asked.

"Trouble sleeping." She waved her hand vaguely and went over to the couch.

This wasn't the first time she mentioned trouble sleeping. I'd said something about it to Ezra once, and he'd explained that insomnia could be a side effect of her cutting down on blood. Drinking that much blood that often had become a sleep aid for her, and without her excessive daily dose, she was having difficulty learning to sleep without it.

"Hello, Olivia." Milo forced a smile at her, doing his best to be polite.

"To what do I owe this pleasure?" Olivia asked. She sat on the couch across from Milo, sprawling out and the robe slipped up over her slender legs.

"What do you know about child vampires?" I asked. I didn't sit down and kept my back to the window. The sun beat warm on my skin, and I tried to ignore it.

"I try not to know anything about them," she answered diffidently.

"Is there a way to… like train them?" I asked.

"Why are you interested in child vampires?" Olivia glanced over at Bobby. "He's young but he's not a child."

155

I exchanged a look with Milo. Olivia didn't know about Daisy. We weren't sure how other vampires would react to a child, and we didn't really think she needed to know. But maybe she did now.

"Mae turned a child," I said carefully, gauging Olivia's reaction. "That's why she's been gone. She's hiding out with the child vampire."

"I'm sure that's turning out marvelously," Olivia laughed dryly but didn't seem surprised.

"Do you know anything about child vampires or not?" Milo snapped. He'd grown very defensive of Mae, even if he didn't agree with her choices.

"Honestly, I've tried to steer clear of the whole thing," she sighed. "Vampires are just as likely as humans to dabble in that particular… fetish, and I know, for awhile, vampires were attempting some kind of child vampire sex trade."

"Are you talking about pedophiles?" Bobby asked, wrinkling his nose in disgust.

"If that's what you want to call it." She smoothed out the silk of her robe and slid deeper in the couch. "There was a time, not that long ago, where it was common for men to marry girls as young as twelve."

"You can't possibly condone that." Milo glared at her and put an arm around Bobby, in case Olivia decided to sell him into the sex trade.

"No, of course I don't," Olivia said, unruffled by Milo's anger. "There's very little I approve of that happened in the past."

"So other vampires were turning children into vampires?" I asked, trying to return to the topic. "They had to have a way to control them."

"Not really." She shook her head. "Most of them are incapable of ever learning restraint. They want to devour everything they see. And even the ones that can learn it, what good is that? Being trapped in a child's body forever is torture. If Peter Pan had been real, he would've gone mad and killed everyone in Neverland."

"Maybe the vampires you encountered were like that just because that's what they were being forced to do," I said. "If they were raised differently, maybe they could turn out better."

"I can't say," she shrugged.

"Do you know anything?" Milo asked pointedly.

"Milo, don't be rude," I said.

"I'm not!" He insisted but his cheeks reddened. As much as he didn't trust her, he didn't want to be impolite. "I just meant that… Olivia never seems to know the answer to anything."

"The more you know, the more you forget," Olivia shrugged again.

"What are you guys doing out there?" A voice shouted from the bedroom next to Olivia's, and Milo tensed up and narrowed his eyes.

"Who is that?" Milo leaned forward.

"It's just me, and I've been *trying* to sleep." Violet opened the bedroom door wearing an oversized tee shirt. Her blond hair was disheveled, and she sounded utterly tired. "But with Olivia getting up and moving around all day, and now you guys talking as loud as you want without regard-"

"What the hell are *you* doing there?" Milo hissed and got to his feet.

"What are you doing here?" Violet shot back, and she snapped awake. She moved like a livewire, and if she wanted to, she'd be over the couch and at Milo's throat before he could even blink.

"Milo, it's fine." I stepped forward, moving in between them. "She's just staying here for a while."

Even though she'd been around and I'd run into her a few times, Milo hadn't seen her at all since she'd had purple hair and hung out with Lucien. The last time he saw her, she'd been trying to kill us. He hadn't seen the transformation from evil sidekick to sad homeless girl, so he was on high alert.

"You knew she was staying here?" Milo asked.

"Yeah, and it's no big deal," I reiterated. I failed to mention it had actually been my idea, but it was probably better if he didn't know that.

"Take it easy, cowboy," Olivia smirked at him. "I don't allow fighting in the penthouse."

"You take it easy," Milo muttered, but he sat back down on the couch.

"Now I'm really awake," Violet sighed and turned to walk back to the kitchen. "If I have to be up, I'm getting something to eat."

"Is there anything at all you can tell us to help us?" I asked Olivia, ignoring the outburst. Milo tried to glare after Violet, but I moved to block his view.

"Stay away from the children." Olivia cocked her head. "Why the sudden interest? Hasn't Mae had the child for a while?"

"Yeah but…" I shook my head. I didn't want to tell her that they'd be in town. "I just wanted to help."

"Sometimes you can't help people," Olivia said, sounding uncharacteristically sad. "That's probably the hardest lesson in life."

Violet came back over to us, sipping blood out of a Big Gulp cup with a straw. The blood perfumed the air, and it smelled like it was pretty fresh. For once, I didn't feel hungry. I was still too full from Jack to even consider eating yet, and that felt nice.

"Oh hey, it's a good thing you're here actually," Violet said. She climbed over the arm of the chair and sat down, curling her knees up to her chest. She pulled the long tee shirt down over her legs and took a long sip from the cup.

"Who? Me?" I pointed to myself.

"Yeah." She took another long drink and quickly swallowed down. "I was working the club last night, trying to keep the riffraff under control, and I saw this bloodwhore with a weird mark on her arm."

"What kind of mark?" I asked.

"At first I thought it was a big 'U,' like the letter 'u,' but I really don't know what it's supposed to be," Violet said. "When I asked the bloodwhore about it, she told me a vampire branded her. It turns out this vampire has been branding a lot of the bloodwhores."

"Branding them? You mean like cattle?" I asked, raising an eyebrow.

"Oh he can't do that," Olivia said disdainfully. "You can't brand girls unless they're in your harem."

"I don't know if they're in his harem or not," Violet shrugged. "I just thought it seemed like suspicious behavior."

"What do you mean?" I asked.

"I don't know." She took another drink, but this time it was to buy herself some time to think about what she meant. "I asked the bloodwhore why the vampire did it, and he'd told her, 'I want everyone to know that you belong to a vampire.' Something about that just sounded off to me. Like everyone would know she belongs to a vampire."

"Huh," I said, but a chill shot down my spine.

"Anyway, I just thought I'd let you know since you were asking about that girl's murder," Violet said off-handedly and went back to finishing her beverage.

I felt Milo's eyes on me as soon as she said it, and I decided that we better get out of there before Violet or Olivia let it slip exactly how interested I was in looking for Jane's killer.

I thanked both Olivia and Violet for their help as nonchalantly as possible, but Milo noticed my hasty exit. He waited until we were the elevator, trapped in the long ride to the basement, before bringing it up.

"What exactly did Violet mean that you were asking about that girl's murder?" Milo asked, his eyes locked on me. Bobby hid next to him, hoping Milo wouldn't realize that he'd been helping me too.

"She was my best friend, Milo." I stared up at the ceiling. "You think I'm not gonna ask at all?"

"No, but you better not be really looking into this," Milo warned me. "The police have it under control."

"I'm not looking into it, but if the police have it under control, what would it matter if I did? If they can handle it, I definitely can," I countered.

"Alice, you don't have the tools or equipment to really solve this," Milo said wearily. "You'd just end up getting yourself in trouble. And what would you do if you did find the killer? You couldn't prove that it was him, and you would never know for sure so you wouldn't want to kill him. What good would it do to track him down?"

"It wouldn't," I said. "That's why I'm not. I just asked a few questions. It's not like I launched an investigation or something."

"Good. That's all it better be."

"Why?" I looked over at him. "What happens if it's not?"

"I'll tell Jack about all those longing gazes you shared with Peter when we were in Australia," Milo said evenly and my jaw dropped.

"We- I- ugh!" I groaned and looked away from him. "That's not even fair!"

"I'm sick of you almost getting yourself killed, Alice!" Milo yelled. "And if you won't wise up on your own, then I'll force you into it! Stay away from this, okay?"

"Fine!" I hit the elevator button, hoping to make the ride speed up somehow.

I didn't need Milo narcing on me for something that didn't even happen, or... barely happened. I mean, it was innocent, but I didn't need another big fight. I promised Jack I wouldn't do anything to hurt him anymore, and I meant it.

At the same time, I wasn't about to let Jane's killer go free. Especially not when I had something new to go on. It may not be a big lead, but Violet's tip had been more than I had yesterday.

"Promise me you'll leave this alone," Milo insisted.

"I promise," I said, knowing I would break that promise as soon as I got the chance.

- 12 -

Every day when I woke up, I found more books added to the stack of my studies. When I saw how few books Milo brought home compared to my workload, I regretted letting Ezra homeschool me instead of going to actual school.

I'd finished *To Kill a Mockingbird* and my chapters in the history book, but I skipped out on anatomy. Turns out, I didn't have much of an interest in becoming a doctor.

Even with all that, I managed to sneak in a moment alone with Bobby. We both thought something was going on with the vampire branding girls. I wanted to check into it more, but we definitely couldn't do anything in front of Milo. He'd made it perfectly clear that he didn't want us involved with this.

Since I'd finished *To Kill a Mockingbird*, I woke up to find *On the Road* by Jack Kerouac and *A Farewell to Arms* by Ernest Hemingway along with a law book added to the growing stack of textbooks Ezra left for me by the couch. *On the Road* wasn't as horrible as I'd envisioned it being, and I sprawled out on the couch to read it.

"How are you finding the book?" Ezra asked when he came into the living room to check on my progress.

"It's okay." I shrugged and sat up more, setting the book aside so I could talk to him. "How do you decide which books you want me to read?"

"I'm picking at random from the most critically acclaimed books of the last century." He picked up the worn copy of *A Farewell to Arms*, flipping through it absently. "This is one of my favorites. I was hoping you'd pick that one first."

"I read *Old Man and the Sea* in high school and almost died of boredom. I'm holding off on Hemingway, if I can."

"Well, you're going to read it." He set the book back down on the couch and crossed the room to sit down on a chair.

"What about the law book? How did you decide on that?" I asked, gesturing to the new textbook.

"You didn't seem that interested in anatomy. I thought law might suit you better."

"So what's your plan? Try everything until you find something that interests me?"

"My plan is to educate you." He smiled. "It's up to you to find out what interests you and what you're passionate about."

"Law might interest me." I leaned forward, resting my elbows on my knees.

"How so?" Ezra asked, sounding hesitant to know why it would interest me.

"The thing is…" I shifted, trying to think how I wanted to phrase it. "There's word going around the clubs that a vampire is branding girls, human girls."

"What reputable source did you hear this from?"

"You know I've been hanging around Olivia's, and I hear things," I said. "What does it matter where I hear it from?"

"It matters because I know you're developing some kind of theory here, and it would be nice to know if that theory has any basis in reality." Ezra leaned back in the chair, looking at me evenly.

"It does. Or at least I think it does." I glanced down at the floor, not wanting to admit to Ezra that I wasn't really sure how much I could trust Violet. Maybe she was just messing with me for the fun of it. I shook my head, deciding that I had to go with the only lead I had. "Look, for the sake of argument, let's just agree that everything I say is true."

"No," he shook his head.

"Ezra!" I groaned. "Just hear me out, okay?"

"I'm presuming this is all about Jane, and I already told you that I can't help you with that," Ezra said, his eyes looking sad. "Nothing can."

"A vampire is branding girls, okay?" I ignored his refusal. "Something about that just feels wrong to me."

"I would hope so."

"No, not just because it is *wrong*, but like…" I shook my head. "It's a gut feeling. I think it's connected, but I might be wrong. Before I go on a hunt for the vampire branding people, I'd like to know for sure."

"And how would you find that out?" Ezra asked.

"If it is the same guy, he probably marked the girls he killed." I took a deep breath. "He probably marked Jane."

"That's a hell of a leap." He pursed his lips and looked down. "A lot of vampires are not nice. They do bad things to humans all the time simply because they can. Just because a vampire is branding

165

humans doesn't mean he's a serial killer. And even if it does, it doesn't mean he left a mark on Jane."

"You're right. I know you're right," I said, but I hated to admit it. "But something about this *feels* like a vampire. I went out looking at the crime scenes-"

"You what?" Jack asked, startling me so much I nearly jumped.

I'd been too focused on my arguments to convince Ezra that I hadn't been paying attention, and Jack had snuck up on me. He stood off to the side of the living room, his blue eyes wide and disapproving. I swallowed hard and smiled sheepishly at him.

"I didn't see you standing there," I said.

"You went to the crime scenes? Why?" Jack asked.

"What do you mean why?" I looked up at him. "I wanna know what happened to Jane."

"And what did you find out?" Jack asked.

"Nothing. I don't know anything." I lowered my eyes for a minute, then looked up, pleading with Ezra. "But you can help. I know you at least know somebody on the police force. You can ask them. I know they withhold some information. If she has any marks, anything at all-"

"You're gonna hunt down the killer? That's your plan?" Jack raised an eyebrow.

"I don't really have a plan," I admitted.

"Yeah, I figured that, since you think it's a good idea to hunt a serial killer on your own."

"I can handle myself, Jack." I stood up. "Milo and I are stronger than you."

"Maybe," Jack shrugged, but he momentarily looked hurt. Physically, Milo had definitely become a lot stronger than Jack, but it wasn't something he liked hearing. "But you don't see me doing stupid stunts like you."

"You would if you liked Jane," I shot back, but he rolled his eyes.

"You know that's not true. I stood up for and helped her every chance I had," Jack said. "I don't want you to get yourself killed or to do something you regret."

The French doors off the patio slammed shut, and Matilda barked a greeting as people walked inside. Jack didn't say anything for a minute, and I knew he was holding something back.

"What's going on here?" Milo asked, noticing the tension between us.

"What is going on here?" Leif repeated. He moved towards Milo and me but kept his eyes locked on Jack. Jack shifted uneasily under Leif's stony glare.

"Your sister thinks it's a good idea to handle Jane's killer herself," Jack said, and both Leif and Milo instantly turned back at me.

"You just promised me you wouldn't!" Milo yelled.

"Yeah but..." I sighed and crossed my arms over my chest.

"Alice, I can't believe you would do that! You lied to me!" Milo sounded genuinely hurt, and I groaned and flopped back on the couch. Any fight I had in me had completely gone out.

"It's not that dangerous. I don't know why you guys keep acting like it is. It's not like I'm human or something," I said, and Milo looked over at Bobby.

"I had nothing to do with it!" Bobby offered up quickly, and I didn't blame him. If I could lie about my own involvement, I totally would.

"You lied about it, so you knew it was wrong." Milo turned back to me. "You knew it!"

"I knew you would be mad, but you've got no reason to be mad! I can handle myself!" I looked up at him.

"Alice, you're just a child," Leif shook his head.

"Whatever. I don't wanna talk about this anymore." I brushed past them, preparing to storm out.

"Alice!" Jack ran after me, out onto the patio. The icy night wind whipped over us, nearly taking my breath away. "Alice!" When I didn't stop, Jack grabbed my arm, forcing me to look at him. "What is going on with you?"

"You already know what's going on with me."

"No, I don't." He furrowed his brow, confused and hurt. "You've been so distant lately, and I know you're hurting over Jane but... this feels like something different. And now you're sneaking around and hiding things from me."

"I'm not hiding things from you!" I snapped.

"Then what do you call a secret murder investigation?"

"You don't understand." I shook my head. "I knew you wouldn't understand."

"What don't I understand?"

"Why I need to have something for myself!" I tried to pull my arm away from him, but he wouldn't let go.

"This isn't the kind of thing you have yourself. It's not 'alone time' or a 'hobby. This is dangerous, Alice, and stupid."

"Let her go," Leif said, his voice startlingly firm. He stood just inside the open French door, watching me and Jack argue.

"She's fine," Jack said, but he let go of my arm. I didn't move away, though. I kinda wanted to leave, to spite him, but I didn't want Leif to think that Jack was actually hurting me.

"I think you should give her some space." Leif walked out onto the patio, his bare feet leaving footprints in the snow.

"Why are you even here?" Jack asked, apparently growing weary of him.

"Give it a rest, Jack," I said. "He doesn't mean anything by it."

Jack looked back at me, assessing me for something I didn't understand. After a moment, he sighed and shook his head.

"Fine. I'm going in the house. Have all the space you want." Jack went back into the house without even glancing back at me.

"Are you okay?" Leif asked, stepping closer to me.

"Yeah, I'm fine." I forced a smile at him. "Jack wasn't hurting me."

"You don't need to make excuses for him." Leif put his hands in his pockets and looked intently at me.

"I'm not. He's… We're just going through something." I shook my head. "I'm going through something, so that means he is too. I just wish I knew what it was."

"Maybe you should talk to him about it. Or Milo," Leif suggested.

"I can't talk to Milo." I wrapped my arms around myself and stared at the black lake behind us.

"He's your brother and he cares about you, a lot."

"I know. This is just... complicated," I sighed. "Forever is a really long time, you know? What do you do with forever?"

"The same thing you do when you don't have forever." He smiled wanly. "Live."

"That's a bit simplistic."

"But at least you have Milo. You know you'll have somebody that will always care about you and always have your back. That's important."

I looked past Leif into the house. In the warm glow of the dining room, I could see Milo and Bobby talking. The wind almost drowned out their voices, but I could barely make Bobby out, denying he knew anything that I was up to. Milo's face was etched with worry, thinking of what kind of trouble Bobby and I could get ourselves into.

"Yeah, I suppose you're right," I said.

"Do you regret becoming a vampire?" Leif asked, pulling me from my thoughts.

"I don't know." I hadn't wanted to think about it. "I love Jack. I love a lot of things about my life. But..." I shook my head. "I can't change it now, anyway."

"It's not something I would've chosen for you," Leif said.

"What do you mean by that?" I cocked my head.

"It's not something I would've chosen for anybody," Leif amended quickly and looked away.

"Why are you here?" I asked, remembering that Leif hadn't answered that question when Jack asked.

"I was with Milo, helping him with his French homework." He took a step back, as if wanting to put distance between us. "He's having problems with the dialect, and I'm fluent."

"You're French?" I asked.

"Canadian," he said. "I lived in Quebec for awhile." He took another step back. "But the two of you seem busy now. I should be going."

"Alright?" I asked, feeling a little confused.

"Tell Milo I'll see him later."

With that, Leif turned and disappeared into the darkness. I looked back in the house. Bobby had apparently convinced Milo nothing was going on, and they were hugging and kissing. I wasn't sure where Jack was, but I was positive our reunion wouldn't be quite so sweet.

- 13 -

"So what did Jack say?" Bobby asked, and I pushed the pedal down harder in the Audi as we whizzed through traffic.

Bobby didn't look nervous about it all, the same way I hadn't been nervous when Jack used to drive me around. He lived under the same fallacy as I had – that because we were immortal, we were infallible. But we weren't.

"I don't wanna talk about it," I brushed Bobby off.

The long, long talk Jack and I had after our fight last night was not something I wanted to repeat. We'd hashed out so much stuff, about Jane, Peter, even me being a vampire, and it had been exhausting. The worst part was that in the end, I'm not sure if I felt any better about anything.

"That good, huh?" Bobby raised an eyebrow.

"Yep."

"So... you're not telling him what we're doing today, are you?" Bobby asked nervously.

"Of course not. There's enough going on with us without him finding out that I'm still trying to figure out who killed Jane," I said.

"Why is he so worried anyway?"

"I have no idea." I shrugged. "It's not like I'm super fragile or anything."

"How do you kill a vampire anyway?" Bobby looked over at me.

"Well, we're not really immortal, per se," I said, telling him what Ezra had explained to me. "Whatever makes us vampires, it's basically just a virus that stops decomposition and promotes healing. Our bones are superior, but not unbreakable. In the end, we still come from a human body, and we can't function without a brain or a heart."

"So the old stake the heart thing, that works?" Bobby asked with a raised eyebrow.

"Sure, if you can get a piece of wood to break through our ribs, but I doubt that," I said. "Stop the heart, sever the head, however you can manage it, and we're dead."

"Good to know," Bobby said.

I pressed on the breaks, and the car skidded to a stop as I pulled over. I stared up at the luxurious apartment complex that towered above us and took a breath. "Well, here we are."

An overcast sky had left the day dim and gloomy, and the sun had just started to set, making the streetlights blink on as I stepped out of the car. I stared up at the building I hadn't been to in months and felt an odd sense of nostalgia.

"Where did she live?" Bobby stood next to me.

"Fifth floor." I pointed to it, even though we couldn't see anything from this angle and distance.

"What's the plan?" He shoved his hands in his jacket pockets as an icy wind whipped over us.

"I guess we go inside." I glanced over at the main door to the apartment building.

Bobby followed me over to the door, where the doorman let me in. I didn't recognize him, but that was because it'd been too long since I'd visited Jane last. It'd been too long since I'd done anything real with Jane.

"Who should I tell Mr. Kress is calling?" The doorman had gone over to the desk to phone Jane's dad. He had to check with him before he could buzz us up, and I really wasn't sure if Mr. Kress would.

"Um, Alice Bonham. I'm a friend of Jane's," I said.

"I see." The doorman gave me an odd look for a moment, then dialed up. "Mr. Kress, an Alice Bonham is here. She says she's a-" He paused, apparently interrupted. "Very good, sir." He hung up the phone and smiled. "Go on up. He's been expecting you."

"Thank you." I smiled thinly at him and walked to the elevator.

"He's been expecting you?" Bobby whispered as he hurried to keep up with me.

"Apparently." I stepped inside the elevator and breathed deeply, trying to hide the nauseated feeling this was giving me. Going back to Jane's apartment. Seeing her father.

"What does that mean?" Bobby asked, and I shrugged. "Does Jane's dad like you?"

"I'm not really sure. Honestly, I don't even know how much he liked Jane," I said.

"Well, then, I'm sure this will go well."

I'd been hoping that Jane's father wouldn't be home. That'd been part of the reason why I picked this time. Mr. Kress usually worked long hours at the office, so I figured he'd still be at work. I wanted to sneak out before Jack woke up and Milo came home from school, but avoiding Mr. Kress was part of it too.

I hadn't even spoken to him or her stepmother at the funeral, and I kinda liked her stepmom Blythe. Even when we'd been close, I'd hated eating supper at Jane's house. Dinner conversation felt so forced and stilted. There was something strangely terrifying about her father.

The housekeeper opened the apartment door before I had a chance to knock. She was new from the last time I'd been here, and I struggled to remember exactly how long it had been since I'd hung out with Jane at her place.

The apartment looked as grand as ever. It wasn't very large, but it had an opulence to it. Everything in it looked lux and expensive, and I'd hated playing here as a kid because it was like playing in a museum. If I touched anything, I'm sure it would shatter, and incur the wrath of her father.

The housekeeper had led us into the entryway, and I heard the click of Blythe's high heels on the wood floors. Jane had gotten her high fashion sense from her stepmother. Her real mother had died before Jane was even in kindergarten, and Blythe had done her best to raise her.

"Alice." Blythe smiled when saw me, but it didn't quite reach her eyes. She stopped several feet in front of me and folded her hands over her stomach, almost as if she was afraid to move forward.

"Hello, Mrs. Kress," I said, unsure of what other greeting would be appropriate.

"You look very well." She smoothed a golden strand of hair back, and her eyes were red-rimmed underneath her makeup.

"Thanks." My cheeks reddened with shame. I know Blythe was only referring to the changes that being a vampire had brought on, but I hated thinking that I looked good right now. I should be a wreck, not looking better than ever before.

"It's been so long since we've seen you." Her smile grew more pained as she spoke. "I saw you at the ... at Jane's funeral, but you didn't stay long."

"No, I, uh…" I floundered and trailed off completely. I had no good reason for why I'd skipped out early, so I just let it hang in the air.

"I'm sure you had other things to do," Blythe said, and I lowered my eyes.

"What's going on out there?" Mr. Kress bellowed from another room, his voice filled with gravel.

"Nathaniel, why don't you come out here and talk to Alice yourself?" Blythe turned her head back when she yelled for him, and she fidgeted with one of the gold earrings she wore.

"I don't want to disturb you," I said quickly and held up my hand. "If you're busy, I don't need to bother you. I just wanted to see Jane's room."

"Jane's room?" Mr. Kress rounded the corner and walked over to his wife. His tie had been loosened around his chubby neck, and he had a lowball glass in his hand filled with Scotch, the same way it had been every other time I'd seen him. "What do you want with that?"

"I wanted to have a look around." I swallowed hard. "I was wondering if I could maybe take some of her pictures of us."

"Take anything you want in there," Mr. Kress said, gesturing with his glass so the alcohol sloshed around. "I don't have use for any of it now."

"Nathaniel," Blythe chastised him quietly and pulled harder at her earring.

"It's true." He ignored his wife and turned his attention to Bobby, giving him a hard look with his steel gray eyes. "Who is this?"

"I'm Bobby. I was a friend of Jane's." Bobby held his hand out for Mr. Kress to shake it, but Mr. Kress just stared at him blankly, so Bobby dropped his hand.

"I didn't know most of Jane's friends," Mr. Kress said, more to himself than us. "I didn't know very much about what went on in her life. But I did know this is where she'd end up if she wasn't careful, and Jane was never careful."

"Nathaniel. Please." Blythe put her hand in his arm, but he shook it off. She turned back to me, smiling that same sad smile. "Go ahead and have a look at her room, Alice. You can take anything that means something to you. I'm sure it would bring Jane happiness to know that you have it."

"It won't bring Jane anything, Blythe!" Mr. Kress snapped, and both Bobby and I shrunk back. "She's dead! She doesn't feel anything!"

"You know the way to Jane's room," Blythe said to me. She lowered his eyes and stepped to the side of the hall, so we could walk passed her.

"Thank you," I mumbled and slid past her, staying as close to the wall as I could.

I wanted to run down to Jane's room, the way we had has children and hid under the bed when her father started yelling. We'd lay under her princess bed with flashlights and tell each other stories about how we'd grow up and be rescued by princes and knights in shining armor. Only Jane's had never come. Nobody ever rescued her.

As soon as we made it to Jane's room, I shut the door behind us, blocking out the sound of her father shouting. Blythe said very little, only quiet words of comfort, but nothing could calm him. Although, for once, I couldn't really blame him. He had just lost his only child.

"This is not what I expected from Jane's room," Bobby said, looking around at the pale pink walls.

The bed in the center was the same four-post princess bed she'd always had, and fairy lights ran around the posts. She had a white vanity against one wall, covered in makeup. Her desk in the corner had a laptop and a few framed photos, but the rest of the décor felt very little girl.

"Her mom decorated the room right before she died, so Jane never really wanted to change it." I gestured to the worn down princess lamp on her nightstand. The pink boa that'd been used as fringe had almost come off entirely.

"I see." Bobby went over to the nightstand and picked up a picture. "Is this Jane with Justin Timberlake?"

"Yeah, she met him after a concert a couple years ago." I went over to her desk and touched a picture of the two of us at a dance from our freshman year. My hair looked ridiculous because I'd let her do it.

"That's pretty fancy." He set the picture down and looked at me. "So… what are we doing here?"

"I don't know." I looked away from the pictures to survey the room. "I thought I might find something here."

"Was Jane even living here before she died?" Bobby asked. "I mean, when she left rehab?"

"I think so." I chewed the inside of my cheek, trying to remember what I'd read on the internet. I could go ask her parents, but from the sounds of Mr. Kress's yelling, now wouldn't be a good time.

"Why did she even leave rehab?" Bobby asked. "Didn't she leave early?"

"Yeah, she did," I nodded. "But I don't know why. The last time I talked to her, she said she was working the program and doing good. Maybe she relapsed or something."

"How can you relapse on vampire bites? It's not like somebody could sneak it in or something."

"I don't know. She left while I was in Australia. I never should've went." I shook my head and went over to her closet. She didn't have one quite as big as mine, but she had shoved twice as many clothes in it. I opened the doors to find shoes and skirts jumping out at me.

"You think if you'd been here, she wouldn't have left?" Bobby asked. I glanced back at him and saw him opening her nightstand drawer and rooting around in it.

"I don't know." I sifted through her clothes, but there were too many for me to really look at. Sighing, I turned around and looked back at Bobby. "The only thing I know is that I don't know what happened to Jane."

"Good news." Bobby reached into her dresser drawer and pulled out a cell phone. "I think I've got her phone."

"Holy shit." I ran over and grabbed it from him. I clicked and touched it all over, but nothing happened. The screen stayed black. "What's wrong with it? It won't turn on."

"Well, it's been sitting in the drawer for at least two weeks, so the battery is probably dead," Bobby pointed out.

I looked around her room and spotted the charger next to the desk. I plugged in the phone and sat down in the chair. By the time I got the damn thing on, my heart felt like it would beat out of my chest. Bobby stood behind me, looking at it over my shoulder.

She had a few missed calls stored up, most of them from people she used to party with, but three were from an unknown caller. She didn't have voicemails, so that didn't help, and I moved on to her text messages. Before the sixteenth of January, she'd received a couple messages, all from people I knew, but she hadn't sent any out.

"Why wasn't she replying to their texts?" Bobby asked, reading over my shoulder.

"She was in rehab until the sixteenth. She didn't have her phone with her," I said. "When she replied, that's when she got out."

The text messages from people she knew were all about going out or partying, and Jane hadn't responded to any of them. The only messages she responded to were from an unknown caller, and those messages made my blood run cold.

Are you out yet? The unknown number had texted.

Who is this? Jane texted back.

You know who this is. I want you to meet me.

Where? Jane replied.

Outside of the gas station on 8ᵗʰ street.

I'll be there soon. Jane texted.

I'll be waiting.

And that was it. There were no more text messages in her phone.

"That's it?" Bobby asked.

"That's it." I stood up, and he reached for the phone, so I handed it to him. "That gas station is only a few blocks from here. She must've been at home."

"So she knew who it was?" Bobby played around on her phone, searching for more hidden messages or some clue that we didn't see.

"Yeah." I walked over to Jane's window, realizing she'd willingly left to meet her killer, and she'd probably died a few blocks from her home. "Call it."

"What?"

"Call the number," I turned back to Bobby. "Call and see who answers."

"What if I don't know who answers?" he asked.

"Then ask who it is. Just call the number and try to sound tough."

"Okay?" He took a deep breath and hit the call button the phone. I watched him, barely able to breathe myself, and waited while he held the phone to his ear. His face fell and he shook his head. "We're sorry. The number you have reached is no longer in service."

"Dammit," I groaned and looked back at the window. "She knew who it was. She left with them. And she got killed right down this street! And I have no idea-"

Then I saw something on the street corner, below her bedroom window. Something moved in the shadows, and I realized that the streetlight was out. All the other lights on the street were lit up fine, but the one outside of Jane's room was out. It didn't mean anything really. Vampires made sure the streetlight was always out outside of V, but a light going out didn't mean anything in and of itself.

But I had this feeling. I couldn't explain it exactly, but it was something inside my veins. Something almost tingly but painful too. As soon as I'd caught sight of something moving outside, I'd felt it.

"Hey, what's wrong?" Bobby asked.

"Somebody's down there."

"Where?" He came up next to me to look outside, and I saw it again. It had moved to the side, so it was almost out of my line of vision, but I knew it was out there.

"Meet me downstairs," I told Bobby as I opened the bedroom window. I pulled out the screen, bending it in half to get it out quickly.

"What? What are you doing?"

"It'll take me too long to go through the apartment. Just meet me downstairs." I climbed through the window, crouching down on the ledge.

"What'll I tell her parents when you're not with me?"

"I don't know. Think of something," I said, and I leapt off her window.

I would've been fine landing on the ground, but I jumped out towards the street lamp. I wanted some element of surprise, even if it was a small one. My hands wrapped around the lamppost, and I looked down at the ground. The figure was looking up at me.

But as soon as our eyes met, I knew who it was, and he knew me. Jonathan began to run, and I pressed my feet to the pole so I could jump off. I landed right behind him. Pain reverberated through my legs, but I was running the instant my feet hit the ground.

I only gave chase for a second because then I was on him. I grabbed his shoulder and threw him into the wall. His skull cracked back against it. He tried to push at me, but I was stronger than him. I'd barely stood a chance against him the last time we tangled, but now I had the strength and I knew how to use it.

"What the hell are you doing here?" I growled. Pressing my arm to his chest, I held him against the wall. Jonathan could keep fighting, but he knew he couldn't win.

"I could ask you the same thing." He glared down at me, his eyes as cold and emotionless as ever.

"Jane was my best friend! And you killed her!" I shouted, and I kneed him in the groin. He grimaced, but only for a second.

"I didn't kill her! She belonged to me, and I want to find out who did kill her!" Jonathan shouted back, and his breath smelled of rotting meat. He'd eaten recently, but smelling it on him was disgusting. Everything about him made me feel gross, and the blood in my veins burned.

"Liar!" I kneed him again, harder this time, and his face twisted for a moment.

"I'm not lying! Why would I kill Jane? She tasted delicious." Jonathan smiled at me, and it took all my restraint to rip out his throat.

"You hated her. You used her, and you treated her like meat. Why would you be loitering outside her apartment unless you killed her?"

"For the same reason you are," he said. "Somebody stole her from me, and I want to find out who it is. Nobody takes anything from me. You know that."

I eyed him up, deciding whether or not he was telling the truth. He was the sort of bastard that would kill Jane, but return to the scene of the crime to get his jollies on remembering killing her. But even if he got some thrill off it, what good would standing outside her window do?

Unless he was telling the truth. He didn't like being stolen from, I knew that much. If he wanted revenge, he had to find out who the killer was, and I'd ended up here because I was running out of places to look.

"You better not be lying to me," I warned him, pressing my arm harder to his chest. "I'll rip out your heart with my bare hands." His dark eyes searched mine, and he saw I was telling the truth, so he nodded.

"I'm not lying."

"So what do you know?" I asked.

"You don't need to pin me here. I'm not running, and you could catch me if I did," he smirked.

Reluctantly, I dropped my arm and took a step back from him. Whether he killed Jane or not, I still didn't like him. He straightened out his clothes and cocked his head at me.

"How did you get so strong?" Jonathan asked.

"Practice." I crossed my arms over my chest.

"But you shouldn't be stronger than me, not yet. You're still a baby." He narrowed his eyes, trying to get a read on me, and I didn't like it. "There's something... different about you."

"Yeah, well, we're not here to talk about me," I snapped. "What do you know about Jane?"

"Not that much." He shook his head. "Not anything at all, really. She was murdered, and when I find out who did it, I'll kill him."

"Do you think it was a vampire?" I asked.

"Doubtful. We conform to human rules." His voice dripped with venom when he said the word *human*. "We don't like to draw attention to ourselves more than need be." He pointed over to the streetlight. "On the subject of which, weren't you worried that you're theatrics would catch some attention?"

"It's dark and cold. Everyone's inside." I glanced around after he said it, realizing he had a point. I'd been lucky that nobody had seen me jumping out of a five-story window and landing unscathed.

"Yes, god forbid a human realize what we are," Jonathan said sardonically. "Then we'd have to answer to their 'higher' authority."

"Yeah, whatever." I ran a hand through my hair and ignored his tirade. "I'm around the clubs a lot, and I'm keeping my eye on you. If you find out anything about Jane, you better tell me."

"Of course," he smiled, and I'm not sure if I believed that either.

I heard Bobby panting behind me, his heart pounding like mad, but I didn't turn around until Jonathan was long gone. I didn't want to take my eyes off him.

"Who was that?" Bobby asked, working to catch his breath.

"That's Jonathan. You remember? He used to 'date' Jane, and he tried to kill you," I said.

"Oh yeah." Bobby rubbed at his side and nodded. "I just never got a really good look at him."

"Well, now, you have," I said and turned to walk back towards the car.

"What was he doing here?" Bobby asked.

"He says he's doing the same thing we are, but I don't know," I shook my head. "I'm not sure if I can believe anything he says."

"Why didn't you just kill him then?"

"Because." I stopped and looked at Bobby. "I don't know if he did it. And even though he's a bastard, I'm not gonna kill him if I'm not sure. I don't want innocent blood on my hands, even if it's a vampire's."

"I understand," Bobby said, and we started walking again.

"What did you tell Jane's parents when you left?" I asked.

"Nothing. They were too busy yelling to notice me, so I just ran out the front door. And then I ran all the way down here, and I couldn't find you for a minute." He took a deep breath. "That's why I'm so short of breath."

"We should hurry home before Jack and Milo realize we're gone," I said. "Then we'll both be in deep shit."

Neither of us said much on the car ride home. I think Bobby was still trying to catch his breath, and I told him he needed to start training with me if he wanted to keep going out like this. I didn't want him getting hurt or killed.

The rest of the time, I was lost in thought. Jane knew her killer. But that didn't mean that much. She'd been running around with all sorts of vampires, and while Jonathan had been her main squeeze, that didn't mean she didn't know other vampires. And if she relapsed and wanted to get bitten again, she would've been desperate to get in contact with anyone.

Or maybe it was something else entirely. Maybe it wasn't even a vampire, like Jonathan said. A human is just as capable of murder.

"Have you decided if you believe Jonathan yet?" Bobby asked as I pulled into the garage at the house.

"No. I don't know if I ever will," I sighed and shut off the car. "I might never know what really happened to her."

"We'll find out who did it," he reassured me, looking at me seriously. "We can do this."

"I hope you're right." I got out of the car and noticed the Jetta was in the garage too. "Milo's home from school. What are you gonna tell him we were doing?"

"What are you gonna tell Jack?" Bobby countered.

"It's a crappy day. I picked you up from school, so you didn't have to take the bus," I said as we walked to the house. "How does that sound?"

"You've done it before, so sure," he shrugged.

"Good."

Bobby was in front of me, and he opened the garage door to walk into the house. Jack was home, so he wasn't worried about deflecting Matilda. Unfortunately, he had a much larger problem waiting for him.

He'd only made it two steps into the house before Daisy flew at Bobby, knocking him backwards before he could even scream.

- 14 -

I lunged at Daisy, burying my fingers in soft blond hair and yanking her head back before she could sink her teeth into his neck. She screamed as I lifted her up, but I didn't care. I wanted to make sure Bobby was safe before dealing with her.

"Whoa! Alice! Easy!" Jack yelled. He rushed over and took Daisy from me, so I let go of her. She buried her face in his shoulder, sobbing, and he held her to him.

I stood there in shock as he rubbed her back, comforting her. Milo helped Bobby to his feet, and he didn't have a scratch on him. Other than scaring the hell out of him, Daisy hadn't hurt Bobby at all.

"Is everything okay?" Mae called from another room.

"Yeah, everything's fine," Peter told her, and I looked over, noticing him for the first time. He stood off to the side, watching Jack and Daisy to make sure everything was okay. "How is she?"

"She's fine," Jack said, stroking Daisy's hair. He tilted his head, trying to get a look at her face. "You're okay, aren't you, Daisy?" She nodded, sniffling.

"Okay. Seriously. What the hell is going on here?" I asked, gaping at them all.

"What do you mean?" Jack asked, pulling his gaze from Daisy to me. "Peter's here." He pointed his thumb back at Peter, who glanced over at me but didn't let his eyes linger. "Mae and Ezra are talking in the other room. We don't wanna disturb them."

"She almost killed Bobby, and you're comforting her?" I gestured to Daisy, who only snuggled deeper to him when I shouted. "You were just as against her as I was!"

"Alice, she can hear," Jack glared at me.

"She wasn't attacking Bobby," Peter said, almost apologetic. "She was just excited, and you... scared her."

"*I* scared *her*?" I snapped.

"She had a long flight," Peter said and stepped towards Jack. "Why don't I take her to lie down?"

Jack carefully untangled her from him and handed her over to Peter. Neither one of them glared at each other or showed an animosity. Jack just handed her off, and cradling her in his arms, Peter carried her upstairs.

"What the hell, Jack?" I asked. "I was gone with Bobby, and it's like stepping into the *Twilight Zone*."

"Where were you, by the way?" Milo asked. He had an arm wrapped protectively around Bobby, and he'd been giving Daisy a wary look, which made me feel a bit better about all of this.

"Alice gave me a ride home from school." Bobby rolled his neck. "I hurt my neck when Daisy knocked me back. I think I should go lie down too."

"I hate that kid," Milo grumbled, leading Bobby away by the hand.

"So what's going on?" I crossed my arms and stared up at Jack. "They've been here for an hour, and now you're all buddy-buddy with Peter and the demon spawn?"

"I thought you'd be happy I was getting along with Peter," Jack muttered. "And she's not a demon spawn. She's just a little kid, Alice."

"You don't know what she's capable of!"

"Yes, I do! Better than you do! I've been a vampire a lot longer than you, remember?" He shook his head and turned to walk to the kitchen. "I know a few things. I don't know why you always think I'm such a moron."

"I don't think you're a moron." I chased after him. "I just want to know what's going on. How come you're all pro-baby vampire, when you weren't before?"

"I'm not pro anything. Mae did a really stupid thing." Jack leaned against the island and lowered his voice, probably so Mae and Ezra wouldn't hear him. "But that's not Daisy's fault. She's still just a child who really can't control her actions. And I'm not saying we should let her run wild without recourse, but there's gotta be something better we can do than treating her like a monster."

"I'm not treating her like a monster. I just don't like it when she attacks me or my friends," I said. "You cared more about her safety than you did Bobby's."

"She wasn't attacking Bobby!" He rolled his eyes. "She was running around and playing with me and Matilda, and then she heard you guys coming and got excited. She likes Bobby, okay? She's thinks he's fun or something."

"Where is your dog?" I asked.

"She's outside now," Jack gestured vaguely to the French doors.

"Did Peter tell you that she kills animals?" I asked him. "She killed a wombat and tried to drink its blood."

"You can't drink animal blood." Jack shook his head and brushed it off.

"No, you can't, but she still tried." I rested my arms on the island and leaned in towards him. "I know she's not evil, but she's really, really dangerous, Jack."

"You sound like Ezra." He sighed and stepped away from me.

"Ezra knows things! He's not a bad person to sound like." I stood up straighter as Jack paced the kitchen. "How did you become such a big fan of hers so quickly?"

"She was just playing with dolls, being a little kid." He shrugged and scratched the back of his head. "And she just seems so small and helpless. I don't know." He shook his head. "I'm not really bonded with her either. She was just scared, and I didn't want to see her scared."

"Don't get attached to her, Jack. She can't stay here."

"I know." He walked over to me, his blue eyes looking sad and far away. Brushing a hair back from my face, he just stared down at me for a minute. "Are we okay?"

"Yeah, we're okay," I smiled up at him.

"Good." He wrapped his arms around me, and I leaned into him, resting my head against his chest. "You're getting pretty bad ass."

194

"What do you mean?"

"The way you pulled Daisy off Bobby. You're getting tough," he grinned. "You don't need me to protect you anymore."

"Maybe not. But I'll always need you." I smiled and pressed him tighter to me. "In other ways."

Ezra had been talking with Mae in their old room, but he came out by himself. He walked into the kitchen and stopped, but he didn't look at either me or Jack. He breathed heavily and his fists clenched and unclenched at his sides.

"Is everything okay?" I asked, pulling away from Jack.

"They need a place to stay," Ezra said, without looking up. "But they can't stay here. We don't have the room or the..." He shook his head.

"Where are they going to stay?" Jack asked.

"I don't know. I have to..." Ezra swallowed hard. "I have to go. Keep things safe here."

"Okay?" I said, but Ezra didn't say anymore. He walked out into the garage, leaving to do something that would hopefully help us sort this whole thing out. I looked back up at Jack. "Have you talked to Mae?"

"Not really," he shook his head. "She's mostly been talking to Ezra since she got here. And..." He shrugged. "I don't have much to say to her."

"You can't still be mad at her." I stepped away from Jack, and he shrugged and walked towards the French doors, where Matilda had started barking.

"I'm not." Jack opened the door. Matilda ran inside, shaking the snow off her fur. Jack stayed by the open door, letting the frigid air into the house. He leaned back against the doorframe and turned the handle back and forth.

"But you're not talking to her?" I asked.

"No, I'm not like avoiding her. I just…" He stared outside and shrugged. "I'm not mad about what happened. Like that she almost killed me. I'm over that. It's just the lying and sneaking around… But I'm not even mad about that." He sighed, as if that's not what he wanted to say at all. "She's just not who I thought she was."

"Jack, come on. She's the same person she always was. She never wants to see anybody hurt." I walked closer to him, petting Matilda when she ran up to me.

"Yeah, I know, and neither do I. But that doesn't mean I can lie and do whatever I want." He looked at me, his eyes grave. "I always thought she'd put everyone before herself, but she's been so selfish about major things. Not just lying to me, but what she's done to Daisy, and Ezra." He shook his head. "What's she done to Daisy is unforgivable."

"You really think that?" I asked quietly.

"Yeah. But luckily for Mae, I'm not the one that has to forgive her this time," Jack said. Matilda went over and jumped up on him, and he scratched her head. "As soon as Daisy's old enough to realize what Mae did to her…" He whistled and shook his head.

"Where is Mae?" I asked.

"I think she's still in Ezra's room. Why? Are you gonna go talk to her?"

"Yeah, I wanna see where her head is at with all of this and what she thinks they're going to do, since nobody else has any idea."

"Alright." He nodded once, but I couldn't get a read on how he felt. Lately, his emotions seemed murky, like he was trying to bury them too deep for me to feel. "I'll be outside with Matilda." He stepped outside, and the dog followed at his heels, even though she'd just come in.

I walked down to Ezra's room, feeling like I was creeping up on a stranger. I'd just seen Mae a few weeks ago, but my visit with her hadn't been that amicable. It had been months since she actually lived here, and it sounded strange hearing her voice as she sang softly to herself.

The bedroom door was slightly ajar, but I pushed it open a little farther, peering inside. Mae had made the bed and moved onto fluffing the pillows and tidying up. Ezra wasn't a messy person, but he'd let things fall to the wayside since she'd been gone. Whenever she cleaned, she always had a song on her lips, and she settled for something low and bluesy by Etta James.

"I see you lurking outside the doorway, you know," Mae said without looking at me. She folded a pair of Ezra's pants that had been crumpled on a chair and set them on the bed.

"Sorry," I mumbled and pushed the door the rest of the way open.

"You all don't need to hide from me. I'm not going to bite." She picked up a few other stray articles of clothing off the floor and began folding them neatly. "I had no idea Ezra would be such a slob

197

after I moved out. And I noticed that none of you have been doing the dishes."

"Bobby's the only one that eats. The dishes are his responsibility," I said, referring to the pile of dishes growing in the kitchen sink.

"He's a guest, and all you're capable of picking up a mess, no matter who made it." She'd folded his clothes and moved on to picking up the books and newspapers Ezra had strewn about the room. "You're all adults here, and you should act like it."

"Milo's not an adult yet," I corrected her and leaned back against the wall.

"How is your brother?" Mae stacked the books neatly, making sure all the edges matched up, and she paused for a moment. "He didn't talk to me much in Australia or when I got here. I felt like he didn't want me to be here, like he might be mad at me."

"He's good," I said. "But... let's be honest, Mae, we're all kinda mad at you."

"Hmm." She stopped straightening the books and touched at a strand of her hair before flitting about the room to pick something else up. "I didn't expect any of you to understand, but I hoped that you'd support me."

"We all understand where you're coming from. I get it completely." I stepped away from the wall, moving towards her, but she had her back to me as she folded a blanket on the chair.

"No, you don't. None of you. You just *think* you do."

"Fine. Whatever. I don't. Nobody understands your pain, Mae. Because it is so unique! Nobody's ever loved something so much they would do anything to save it, except for you, Mae. You cornered that market!"

"Don't condescend me!" Mae whirled on me, looking at me for the first time. "I didn't do anything to deserve your contempt! I've made a choice that doesn't even affect you!"

"How does it not affect me? You and 'your choice' are hiding out in my house, putting my family and friends in danger!"

"We'll be out of here first thing-"

"That's part of the problem too, Mae!" I cut her off. "We didn't want you out of our lives, but you left us with no other choice. You know she can't live here, not with us. So that means we can't live with you either."

"You know I didn't want to leave you." She tilted her head, tears filling her eyes. "I love you all so much, and I did want to spend the rest of my life with you. But I have let my family down too much. I had to save her."

"But at what cost, Mae?"

"I know." She wiped at her eyes and looked away from me, smoothing out nonexistent wrinkles on the bedspread. "I know what I've done. I know what she is." She swallowed hard and looked at me, meeting my eyes. "I won't leave her. I can't."

"Nobody's asking you to," I said finally.

"Thank you." She nodded and picked up Ezra's clothes to put them in the hamper. "How has Ezra been?"

"He's been doing better." I sat down on the bed, relieved to be talking about something lighter. "He's helping me with school now."

"Oh? I didn't realize you were going to school." Mae sounded surprised but happy.

"I'm not. At least not yet, but Ezra doesn't want me getting stupid. Or stupider, anyway." I shrugged. "I think I might go to high school next year. It's gotta be easier than what Ezra's having me do."

"Well, good. I'm glad to see you applying yourself." She smiled at me and sat down on the bed next to me. "I do worry about you, love. You and Milo and Jack. I care about you all a great deal."

"I know. Nobody's ever doubted that," I said.

"I'm happy to hear it." She reached forward, brushing a strand of hair back from my forehead.

"Can I ask you something?"

"You can ask me anything." Mae dropped her hands to her lap and sat up straighter.

"Before you turned Daisy, you had a big argument with Ezra." I looked down at my jeans and picked absently at them. "You said something." I squirmed, thinking of how I wanted to phrase it. "You implied that... I don't know. That Ezra might... treat me special, or something."

"Oh, that." She sighed and looked straight ahead. "Ezra does treat you special, both you and Milo actually. But so do I. So does everybody. Peter should've killed you, and I'm glad that he didn't, but... other vampires would've. Or maybe they wouldn't. I don't know with you."

"What do you mean?" I asked.

"There's something... different about you." Mae furrowed her brow. "I've never known what it was, but I've always felt it. The boys

200

had a harder time recognizing it because they already had a connection with you. Your blood bond makes it's harder for them to see that it's different, even though it should be obvious."

"I don't understand," I shook my head.

"Vampires in general seem drawn to you." She looked over at me. "And you're stronger. You adapted faster to being a vampire than anyone should."

"Milo adapted faster than I did," I said.

"Which only proves my point. There's something very different about you both." Mae eyed me, almost as if she was looking at me for the first time.

"I didn't adapt that fast," I shook my head. "And I had to fight to keep my bloodlust in check."

"Not as much as us. Ezra's told you the stories of when he first turned, of how other vampires had to be chained to keep from killing each other?" Mae asked, and I nodded. "We're all like that in the beginning. You know how Daisy… gets out of hand?"

"Yeah?" I nodded, surprised she was bringing it up.

"The only difference between Daisy and any other new vampire is that she gets hungry more often. That's what a new vampire is supposed to be like," Mae said. "And that's not what you were like or Milo. But Jack…" She shook her head. "Ezra had to hold him down once to keep him from killing the mailman."

"Seriously?" I raised an eyebrow.

"Seriously. You've adapted to this much better than anyone I've seen before."

"But why? Why are we different?" I asked.

"I don't know," Mae admitted wearily. "And in a fit of anger, I threw it Ezra's face. I wanted to get him to side with me, but I understand now that he can't and he never will. But I don't hold it against you. You're special, love." She smiled and put her hand to my cheek. "That's something good, not something to fear."

"Thank you. I think."

"How is Daisy doing?" Mae dropped her hand and stood up.

"Uh, good. I guess. She's lying down, with Peter."

"Good. She needed a nap after that flight." Mae went over to her luggage and flipped it open. "And I need a shower. That flight from Australia is unbearable."

"Oh, right." I stood up. "I'll let you... get to it."

"Sorry." She smiled sheepishly at me. "I should just shower while Daisy is calm and asleep."

"Yeah, that's a good idea," I nodded.

"It was nice visiting with you, though," Mae said as she pulled out clean clothes.

"Yeah," I nodded again and backed towards the door. "Do you guys know when you're leaving?"

"Not yet, but soon. Probably in a day or two." She looked sadly at me. "But you'll always be welcome, anywhere we end up."

"Thanks." I smiled and slid out of her room.

I missed Mae, but I didn't like having her here. It made everything feel tense and precarious, like at any minute it could all fall apart.

- 15 -

I started up the steps to my own room, thinking about how a shower would feel good myself, but I stopped when I heard something strange coming from the bedroom. Not strange *strange*, just completely unexpected. It sounded like Peter and Jack were being nice to each other.

"I'm just saying *Apocalypse Now* isn't the best war movie," Peter said.

"You can't say *All Quiet on the Western Front*! That movie is so boring!" Jack groaned.

"Just because something is in black and white doesn't make it boring," Peter said.

"Well, it doesn't matter. I don't own it so you can't borrow it. *Apocalypse Now* is the best war movie I own."

I climbed up the stairs and stopped outside the doorway, spying on them before they noticed me. Jack had opened the pocket door that hid his thousands of DVD's, and he stood in front of it, inspecting his collection. Peter sat at the end of Jack's bed while Daisy lay curled up in the bed, sound asleep next to Matilda.

"Don't you have *Saving Private Ryan*?" Peter asked, looking up at Jack.

"No. I'm not obsessed with war movies like you." Jack reached up and pulled one off the shelf. "I have lots of ninja movies, though. Or movies with robots. Those are good."

"I should be happy you're not pulling out something with ninja robots," Peter rolled his eyes.

"What are you guys doing?" I asked, tentatively stepping into the room.

"Just trying to find something for Peter to watch, but he's picky as all hell," Jack said.

"I'm not picky. I just don't love something just because it has explosions," Peter said.

"What's not to love about explosions?" Jack scoffed. "And besides that, I love lots of movies without explosions. Here." He grabbed a DVD from a shelf and held it out to him. "*Edward Scissorhands*. Nothing blows up the whole movie."

"But you have a crush on Johnny Depp, so that doesn't count," Peter shook his head.

"I do not have a crush on Johnny Depp." Jack rolled his eyes. "And whatever. Do you want a movie or not? You only have like a day to watch this thing. Do you want to spend all the time arguing about what movie it is you want?"

"Hey, don't rush me." Peter got up and went over to the rows of DVD's, brushing past Jack without comment from either of them. "I need to enjoy technology while I have the chance. Who knows where we're gonna end up after this."

"Where are you going?" Jack asked, taking a couple steps back so Peter could peruse his DVD's more easily.

"I honestly don't know. I'm hoping Ezra can figure something out." Peter grabbed a movie and flipped it over, reading the back. "I don't really want to think about it. My plan is to shower, relax, and sleep, because I'm not sure how much I'll get once we go."

"I see." Jack crossed his arms over his chest, and his face tightened a bit. He was worried about Peter, concerned about where the three of them might end up, but he didn't want to show it.

"Anyway, I think this one will do." Peter held up *Blade Runner*.

"That's what you picked?" Jack raised an eyebrow. "You were just mocking me about my robot movies. And I thought you wanted something about war."

"I like this movie." Peter shrugged. "I'm going to go downstairs and watch it, since that's where I'll be crashing tonight because my room is dismantled."

"I have some extra blankets if you want to crash in your old room," Jack suggested.

"No, I'm good." Peter walked past me, giving me a small smile, and paused at the doorway. "Is Daisy alright in here?"

"Yeah, she's fine for now," Jack nodded.

"Thanks." Peter waved at him with the DVD and headed downstairs.

I waited until I heard his footsteps disappear into the living room before I went over to Jack. "What was that about?"

"What?" Jack put back his movies on the shelf and glanced back at me. "I just lent Peter a movie. Most of his stuff is still in Australia."

"Yeah, but you were being... *nice*."

"I'm a nice guy," Jack laughed and pushed a button so the closet door slid shut, hiding all his movies. "And I don't hate Peter."

"That's not what you've been saying for like the past year," I pointed out, crossing my arms over my chest.

"Do you want me to hate Peter?" He looked at me, his eyebrows arched.

"No, of course not!" I said quickly. "It's great to see you getting along. It's just… strange."

"I know." He sighed and looked down at the floor, rubbing his feet along the carpet. "I hate the way Peter feels about you, and I *really* hate the way you feel about him-"

"I don't feel anything for him!" I interjected. Jack glanced up at me, and I knew I protested too loudly.

"Well. Whatever. I still don't like it." He shrugged. "But you spent two weeks alone with him in Australia, and that turned out fine. I think I can trust you to be around each other for like two days." He ran a hand through his sandy hair, disheveling it more. "And even if I can't, he's my brother, and he's in trouble. I don't want the last things I say to him to be in anger."

"That's really sweet, Jack." I touched his arm. "And it's really mature."

"No, it's not mature," he sighed. "I just can't hold a grudge. I'm a sucker."

"You're sweet, and I love you." I wrapped my arms around him and smiled up at him.

Jack leaned down and kissed me, his lips pressing warmly against mine. It started out gentle, but quickly worked its way into something more. His arms wrapped around me, pressing me hard against him. His skin burned hot against mine, and his emotions flooded me with their fervor.

"Jack," I breathed, putting my hand on his chest.

"Oh, right." His eyes went over to the bed, where Daisy lay buried amongst his navy comforter. He grinned when he looked back, but I felt how disappointed he really was. "If only there wasn't a small child on the bed, I would totally ravish you."

"I'm sure you would," I smiled.

"Too bad." He gave me a kiss on the forehead and pulled away from me. "I'm gonna hop in the shower."

"I was just gonna take a shower."

"I need the cold shower more." He walked backwards toward the bathroom. "Unless you wanted to join me."

"That would defeat the purpose of a cold shower, wouldn't it?" I asked.

"Maybe." He shrugged and pulled off his shirt, revealing the perfect hard contours of his chest and stomach.

He disappeared into the bathroom. I heard the water turn on a moment later, and he tossed his shorts out into the bedroom, enticing me to join him. I probably would've, if it weren't for Daisy in the room and Peter in the living room below us.

I shut the bathroom door without even peeking in on Jack, and he laughed. I looked over at the bed, and I knew I didn't want to hang out in here with Daisy. She still creeped me out. I didn't trust her alone with the dog either, so I called Matilda as I left the room, and she ran after me.

Peter was in the living room, sitting on the couch with his feet propped up on an ottoman. *Blade Runner* played on the TV, but he didn't seem to be paying attention to it. He had his fingers laced behind his head and he stared off at nothing.

"Are you okay?" I asked.

"What?" Peter looked over at me, as if he'd just realized I was there. "Uh, yeah. I'm great." He lowered his arms, crossing them over his chest, and sat up straighter so his feet were on the floor.

"You seem kind of spacey."

"Got a lot on my mind," he shrugged.

Matilda jumped on the couch next to him, and he scratched her head. I sat down at the opposite end of the couch, putting as much room between us as I could.

"I thought you said you weren't gonna think about it," I said.

"Trying not to." He gave Matilda one final pat than dropped his hand. He looked over at me, letting his emerald eyes linger on me just long enough where I had to look away. "How have you been?"

"Good, I guess."

"Even with Jane's murder?" Peter asked, and I shook my head. "She was murdered, right?"

"Yeah, she was. And they don't know who did it."

"I'm sorry to hear that," he said, and it really sounded like he meant it. I don't think I could ever get used to him sounding so kind. It added something to his already velvet voice that never failed to startle me.

"Me too," I sighed.

After that, we watched the movie in silence. I sat stiffly, afraid to move or do anything. I could feel Peter sitting next to me, doing the same thing. I'm not exactly sure what I was afraid would happen, but I knew I didn't want to risk it. I'd already hurt both Peter and Jack enough.

Jack bounded downstairs a little while later. His hair was still damp from the shower, and he ran his hand through it absently, sending little droplets sprinkling all over the room.

"How's the movie?" Jack asked, glancing back at the TV.

"Fine," Peter and I both answered quickly.

"Great." Jack pushed Matilda off the couch and sat down next to me, but he turned to Peter. "I was thinking. Why are you going with them?"

"What?" Peter asked.

"Why are you going with Mae and Daisy when they leave?"

"Because." His eyes flashed to me for a moment, then he looked away from both of us.

"Mae and Daisy don't need you," Jack went on. "And I know me and Bobby have a lot of crap in your old room, but we could clean it out. Well, we're gonna move soon anyway, but that's not the point."

"What is the point?" Peter asked.

"Why don't you stay here?" Jack asked. "This isn't your fight, the thing with Mae and Daisy. Neither of them are your responsibility."

"Thanks." Peter swallowed and stared down at the floor. "I mean, I appreciate it, Jack, I really do. Especially coming from you. But you know why I'm going with them."

"Come on, Peter." He gestured to himself and glanced back at me. "This thing between the three of us, it's stupid. I didn't realize how stupid it was until I saw you today. It's over, you know? I'm with Alice, and you're fine. We can just be... normal, again."

"I think you're being overly simplistic, Jack." Peter lifted his head to look at him.

For a minute, they only stared at each other. Finally, Jack nodded and looked away.

"Hello?" Leif called as I heard the French door swing open.

"Who is that?" Peter asked, and Jack rolled his eyes.

"It's *Leif*," Jack sighed and got up. "He practically lives here now."

"Oh, he does not." I stood up and went out to the dining room to meet him.

"Sorry. I didn't mean to just barge in." Snow clung to Leif's hair, and he brushed it out.

"You didn't barge in. You know it's never a problem when you visit," I smiled at him.

"Nope, no problem at all," Jack said. He shoved his hands deep into his pockets as he came into the dining room, and Peter followed more slowly behind.

"Peter." Leif's brown eyes widened at him. "I didn't know you were back."

"It's only temporary." Peter rubbed at his arm, but his eyes had hardened at the sight of Leif.

He'd spent some time with Leif when they'd both been part of the lycan pack, and as far as I know, they'd gotten along. Neither of them ever really talked about what happened there, but like Jack, I don't think Peter trusted Leif or his intentions here.

I moved closer to Leif. It'd been bad enough when just Jack had been around glaring at Leif, but with him and Peter both doing it, I felt like I had to move to defend Leif somehow.

"Really? Why is that?" Leif asked.

"We have to lay low. I don't want to trouble the family here," Peter said, giving away as little as possible.

"You're in trouble again?" Leif raised an eyebrow.

"Well, Peter isn't this time." I cut in with a nervous laugh, attempting to lighten the mood. "He's just helping out people who are in trouble."

"Alice, I don't think he needs to know our problems," Peter said.

"No, I don't," Leif agreed. "But if you need a place to hide out, I might know somewhere."

"Really?" Peter crossed his arms over his chest. "You know a place here?"

"Yes," Leif nodded. "I've had to hide out myself."

"What kind of trouble have you gotten yourself into, Leif?" Jack asked, his tone only pretending to be light.

With Jack and Peter standing there, glowering at Leif, I decided that I didn't like them getting along. I'd never really seen them agree on something before, but they'd apparently both decided to hate Leif, and it was really annoying.

"Hey, guys, Leif is offering to help out." I stepped closer to Leif, almost standing in front of him now to block Jack and Peter's unflinching stares. "And we need help. I think we should hear him out."

"Where is this 'hide out?'" Peter asked, doing air quotes with his fingers, and I rolled my eyes.

"Underground," Leif said.

"You mean like 'underground railroad' underground? Or like six feet under underground?" Jack asked.

"Actually under the ground." Leif pointed to the floor. "In tunnels."

"You want us to stay in tunnels?" Peter asked skeptically.

"No. I want you to stay wherever you want to stay," Leif corrected him. "I'm merely offering a place you can hideout. I'm not sure how much trouble you're in or how deeply you need to hide, but I know that this will work for whatever your troubles might be."

Peter didn't say anything for a minute and exchanged a look with Jack. Peter sighed and nodded.

"Let's check it out," Peter said. "We don't have anything to lose at this point."

Without bothering to tell anyone where we were going, we all left in the Jetta after a small argument. Jack wanted to take the Delorean, but that would mean taking two cars since it only sat two people. Peter told him to shut up and get in the Jetta, and to my surprise, he did.

I sat in the back with Jack while Leif gave Peter confusing directions to the entrance of the tunnel. Leif didn't drive, so he knew where things were by foot – cut through lawns and back alleys. Eventually, Peter figured out that Leif was directing him to an area underneath a bridge.

We parked next to the river and had to scale the icy slope to get below the bridge. Leif led us to a narrow hole in the cement wall of the underpass. He went in first, sliding through with ease, but Peter and Jack stood outside, staring at the hole.

"Do you think it's a trap?" Jack asked, his words barely audible over the sound of the river rushing past us and the cars rushing on the bridge above us.

"I don't know. It's a weird trap, if it is," Peter said, staring thoughtfully at the hole.

"Oh you guys are idiots," I scoffed. I pushed past them and crawled in through the hole. A chunk of concrete scraped against my back, but I just kept going.

"Alice!" Jack called after me, surprised I'd just gone in, but I didn't stop.

The tunnel had no light, other than the bit that came in from the hole. I could see, but not as well as I'd like. The walls were brick lined with several rows of thick, black wires. The floor was dirty concrete, and when I stepped inside, I saw vermin scatter, but I couldn't be sure if it was insects or rats.

"Well, this is sexy," Jack said once he'd climbed inside. "I can totally see Peter living it up here."

"This is just the entryway. I've got much more to show you." Leif turned and walked forward.

Peter had barely made it inside, but I followed Leif. Jack stayed right behind me, muttering things about rats and the smell, as we let Leif lead us through the twists and turns of the tunnel.

The brick walls eventually gave way to sandstone halls with arched ceilings. I ran my fingers along the walls, surprised to find that they'd been carved right from the earth. We climbed up a makeshift set of stairs carved into the stone, and we made it to an area that seemed much more habitable.

The floors were smooth concrete, with a small stream running down the center. From the smell of it, I'd guess it was a sewage line. The ceilings were rounded brick, but the halls were much wider than the narrow ones we'd walked through to get here. Dim yellow lights were spaced out along the ceiling, the only lights we'd encountered since we got here.

"I feel like a Teenage Mutant Ninja Turtle," I said, stepping over the sewage stream to follow Leif down the tunnel.

"Cowabunga," Jack said, and I smiled at him. He stepped after me and took my hand in his.

"And here we are." Leif gestured to an entrance off the side of the tunnel.

Jack squeezed my hand as we walked through the entrance. I think part of him still expected this to be some kind of trap, although I'm not sure why. Leif had been nothing but kind to us, and just because he couldn't explain it, it didn't mean Leif was bad.

The ceilings were shockingly high, at least twenty feet above us. Three of the walls were the same brick as the tunnel, lined with a few dim lights and a couple electrical boxes. The cement floor ended in a cliff, but I could see the smooth concrete wall thirty feet across from it.

I walked to the edge and stared up and down, but the wall across from it seemed to have no beginning and no end. A few pipes jutted out from it, letting water flow from it, pouring like never ending waterfalls into the bottom. The water smelled fresh and chlorinated, so I guessed it was clean water here, not the sewage from the tunnel.

"Wow. That's an impressive drop," Jack whistled, looking over the edge with me. He leaned farther forward than even I did, and his foot slipped on the moss that grew over the edge. I yanked him back from certain death, and he smiled sheepishly at me. "Sorry."

"I'm not sure how Mae would feel about that," Peter said, nodding towards the cliff. He turned and admired the cavern. "But the rest of this is good."

In one corner, a few blankets were piled up, next to a stack of books and a few items of clothing. Peter stepped closer to inspect it, but before he even got to it, he realized what it was. He looked back at Leif.

"You stay here?" Peter asked him.

"Yes." Leif shrugged. "It's quiet and dry here. Nobody bothers me."

"So, you're inviting us into your home?" Peter asked.

215

"You can say that, I guess." Leif turned away from Peter's apologetic expression and his bare feet padded on the concrete as he went over to the edge of the cliff. "It's a nice place to hide out."

"It is nice," Peter agreed. "But there are no showers or bathrooms."

"The sewer is in the tunnel," Leif nodded to the door. "The river is right outside for a quick wash up, but it's not that hard to leave if you need to do laundry or shower."

"But there aren't any people around," I said. "It'd be impossible for Daisy to get into trouble here."

"I don't know." Peter chewed the inside of his cheek mulling it over. "But we can't stay at home. Ezra won't let us even if it wasn't dangerous. This would work better than your place until we find a house that suits our needs."

"You think you can sell Mae on this?" Jack asked.

"I don't have much of a choice. I need time to find somewhere even more out of the way and uninhabited than where we lived before," Peter said. "That'll take some time. This will keep Daisy under wraps until then."

Peter and Jack started talking about what they could do to it make it more homey down here. Peter was good with home improvements, and Jack liked to pretend he was, so he joined in the discussion with unfounded enthusiasm.

I walked around, admiring the surprising detail in the architecture of the cavern. It was strange to think that a hundred years ago, people put more detail in building their sewers than they do in building most homes anymore.

Leif's pile of belongings looked sad in the corner. It consisted almost entirely of things we had given him. The comforters he had spread out were actually a Christmas gift from Milo to him. I'd thought they were a horrible gift since we didn't know if Leif even had anywhere to live, but Milo said that was all the more reason he'd need blankets.

The books had most likely come from Milo or Ezra. A thick copy of *Crime and Punishment* by Fyodor Dostoevsky was stacked on top of *War and Peace* by Leo Tolstoy. A few other Russian books were in the stack, and that made the copy of *To Kill a Mockingbird* sitting next to it stand out.

Before I'd even picked it up, I knew it was the same copy that I'd just finished reading. I flipped through the dog eared pages, and a makeshift bookmark slipped out. I snatched it before it fell to the ground, and my breath caught in my throat.

Leif had been using a picture of Milo and me as his bookmark. It'd been taken on New Years of this past year, and we both had on too much silver glitter. Milo had stuck it on the fridge because he loved the way his cheekbones looked in it, but it had gone missing a few days ago. I'd assumed it had fallen off and slipped under the fridge or the stove, but here it was. Leif had taken it.

"What do you think?" Leif asked from behind me, and I shoved the picture back in the book, afraid that Jack might see it. I had no idea what Leif would want the picture, and I tended to think his motives were more innocent than Jack did.

"Um, of what?" I turned to face him, forcing a smile so I didn't look as flummoxed by his picture thieving as I really felt.

217

"The cave." Leif smiled faded from bemused to concerned. "Are you okay?"

"Yeah." I smiled wider. "Yeah. I was just, um, admiring your books." I pointed to his pile of Russian literature with the copy of *Mockingbird*.

"I'm going through a Russian phase," Leif said, then gestured to the book in my hand. "I decided to take a break with some lighter reading after I saw you reading it."

"Oh. Well… it's a good book." I handed it to him. Part of me wanted to take the picture from it, but I really didn't think he'd do anything bad with it. It just felt weird that he'd stolen it.

"Ezra knows I have the books," Leif explained, misreading my reaction. "He lent them all to me."

"Ezra has a really big library," I nodded my head more quickly than I needed to. "He has a lot of really good books, and he loves to share them. He's really… good like that."

"Yes, he is." Leif paused. "Are you sure alright?"

Thankfully, I didn't have to answer that question again. A bat flew over ahead, distracting us all momentarily, and after that, Peter decided we should go. He'd already made a lot of plans of what he wanted to do with the space so Mae wouldn't freak out, and he had to get started on them.

Leif stayed behind when we left, and I took Jack's hand as soon as we stepped out into the tunnel. I'd never felt weird about anything Leif did before. As soon I'd met him in the forest of Finland, I had liked him, even though he was a member of the brutal lycan pack.

But something about stealing a picture of me and Milo. It felt personal in a weird way. Maybe it was because Milo was in the picture, too.

I understood a bit more the way Jack felt now. I knew that whatever connection I had with Leif, it was harmless. But when it came to my brother, I felt more protective. What exactly did Leif want with Milo?

- 16 -

"The promise I made to my parents," Bobby said, his voice low and gravelly, "the promise to rid this city of the evil that took their lives, may finally be within reach." He crouched low on the bars that surrounded the roof above Olivia's penthouse, surveying the city lights of downtown Minneapolis.

"What are you talking about?" I asked, pushing Violet off me. She'd nearly had me pinned to the ground, but I had put my hands flat on the ground and pushed up, almost doing a hand stand, and used my legs to kick her back.

"Are we gonna do this or are you gonna goof off with that idiot?" Violet asked, pushing a strand of her blond hair behind her ears. She hadn't even fallen back when I pushed her, and she stood in front of me, ready to pounce.

"Can't we do both?" I asked as I stood up.

"Alice, you're not even trying tonight," Violet said and her stance relaxed. "You shouldn't have brought him with you. He's just a distraction."

"No, he's not the problem." I shook my head and brushed gravel from the roof off my jeans. "And even if he was, that's good. I need to learn to fight with distractions."

"I guess," Violet muttered, kicking a stone with her foot.

She hadn't been happy that I'd brought Bobby with me tonight, but after we'd run into Jonathan the other night, I decided that Bobby needed to work on his defense training. Unfortunately, he wasn't really feeling it either.

"What are you going on about?" I asked Bobby as I walked over to him. He had one leg resting on the bar as he leaned over, and if Milo caught him doing that, he'd probably freak out and kill us both, but I didn't say anything.

"I'm Batman," Bobby repeated in that same gravelly voice.

"Oh, you're an idiot," I rolled my eyes and leaned on the bar next to him.

"Don't you ever feel like a superhero up here?" Bobby asked, his voice back to normal.

"Nope."

"Not even a little bit?" Bobby stepped down off the bar, probably tired of crouching, and pulled his Member's Only Jacket tighter to him. "Or how about a superhero with hypothermia?"

"I like the cold," I reminded him.

"So neither of you are gonna practice at all?" Violet put her hands on her hips and glared at us. She wore a tank top and yoga pants to train, and her pale arms had a bluish tint from the cold.

"Guess not." I turned to face her, leaning my back on the bar. "Where did you say Olivia was again?"

"I don't know." Violet shrugged. "She just left and said she'd be back in a few days. But she doesn't tell me much. I don't think she likes me."

"She left you alone in her penthouse and her club," I said. "I'm pretty sure she likes you."

From the way Olivia had been looking at Violet, I'd say she liked her a whole hell of a lot, but I didn't want to be the one to say that. I wasn't sure if Violet reciprocated those kinds of feelings, and I didn't want to screw up the arrangement they had if Violet felt weird about her benefactor having a crush on her.

"Since we're not training, do you think it'd be okay if we went inside?" Bobby asked through chattering teeth. He wore a knit cap, which kept his hair pinned back out of his eyes for his change, but the narrow scarf around his neck didn't do anything for him.

"Yeah, come on," Violet said and went over to the door that led downstairs to Olivia's place. She trudged down the steps, and Bobby scampered ahead of me, eager to get out of the cold.

"You still need to do combat training eventually," I told him as he pushed past Violet to get into the warmth of the apartment.

"I know. And next time I'll wear a cape!" Bobby declared. He ran into the apartment, rubbing his hands together. Olivia kept the place at about sixty degrees year round, but after the roof, it had to feel pretty good for him.

"You're gonna wear a cape?" Violet laughed, raising an eyebrow. "Oh yeah. Combat training is so gonna work for you."

"I'll take it off to fight," Bobby said defensively. "I just wanna survey Gotham with my cape flapping in the wind."

"Okay, I'm ignoring you, because you're just too stupid," Violet said and turned to me. "Hey, you have a car, right?"

"Oh, it's more than a car." I grinned broadly.

Peter was back and using his Audi to run around, Milo had the Jetta for school, Ezra was using the Lexus to do lord only knows what, and Jack wouldn't let me drive the Delorean. Which meant I finally got to take the bright red Lamborghini out on my own.

"Excellent. I don't have a car, and we're low on blood." Violet walked towards her bedroom. "Just let me change real quick, and we can run to the blood bank."

"It's only a two-seater," Bobby said, but Violet ignored him as she went into her room and shut the door behind her. "There's only room for two."

"You can make it work, or you can stay here," I shrugged.

"I don't wanna stay here," he scoffed. "I've never been to the blood bank."

"It's not that exciting."

"I don't care. I've never been, and Milo won't let me go." He looked at me severely. "I'm going."

When Violet came out, she informed Bobby that he would be sitting bitch. He tried to argue it, but she glared at him, and then he shut up. In the car, he sat in the middle over the hump, which proved to be quite problematic with the low ceiling. He had to crunch up, almost in the fetal position to manage it, and his feet were on Violet's lap, which did not make her happy.

Luckily for him, the blood bank wasn't that far away from Olivia's. It was a small, white box of building with an even smaller parking lot next to it. I had to park half a block down in front of a meter, but Bobby didn't mind the walk because he got to stretch out his legs.

224

Inside the building was white and sterile. Plastic chairs filled the waiting room, with battered magazines lying on a few. The posters on the wall of red crosses were purposely misleading. The vampire blood bank did everything it could to associate itself with the real blood banks.

To the casual observer, the only thing really strange about the place was that it was open 24-hours. Of course, it actually helped draw in donors, and the location helped too. The blood bank paid their donors, so a lot of them were junkies and drunks who needed fast cash.

A nurse sat at the reception desk in the center. She had bulletproof glass around her to protect her in case people tried to rob her, and from the scratches on the glass, I'd guess that people had tried.

"Hello." I smiled at her and leaned up against the desk.

"It's nice to see you again, Miss Bonham," the nurse smiled brightly at me, making me feel guilty for forgetting her name. I think it might be Janice or Francine.

"It's nice to see you," I nodded. Her skin looked too white under the fluorescent lights, and her blond hair was hidden under one of those nurse's hats that always come with Halloween costumes but nurses never wear in real life.

"How many bags will you be needing tonight?" Nurse Janice or possibly Francine asked.

"Um…" I tried to think. We weren't completely out at home, but we could use some. "Like… ten bags?"

"Very good." She punched something in on the computer. "And for you, Miss Williams?"

"Like twenty," Violet said.

"Very good." The nurse punched in a few more things, still smiling so wide. She reminded me of a *Stepford Wife* sometimes. "Will you be paying together?"

"Nope," I shook my head.

"Will you be charging to the Townsend account, then?" she asked, and I nodded. "Miss Williams, will you be charging to Olivia Smith's account?"

"Yes," Violet nodded.

"I just wanted to remind you that I sent an invoice out to Miss Smith last week," the nurse informed Violet, and then looked to me. "The Townsend account has been settled as of the fifteenth of January."

"Alright," I shrugged. "Good to hear."

"I'll be right back with your orders." Nurse Janice or maybe Francine got up and went through a door in the back to get our blood.

"How much does the blood cost anyway?" Bobby asked. He leaned on one of the plastic chairs behind us, and I turned back to him.

"I really have no idea. Ezra pays for it," I shrugged.

"I think it's kinda expensive," Violet said. "I know, before, I could never afford it. But I couldn't afford much of anything."

"This place isn't as exciting as I thought it'd be," Bobby said, looking around. "It's all kind of... ordinary. It reminds me of the Planned Parenthood where I get tested at."

"I told you." I leaned against the desk with my back resting on the glass, so I faced the front of the blood bank. "Was it worth sitting bitch for?"

"Maybe." Bobby picked up a nearby magazine. "Ooo, one of the Olsen twins might be pregnant!"

"I don't think they like being called the Olsen twins anymore," Violet said. Using her long fingernails, she carved a heart in the glass next to where she stood.

A bell chimed as a vampire pushed through the front door, and I smacked Violet's arm so she would stop making graffiti. I wasn't sure that anybody would care, but I didn't want to start trouble. The vampire was followed by two more, so I straightened up. Vampires in groups always scared me.

The first one that came through was tall with black hair and black eyes. He wore a leather jacket with a black shirt underneath. He might've been attractive, but all that black made him look like he was trying too hard to be a vampire.

The vampire that followed right behind looked like a young James Spader, like when he was being a dick in *Pretty in Pink* before he got all bloated like on *Boston Public*. He dressed like 1980's James Spader too, with the popped collar on his blazer.

The only female vampire in the trio looked oddly proper next to the two of them. Her hair was shoulder length and smoothed back, and she wore sensible flats with a pencil skirt. If she had a day job, I would peg it as a court stenographer.

"Hello," the black haired one said, and I decided that he was probably their leader.

Then I wondered if they even had a leader. Just because the three of them were together didn't mean they were a gang. Violet, Bobby, and I weren't a gang, but they didn't know that either. Maybe he thought I was our leader, or maybe Violet looked tougher.

"Hi," I said, because I wanted to establish myself as the leader, in case they thought they we had one.

"What you got there?" Young James Spader asked and stole the magazine out of Bobby's hands.

"Hey!" Bobby stood up to defend his magazine's honor, and I stepped forward.

"It's a rag mag. Like I care." Young James Spader tossed the magazine back at him. Bobby caught it, but he crumpled it up in the process.

"That wasn't very nice," I said, and Violet rolled her eyes at my attempt at standing up for Bobby.

"What are you gonna do about it?" Young James Spader stepped towards me.

"Dane." The dark haired vampire put his hand on young James Spader's chest, and I assumed that his name was Dane, and not Young James Spader.

"We don't mean any trouble," the woman said, stepping out from the shadow of the other two. Her eyes were large and innocent, but I sensed something sinister about her despite her button down appearance. "We just want to know if you've seen anything."

"Seen anything what?" I asked. Bobby had taken a few steps back, standing more behind me and closer to Violet. I'm not sure that he really needed to, but it made me feel safer.

"We're looking out for you. That's our job," the dark haired vampire gestured to himself and his comrades. "We just want keep you safe."

"I have no idea who you are or why you'd want to keep me safe," I said, but I stood taller. Out of the corner of my eye, I saw Violet tensing up too.

"I'm Thomas," the dark haired vampire said. "And this is Dane and Samantha."

"So?" Violet asked.

"We've seen you," Samantha said. Her eyes were on me and only me.

"You've seen me what? What are you talking about?" I asked, and I hoped I kept the fear out of my voice.

"We want to know what you've seen," Samantha said.

"Okay, look. I seriously have no idea what you're talking about." I held my hands up, palm out. From the look on Dane's face, it wouldn't take much to set him off. "I was here, with my friends, getting some food. That's it. We didn't see anything. We don't want to see anything. We're all good here."

"Yeah, well, we know that's bullshit," Dane said derisively, and he wouldn't even look at me when he spoke. Not out of fear but like looking at me was beneath him.

"We believe you're involved with the serial killer," Samantha said, ignoring her friend's inappropriate outburst at me.

"What?" My jaw dropped. "No, no. I'm not. I'm trying to find them, but I don't know who it is." Thomas and Samantha exchanged a look but neither of them said anything, so I blundered on. "And what do you even care? I was told that vampires don't give a shit because only humans were killed."

"We take life very seriously," Samantha looked at me gravely. "All life is sacred, even humans."

"Thanks," Bobby muttered when she smiled at him.

"If vampires don't care about human murders, then why do you?" Dane asked, picking at something on his fingernail.

"My friend was murdered," I said.

"You're friends with a human?" Thomas sounded surprised and eyed me up.

"Yeah. I am." I gestured to Bobby to emphasize my point.

"Interesting." Samantha's eyes flashed with something, and I saw a darkness flicker underneath.

"Whatever your involvement is with the serial killer, you need to let it alone. Now," Thomas said.

"Why should I?" I asked.

Before he could answer, Nurse Janice or Francine came out from the back room, carrying two coolers for Violet and me. Thomas wanted to say something, but when he saw her, his mouth closed. I glanced back at her and saw the same *Stepford* smile she always had.

"Hello, Mr. Hughes," the nurse said, setting the coolers on the counter. "Will you be needing anything from us?"

230

"Not today." Thomas smiled back at her, but it looked strained. He nodded to his associates, and the three of them turned and walked out of the blood bank, the bell above the door chiming behind them.

"Okay. That was weird, right?" I looked over at Violet.

"Yeah. Were they following you?" Violet narrowed her eyes at me.

"I don't know," I said, and my mouth felt dry. They had just walked in here, saying they'd seen me, and left without buying anything.

"They might be following you," the nurse said. We'd been staring at the front of the shop to watch the vampires as they left, but all three of us wheeled around to face her.

"Do you know who they are?" I asked.

"Yes, of course." She smiled and blinked her eyes, but said nothing more.

"Can you tell us who?" Violet asked, her words much snippier than I would've gone for.

"No. Confidentiality." Her smile turned apologetic, and she gave a helpless shrug.

"So there's nothing you can tell us about them?" I asked.

"Oh, no, I can tell you something." The nurse lowered her voice and leaned closer to the glass. "They aren't people you want to mess with. They're vigilantes. Miss Smith is familiar with them."

"Of course she is," I sighed. "And she's not here right now."

"Wait." Bobby pushed in between Violet and me to get closer to the glass. "Vigilantes? You mean like Batman?"

231

"What is with this kid and Batman!" Violet groaned.

"He's only the most awesome thing ever," Bobby shot back, glaring at her.

"Hey, you guys shut up!" I snapped, and they fell quiet as I turned my attention back to the nurse. "What are they vigilantes against?"

"Why, vampires of course." She stood up straighter and scanned the UPC symbol on the cooler. "Vampires can act out if someone isn't watching."

"And they're watching?" I asked. She punched something in the computer after she scanned the coolers. "Are they part of an organization?"

"No." The nurse opened the slide glass window and set the coolers in front of us. "You're all set."

"Is there anything else you can tell us?" I asked, and Violet grabbed her cooler off the counter.

"No, I'm sorry." She did the apologetic smile again. "Miss Smith probably knows more than I do, anyway. She used to work with them."

"Awesome. Thank you." I sighed and grabbed my cooler and turned to start walking out.

"Oh, you, sir!" The nurse pointed to Bobby. "Were you going to donate today?"

"Um, no, sorry," Bobby said, following us out. "I already give away too much for free."

As soon as we pushed the doors, I looked around. I half-expected the trio of vigilante vampires to be waiting outside to jump us, but they weren't. I wanted to walk quickly to the car, but I had to slow down to match Bobby's pace. Milo would kill me if I let something happen to him.

"Did Olivia leave any number for you to get a hold of her?" I asked Violet as I popped the trunk.

"No. She doesn't believe in cell phones." Violet tossed her cooler in the trunk, and I did the same.

"But this isn't necessarily a bad thing," Bobby said. "I mean, most vigilantes are good guys. They're on our side. They're trying to stop the same killer we are."

"Maybe." I slammed the trunk shut and got in the car. Bobby climbed in before Violet and arranged himself on the hump in the center, and then Violet got in. "But if these vampires think *I'm* with the killer, and they're out to get him, then they're out to get me too. And that's not good."

"Yeah," Violet agreed as I started the car. "And besides, that Dane guy seemed like a major douche."

"Yeah, and what was with his clothes?" Bobby asked. When I floored the car, he flew backwards, hitting his head on the glass.

"Hang on," I told him belatedly.

"That happens sometimes with the older ones," Violet said, referring to Dane's sense of fashion. "They get really, really out of touch with trends, especially if they live off the grid. Olivia's told me some about what she used to do. When she was working, she'd move around a lot. She usually only reentered society when she got called in."

"You mean somebody like summoned these guys to come here and take care of this?" I asked.

"I would guess so," Violet shrugged. "If they really are friends of Olivia's, they're probably more familiar with the area."

"Do you think she would've called them?" I asked.

"I doubt it. I mean, not without telling you at least."

"But why would anybody call them?" I rounded a corner fast, and Bobby flew into Violet.

"Get off me!" Violet shoved him back roughly.

"It'd be nice if you could take it easy," Bobby said, readjusting his hat.

"Sorry." I slowed down a bit as we got closer to Olivia's building.

"It's a vampire," Bobby said.

"What?" I glanced over at him.

"I said that earlier that a vampire is the serial killer," Bobby said. "That's the only reason those guys would get involved, right? I mean, assuming they are what that chick said they are."

"Holy shit." I stopped in front of the building, almost slamming on my breaks, and Bobby reached to brace himself on the dashboard. "You're right."

"You know, Olivia has never called herself a vigilante," Violet said, looking over at us. "She's a vampire hunter. And so are they." Her purple eyes met mine. "And we're both vampires."

"Oh, that's real deep," Bobby said sarcastically.

"You're lucky you're with her, or I would kill you," Violet said flatly.

- 17 -

I popped the trunk, and Violet got out of the car. She grabbed her blood from the back, and giving me one final wave, she went into the building. Bobby adjusted himself more comfortably in the seat and clicked on his seatbelt, and I pulled away from the curb.

"Do you think it was her?" Bobby asked as I drove us home.

"Who?"

"Violet. Do you think she's the serial killer?"

"No, of course not," I scoffed.

"Why not?" Bobby asked me directly. "She tried to kill you once before. You did kill her boyfriend. She just threatened my life. And she knows Jane."

"She didn't really threaten your life," I shook my head.

"Yeah, but she fits everything else." He got more excited and turned to face me. "The only thing we know about Jane's killer is that they knew Jane and they were a vampire."

"What about that branding thing?" I asked. "Violet was the one that told us about that."

"Exactly!" Bobby said. "She told us! It could be a total red herring. And we don't even know if Jane was branded. Even if it's true, it could be completely unrelated."

"Come on." I shook my head, but I couldn't refute his logic. I looked over at him. "You don't really think its Violet, do you?"

"No. I don't know." He shrugged and leaned his head back against the seat. "It *could* be her, though. You can't discount that."

"No, I guess I can't," I sighed. I didn't want to agree with him, but at this point, I couldn't cross anybody out.

"Well, who else do you think it could be?" Bobby asked.

"I don't know," I admitted. The truth is, I didn't really want to think it was anybody.

"What about that Jonathan guy?" Bobby asked. "He's a douche, right?"

"Yeah, he is, but being a total douche doesn't make you a killer," I said. "And right now, that's all I have on him. That he's douche."

"What about those three assholes we met tonight?" Bobby asked.

"Nah." I sighed. "I don't know. Maybe. I mean… maybe they're… I don't know. They might've, I guess, but since I know nothing about them, I can't say anything for sure."

"How about Leif?"

"What?" I looked at him and jerked the wheel.

"Hey, take it easy!" He held up his hand. "Watch the road. I'm just saying stuff."

"You can't possibly think Leif did it," I shook my head. "Why would he have any reason to do it?"

"He was part of a totally sadistic pack of lycan that already tried to kill you and Jane before," Bobby said. "Or did you forget that?"

"No, I didn't forget, but he did fight against them to save us." I gave him a hard look. "And he saved your life, too."

"Well, maybe he killed Jane for altruistic reasons. Like to protect you and Milo cause Jane is a bad influence."

"Why would he want to protect me and Milo?" I asked.

"I don't know." He shrugged. "But Leif does it all the time. Whenever I'm fighting with Milo about something stupid, he always comes in and defends Milo's honor, even if Milo's wrong. And I've seen him do it with you and Jack before. He's always protecting you guys."

"Well, that means he wouldn't kill Jane, because he'd know that hurts us," I argued lamely.

"Maybe." Bobby didn't sound convinced when he looked at me. "But you can't say for sure it's not him."

"I can't say for sure it's not anybody!" I wanted to throw my hands up in the air, but I was driving, and it would be better if I didn't kill Bobby. "It could be you, for all I know."

"No, it can't. I was in Australia with you when she was killed," he said. "The only people you know for sure didn't do it were me, you, Milo, Mae, Peter, and that brat of theirs." He shrugged. "Maybe Jack did it."

"Oh, Jack did not do it," I rolled me eyes. We rounded the turn getting closer to our house. "You can't tell Milo about those vampires we saw tonight, okay?"

"Well, duh," Bobby said. "And you can't tell Jack."

"I know." I hated having secrets from Jack, but he didn't need to freak out and worry.

When we got home, only Milo and Jack were there. Peter had taken Mae and Daisy down to show them how things were coming in the tunnel, and I wasn't sure if they were coming back to the house or not.

We found Milo in the living room, sitting on the floor next to the couch with a few of my textbooks lying around next to him. Jack had taken to the X-box, and he appeared to battling some kind of horrific demon in *Dante's Inferno*. He'd already beaten the game twice, but he kept coming back to it.

"Are you even reading any of these?" Milo asked, not bothering to look up from the law book he had opened on his lap.

"I've read some of it." I flopped down on the couch behind Milo. "I haven't yet today, but today's been busy." I reached over him and grabbed the book from him.

"How did training go?" Milo asked, looking back at me.

Bobby sat down on the floor next to him, snuggling up to him already, which was good. If Bobby distracted him with affection, Milo would be less likely to lecture me about my schoolwork or pry too much about what happened tonight.

"Great," I shrugged and flipped through the book.

"Did you kick Bobby's ass?" Jack asked, keeping his focus on the video game on the screen.

"Nah, Bobby didn't do a lot," I said. "He was too busy pretending to be Batman."

"If Batman were real, that's exactly where he'd hang out!" Bobby turned back to glare at me. "That building is like Wayne Industries!"

"You're just deflecting because you can't fight." Jack glanced away from the game to laugh at him.

"You're one to talk," Milo scoffed. "It's not like you can fight either."

"I can fight." Jack paused the game when Milo and Bobby laughed at him, and he looked back at us. "You guys really think I can't fight?"

"We've seen you fight, Jack," Milo said with a smirk. "We know you can't."

"Oh, it's on." Jack shut off the X-box and tossed the controller in the chair and stood up. "You wanna fight, little man?"

"Really?" Milo arched an eyebrow.

"Yeah. It's go time!" Jack pointed to his chest in some kind of weird dominant gesture, trying to stifle his own smile.

"Jack, you're really no good at trash talk," I said.

"Come on." Jack grinned at Milo. "Let's do this."

"Alright." Milo shrugged and got up, and I rolled my eyes.

Jack bounced around on one side of the room, rolling his neck, like he thought he was Muhammad Ali. Milo smiled and went about pushing all the furniture to the side of the room so they'd been less likely to damage things if they tussled.

"Bobby, you should probably move," I said, flipping a page in the law book that I was only half-reading.

Bobby did what he was told, climbing up on the couch next to me. I'm not sure exactly why Milo and Jack were fighting, since they'd never been the kind of boys that even play fought. It probably had something to do with the fact that Jack was all riled up from video games, and both of them were bored.

They both eyed each other up, grinning like idiots, and neither of them really knew how to start a fight. Any time they fought, somebody else had started it.

"You ready?" Milo asked, suppressing laughter.

"I was born ready!" Jack declared.

Milo rushed Jack half-heartedly, but Jack responded with as much intensity as he could muster. He sidestepped Milo and tripped him, but Milo caught his balance before he even stumbled. He turned on Jack, swinging his leg around, so he knocked Jack's feet out from under him.

Jack fell to the floor with a bit of a bang, smiling up at Milo and looking surprised. Matilda barked and wagged her tail. I didn't want her getting hurt in the fray, so I got up and let her out the back patio.

On my way back, I heard a horrible crashing sound, and I ran to the living room. Jack lay sprawled out in a pile of a broken chair, with a broken picture shattered on the floor behind him. Milo stood on the other side of the room, looking rather proud of himself.

"You guys! Mae's gonna be-" I stopped myself before I finished the sentence. Mae didn't live here. She wouldn't be mad about anything we destroyed because she would never know about it.

"Are you okay?" Bobby asked, his eyes wide. He got up off the couch to help Jack.

"Yeah. I'm fine." Jack shook his head to clear it, and a few bits of broken glass fell from it.

I went past Jack to pick up the picture. It looked like all squiggles and lines to me, but it was probably some kind of priceless work of art, so I worked to rescue it. Brushing glass and splintered wood from it, I scowled at the mess.

Bobby gave Jack a hand, and even though he didn't need it, Jack let him help him to his feet. Jack shook his head again, dismayed by what had happened.

"When did you get so strong?" Jack asked Milo, brushing debris from his tee shirt. "I used to be able to take you."

"We never really fought. You never really took me," Milo shrugged.

"Well, I could at least hold you back." Jack cocked his head, looking over Milo in a different light. "Now I don't think I could even do that. And you should still be pretty weak. You're only a baby."

"What does that mean?" I asked. Jonathan had said almost the exact same thing to me the other day, and I didn't fully understand it.

"He's only been a vampire for six months," Jack gestured to Milo. "He should be still getting his sea legs. Usually, the older you are, the stronger you are, but Milo slammed me like that." He snapped his fingers to demonstrate.

"You always said you're a lover, not a fighter," I said.

I stood up and held the painting out in front of me. It had a tear down the center, but maybe I could salvage it with some creativity and glue.

"What are you doing?" Jack asked, standing behind me.

"I'm trying to see if I can fix this."

"Why?" Jack asked.

"Cause you destroyed an expensive painting," I shot him a look.

"It's not expensive," he shook his head. "That's a reprint from Target. It cost like twenty bucks."

"Well…" I floundered for a minute. "You still shouldn't destroy stuff."

"What happened in here?" Ezra asked. His voice always boomed, so it made me nervous, even though he sounded more perplexed than he did angry.

"They were screwing around," Bobby answered quickly and pointed at Milo and Jack.

"Way to throw us under the bus," Jack said.

"Sorry." Bobby lowered his head as he cheeks reddened. "Ezra scares me."

"We were just playing around," Milo told Ezra. "We'll clean up the mess."

"I see." Ezra surveyed the damage and nodded once, then his russet eyes landed on me. "Alice, may I speak to you for a moment?"

"What?" I exchanged a look with Jack, who just shrugged. "Uh, yeah. Sure. Of course."

Ezra turned and walked back to his den. I handed the painting to Jack and stepped over the rubble. Tucking my hair behind my ears, my mind scrambled to think of what I had done wrong. I had fallen a bit behind in the schoolwork Ezra assigned me, but I'd been really busy lately.

Well, maybe not *really* busy. But Peter and Mae had thrown everything off, and I was still training and trying to find Jane's killer, and I'd been hassled by those vampire hunters tonight. So, Ezra couldn't blame me for being ten pages behind in a law textbook meant for college students.

Maybe he was angry at me for not keeping the boys in line. Mae had always done that, or at least tried to. Since she'd been gone, I'd tried to step up and do my part, but it was hard being the only girl in a house filled with adolescent males. Even if they weren't really adolescent, they sure acted like it most of the time.

By the time I reached Ezra's den, I'd thought of a million apologies and excuses I could give him.

"So… you wanted to see me?" I said, barely stepping into the office. I hid by the door, my hands folded behind my back.

"Would you close the door behind you?" Ezra gestured to the door and sat down at his chair behind his desk.

"Uh… yeah." I shut the door and swallowed hard.

"I'm assuming you don't want Jack to know you're tracking that serial killer?" Ezra asked. He looked up at me with a bemused expression, noticing my anxiety.

"No. Why?" I narrowed my eyes at him.

"Well, I've been doing some digging around, like you asked," Ezra said.

"Really?" I hurried the few steps forward so I was right in front of desk. "What'd you do?"

"I found out this." He typed something on the keyboard in front of him, then turned the monitor around so I could see it.

The screen showed a red mark, so swollen it was hard to decipher. I leaned in closer, squinting at it. It was shaped in a U, just like Violet had said. I could tell there were more details in the marking, even if I couldn't make out what they were.

"Is that a horseshoe?" I asked.

"Not exactly." He clicked the screen and a different picture appeared.

This one was the same as the first, expect it had healed up more. The U had some kind of design on it, like a crosshatch pattern. The left side of the U was thinner than the right, and the right had some kind of disfigured knob at the end.

"Is it a serpent?" I tilted my head, hoping viewing it from a different angle would help.

"It's a dragon." Ezra pointed to the screen, touching on the underbelly of the U. "The wings are tucked into the sides there." The crosshatch pattern I saw were scales, and the disfigured knob was the head. "The design doesn't hold up well when it's been seared into flesh, but whatever made the brand was quite detailed."

"This is the brand?" I leaned in even closer, as if getting nearer would solve anything.

"Yes. This one here-" he nodded to the second picture that was displayed, "- is a picture taken from a girl that was picked up downtown for prostitution."

"The police know about bloodwhores?" I stood up straighter and walked around the desk, so I could sit on the edge of it next to Ezra. He turned the screen back to face himself more and leaned back in his chair.

"Most of them, no," he shook his head. "She was picked up for the old fashioned kind of prostitution, but she's definitely a bloodwhore."

"Did she say anything about the guy who branded her?" I asked.

"Not that I could find out, but I doubt she said anything. Bloodwhores are loyal to a fault." He exhaled deeply and stared at the screen. "The first picture I showed you, that was from a body of one of the slain girls."

"Jane?" I whispered, a lump swelling in my throat.

"No. I wouldn't show you that." His dark eyes met mine, and I nodded my gratitude.

"But this is good, right?" I pushed any sadness I had about Jane out of my mind. "This is the link I wanted. Whoever is branding the girls is the killer."

"It seems that way," Ezra agreed. "It could be a coincidence, but the reason the marks are so hard to see on the dead body is because they were fresh. He did it right before he killed them, so they didn't have a chance to heal."

"Do you know that it's a 'him' for sure?" I asked.

"No," he shook his head. "But I do think it's a vampire."

"Why?"

"For one thing, they all had scar tissue from repeated bites."

"How do you know that?" I asked.

"I saw the autopsy report," Ezra said offhandedly.

"How did you manage that?"

"I know people," he shrugged and leaned more to the screen. "But the big clue is this symbol."

"A dragon?"

"It was long believed to be a symbol for Dracula. 'Dracul' means dragon." Ezra nodded at the dragon brand on the screen.

"Wait. You're saying *Dracula* killed Jane?" I scoffed.

"Of course not." Ezra shot me a look like I was a moron. "I'm saying that whoever did is marking his girls with the symbol of a vampire. They want people to know a vampire did this."

"Is that how they died, then? By vampire bite, I mean?"

"No. They were all stabbed." His brow furrowed.

"Wouldn't it make more sense for him to kill them like a vampire if he wants people to know that is a vampire?" I asked.

"One would think so, at first. But it's a clean death." He looked back at me. "No blood. No nothing. If he wanted to make an impact, he needed a violent death."

My mind flashed back to the crime scene photo I'd seen in the newspaper. All the blood staining the sidewalk from Jane's body, and my stomach twisted.

"Why?" I stared down at the oriental rug on the floor and swallowed. "Why would he want to do that? Why would anybody want to do that?"

"I honestly have no idea." Ezra watched me, and he put his hand gently on my leg. "Are you alright? I didn't tell you this to upset you. Maybe I-"

"No, thank you." I shook my head and smiled wanly at him. "I needed to know. I'll be fine."

"I shouldn't have told you that. I looked into this a few days ago, but I've been debating telling you." He chewed the inside of his cheek, his dark eyes going far away. The pressure from his hand on my leg intensified. "You can't go after him alone, do you understand me?"

"Yeah, of course not," I said. In the back of my mind I wondered if Ezra would count Bobby as back up.

"Search all you want, but if you get close, call me." His dark eyes never left mine, and the severe expression on his face made me too nervous to do anything but nod. "You cannot take him on your own. He is a vampire without a conscience, and we have no idea what his motivations are. That makes him a very dangerous adversary."

"I understand," I nodded. When he looked away and his hand loosened on my leg, I let out a deep breath.

"I shouldn't even have looked this up for you." He leaned back in his chair, his head resting on the back, and he swiveled the chair slow from side to side.

"Why did you?" I asked. "I mean, thank you. I appreciate it. But I didn't think you would."

"I don't know." He fell silent for minute. "I wanted a reason to be away from here, and helping you on your goose chase seemed like a viable option."

"Oh." I realized I hadn't talked to him that much lately, and not at all since Mae came back. "How are you holding up with everything?"

"I've been through worse." He smirked, but it didn't hide the pain in his eyes. He must've known that because he turned and faced the monitor.

"Have you talked to her since the first night she got here?" I asked, and Ezra shook his head. "Why not?"

"Alice, you know why not," he sighed. To avoid the conversation, he began clicking things on the computer, zooming in and out on the dragon brand on the girl's arm. "I didn't have anything to say to her while she was gone, and I don't have anything to say to her now."

"She's your wife, Ezra."

"I am fully aware of who she is." His words were clipped, and when the mouse didn't move the way he wanted, he slammed it on the desk. "Damn thing is never working."

"Don't take it out on the computer because you're mad at her," I said.

"I'm not mad at her. Right now, I'm rather annoyed with this conversation." He glanced over at me, but I wouldn't be deterred.

"Why don't you go with her?"

248

"And live in a sewer?" Ezra scoffed. "No. She and the child can live happily after like a sewer rat. They don't need me."

"Don't get bitter." I wanted to reach out and touch his shoulder, but I wasn't sure how he'd react. "I get you're angry and hurt and sad and you still love her, but... don't get bitter over this."

His shoulders slacked a bit, and his expression softened. Turning his head toward me, he didn't lift his head or look at me.

"I wasn't lying, Alice. I have been through worse, and I'll make it through this. I appreciate your concern, though."

"No problem."

Ezra had gone back to staring at the computer screen, so the conversation seemed to be over. I thought of telling him about the vampire hunters we'd run into at the blood bank, but he didn't need to worry about that now. The drawn look on his face let me know he already had too much on his mind.

I'd made it over to the door and opened it when he stopped me.

"Alice, remember what I said. Don't go this alone."

"I won't." I smiled, and even I wasn't sure if I was lying.

Jack stood in front of the full-length mirror, holding his tee shirt bunched up in his hands. With his back to the mirror, he kept twisting and turning, trying to get a good view of his back. After watching him for a few seconds from the hallway, I went into our bedroom.

"What are you doing?"

"Something hurts." He craned his neck around, stretching it so far it looked uncomfortable. "In my lower back. But I can't see what."

"What do you mean something hurts?" I walked over to him. Vampires feel pain, but it usually only lasts a few seconds, unless it's a major injury that takes a long time to heal, or we're really low on blood, which slows the healing time.

"I don't know. But it hurts." He kept moving around, so I put my hand on his back.

"Stop. Let me look."

When he finally quit moving, I saw it. In his lower back, just above the waistband of his pants, he had a large bump. A wooden splinter from the broken chair downstairs had gotten lodged in his smooth muscles, and it looked angled like it was digging in is spine.

Only a bit of the end was sticking out, but I grabbed it with my fingers and yanked it out.

"Ow!" Jack winced. I held the splinter up to him. It was about half an inch thick and three inches long. "That was in my back?"

"Sure was."

"That sucks." He inspected it for a minute, then set it down the dresser behind him. When he started pulling on his shirt, I stopped him.

"What are you doing putting on your shirt?"

"What are *you* doing?" Jack grinned, raising an eyebrow.

"I don't know. After I saw the way my kid brother whooped you tonight, I thought I'd see if you wanted to try your luck against me."

"Sorry. I can't fight you." He bit his lip when he smiled, his blue eyes appraising me.

"Cause you know I'll win?"

"I don't hit girls." Jack shrugged helplessly.

"That's probably a good policy." I stepped towards him, and he laughed. "Too bad that won't stop me."

I put my hands on his chest. He reached up to wrap his arms around me, but I pushed him back. Not hard, but he stumbled back and fell onto the bed. I climbed on top of him, straddling him between my legs, and he put one hand on my hips. My hair fell into my face, and using his other hand, he tucked it behind my ears.

"What's all this then?" Jack asked, smiling up at me.

"I don't know. I feel like I haven't seen you much lately."

"You haven't," he agreed. "You're gone all the time." He tilted his head, his expression growing more serious. "What have you been doing, Alice?"

"Training a lot," I said. I didn't want to talk about this, not now. This wasn't the time when I wanted to lie to him. "I don't know. I've been around."

To silence anymore questions, I leaned down and kissed him. His lips felt hesitant on mine, so I pushed against him, but his skin remained cool.

"What?" I stopped kissing him.

"Are we okay?" Jack asked.

"Why wouldn't we be?"

"I don't know." His forehead crinkled with confusion. "I feel like we've been fighting a lot lately, and I don't know where you go." He swallowed. "I feel like... something's wrong."

"Nothing's wrong," I reassured him. "I love you, remember? I chose this life to spend eternity with you, and it's only just begun. You can't start questioning it already."

"No, I'm not questioning it." His smile came more easily now. "And yeah. I know you love me. I just... you'd tell me if something was going on, wouldn't you?"

"I tell you everything, Jack," I lied, and it hurt a little to say that. It used to be true, and it would be again, but right now, I just couldn't tell him everything.

"Good."

He reached up, burying his fingers in my hair, then pulled himself up to kiss me. This time, his kisses felt like they always did. I loved the desperate way he kissed me, like he was afraid to stop. Hot tingles spread over my skin, and my stomach fluttered.

When he sat up, he kept his hand on the small of my back, holding me to him. Barely taking his lips from mine, he slipped off my shirt, pulling it over my head. With surprising dexterity, he unhooked my bra, and pressed my bare skin against his. My flesh seared against him.

His heart pounded hard and fast, echoing over my own. He flipped me on the bed, so I lay on my back, and somehow, he slipped my pants and panties off in the process. He struggled to undo his own, and my fingers worked quickly to unfasten the button.

He laughed, sending fresh tingles through me, and then his lips were all over me. Kissing my belly, my chest, my shoulders, my neck. I raised my chin, allowing him to bite me if he wanted, but he didn't. He hovered over me, his faded blue eyes meeting mine.

"Not this time." Something in his smile looked sad, and his regret came off faintly, buried underneath his excitement. "For once, I want to love you the way you were meant to be loved. Without all the… vampire stuff."

"I don't understand." I reached up, running my fingers through his hair and my thumb on his temple.

"I know." He laughed, but it had a strange hollow sound to it that broke my heart. He looked at a spot above me instead of at me. "I turned you into a vampire without giving you a chance to learn what it really meant. And I said I did it to protect you, and I did, but maybe…"

"I know you did it because you loved me and you wanted me with you always."

"Yeah." He lowered his eyes and swallowed hard. "You regret it. I know you do, and… I did this to you."

"Jack, no," I shook my head. He had has arms on either of side of me, holding himself up, and I ran my hand over his arms, trying to comfort him.

"You rushed into something you didn't understand because it was what I wanted, and you can't take it back."

"I don't want to take it back," I insisted, but I wasn't sure of that anymore.

"Come on, Alice." He shook his head. "That's why we've been fighting so much. Everything we've been arguing about, it all boils down to the fact that you don't want to change. You don't want to be this *thing* that drinks blood. I made you into a monster."

"No, Jack! You did not! I'm not-" I stumbled, trying to think of what I meant. "We're not monsters. Okay? You just gave me forever with you. I want to be with you. I love you."

"I know you do. That's what makes this so much worse." When he looked at me, he had tears swimming in his eyes, and I gaped at him.

"I'll never regret being with you," I told him honestly.

"And I'll never stop regretting doing this to you."

Lying there naked, as close as two people could be, I had never felt such distance between us. The problem was that Jack was right. While I loved him and I did want to be with him for as long as I was alive, I didn't want to be a vampire. I didn't want to be a monster that hunted and hurt people, that lived an endless life without purpose, wandering the earth without ever contributing anything.

But I didn't blame him for that. I had made a choice, and even if I'd rushed into it, that had been my fault, not his.

I couldn't say anything to ease his guilt, so I leaned into him and kissed him again, this time hungrier and more intense. I wanted to make his pain go away, I wanted him to feel how much I loved him, how desperately I needed him, and how I never, ever wanted to live without him.

He slid inside of me, and I buried my fingers in his back, pressing him close to me. His love surged through me, but it was tinged with something else. His own regret held it back, and even when he kissed me, the closeness I desired escaped us.

Afterwards, Jack held me in his arms, but he pretended to be asleep, even though I knew he wasn't.

I couldn't sleep, and I felt too restless to even pretend. I got up, took a shower, and got dressed. In the bedroom next door to mine, both Milo and Bobby were sound asleep, and I hated them for it. Milo'd been going to bed earlier because he had to get up for school, and Bobby had apparently beaten his insomnia for once.

Since I had nothing to do, I thought I would eat. Drinking blood didn't knock me out the way it did before. In fact, other than when I drank fresh blood, like when I bit Jack, the blood had been energizing me lately. I'm not sure if that's exactly what I wanted right now, but my veins felt a little dry and my stomach grumbled.

It wasn't until I opened the fridge that I realized it had been over a week and a half since I ate last. And I was barely even hungry.

Feeling rather stunned by this realization, I thought about ignoring my phone when it rang in my pocket. But it could be important, so I shut the fridge door without getting a bag of blood and got the phone.

"Hello?" I answered.

"Alice?" Mae said. Or at least I think that's what Mae said. Her end of the phone crackled with static. "Al-" The phone cut out for a second. "-glad I finally-" A loud blast of static cut her off.

"Mae? What's going on? Where are you? I can barely understand you."

"-damn tunnel! I've been trying but the call-" She cut out again, and I sighed.

"Mae! I can't hear you! What do you need?" I asked.

"Towels! We need-" Static. "-bring them here?"

"Yeah, fine. Sure. I'll bring you towels," I said. Mae started to say something else, but the call dropped, which was just as well. I didn't want to listen to the static anymore.

I had nothing better to do, so I went to the bathroom and gathered up a bunch of towels. I'm not sure how many they needed, so I just grabbed a lot. I thought about grabbing more stuff, like blankets and pillows, but Peter had already gotten a lot of stuff to make the place livable.

Since no one was around to stop me, I took the Lamborghini, but I parked it out of the way when I get to the bridge. A bright red sports car parked right by the underpass would stick out. Carrying a stack of towels down a slippery ravine proved more difficult than I had thought it would be, but I managed.

Peter had torn out more of the concrete, so the hole into the tunnel was much larger than it had been before. I could stand up and walk in, and there was still plenty of room around me.

Before I even got to the cavern where they were staying, I could hear Daisy's voice echoing off the walls. She had a lovely singing voice, especially for a small child, but she was butchering the lyrics to "Hey Jude."

I found her in the tunnel just outside of the entrance to the cavern. Her blond curls were tied back in a ribbon, and she crouched down on the concrete. A tub of fat sticks of colored chalk was spilled out next to her, and she scribbled furiously at a picture on the ground.

"Hey, Daisy," I said, walking over to her. She appeared to be coloring a picture of a flying, purple hippo, but I could be wrong.

"Hi, Alice." She glanced up at me, but her concentration was clearly on the picture.

"How are you doing?" I asked.

"Good. I got new chalk today cause I was bored. Mae says we can't have music or Sesame Street down here. I hope we move soon."

"Yeah, that'll probably be good," I agreed. "Is anyone else around here?"

"Peter's inside." Daisy pointed to the entrance. "Mae is gone, and I don't know where that other guy went."

"What other guy?" I asked, tensing up.

"I don't know," she shrugged. "The other guy that lives here."

"Oh, Leif?" I had actually forgotten that he'd be staying here too, and my stomach twisted. I hadn't talked to him since I found that picture of Milo and me. Then I remembered what Bobby had said about Leif being a killer, and that didn't make me feel any better.

"That's a silly name," Daisy commented.

"It sure is. Well, I'll let you get back to your coloring," I said, and she just nodded.

The cavern looked much better than it did before, but you could only dress up a sewer so much. Mae had draped brightly colored curtains all over to add separations and to cover up the walls. In one corner, Daisy had a massive pile of toys and coloring books. Three mattresses had been made up and sat in different areas, and Peter laid on the one closest to the cliff, reading a book.

"Hey, Peter." I walked over to him and dropped the towels by the bed. "I brought you some towels."

"Oh. Thanks." He set aside his book and sat up. "Mae didn't think you heard her. She ran to Wal-Mart to pick up more supplies."

"Why didn't she send you?" I asked.

"Apparently, I forgot too much stuff the last time I went."

"I see." I looked around the cavern. "You've really dressed up the place."

"It's better, I guess," Peter shrugged. "I was busy all day looking for somewhere to else to move."

"Did you find anywhere?" I asked, sitting next to him on the mattress.

"Not yet. But we will soon."

"That's…" I leaned forward, resting my arms on my knees, and didn't know what to say. It felt mean saying it was good that he was leaving soon. "Why are you leaving with them?" He gave me a look. "No, I mean, you can go anywhere. Why are you leaving with them? As opposed to anywhere else on earth."

"Contrary to popular belief, I don't want to wander the earth alone," Peter said. "Mae and I were never as close as even she and Jack were, but I've always cared about her. I want both her and Daisy to be okay.

"And I'm doing it for Ezra too," Peter went on. "Ezra's done everything for me, for Mae. He's been the rock that held together a lot of shit." His voice went low as he thought of what they'd been through together. "But he can't protect Mae from this, and I know it kills him. So I'll go with her, I'll take care of her, because he can't."

"How is Daisy doing? Is she better here?" I asked.

"Not really." He glanced towards the tunnel, where Daisy had begun to sing the theme song to Sesame Street. "She wakes up screaming all the time because she's in so much pain."

"Pain?" I asked. "Her transformation is long over. She shouldn't be in pain."

"It's not from that," he shook his head. "She's so hungry, all the time, and it leaves in her almost constant agony. A child's body really isn't meant to handle the change."

"Oh my gosh." I swallowed hard, listening to her sing. "What does Mae think about all of this?"

"I don't know," Peter sighed. "I think she's just starting to realize exactly what's she done to Daisy. Up until now, she's been able to justify it that she saved Daisy, that the life she gave her would be better than death. But with Daisy being in so much pain, I don't think Mae can say that anymore."

"I'm sorry," I said, unsure of what else to say.

"Not everything with Daisy is horrible, though," he said. "Some of it's just weird. She keeps trying to chase down rats and kill them, so I have to stop her from doing that." He raised his eyebrows. "She eats cockroaches."

"*What?*"

"She catches them and eats them whole, and then she gets really sick and throws them up because she can't digest a bug. That's why we need the towels." He ran a hand through his hair and exhaled. "Along with the bugs, she throws up blood, so we have to feed her two or three times a day to keep her to keep her hunger down and her pain at a tolerable level. We're going through so much blood."

"I'm sorry," I repeated.

"Well, on a positive note, she's learned to say the alphabet in French," Peter said.

"What? Why?"

"Mae thinks it's good for her brain." He shrugged. "Daisy's actually really smart. She's just... uncontrollable and blood thirsty."

"Well, that's always fun."

"What about you?" Peter turned to me, his green eyes staring through me the way they always seemed to. "How are things in your life?"

"Great," I lied. I could never tell him about what's going on with me and Jack, especially since the two of them were actually repairing their relationship. "I've been training a lot, so I'm getting pretty strong."

"Good." He smiled, and it made me feel weird. Peter smiled so rarely, so when he did, it felt sorta magical, like a shooting star. "Now that's one less thing I have to worry about."

"What?" I rested my head on my arms and watched him.

"You." He looked away and picked at something on the concrete by his foot. "I still will, I'm sure, but at least in some part of mind, I'll know you're safe."

He picked up a stone and tossed it off over the cliff. We listened for it to hit, but we never heard a sound.

"How far do you think it goes?" I leaned forward, straining to see the edge.

"I have no idea. But if Mae asks, it's not that far," he said. "She started freaking about Daisy falling to her death, but I think Daisy's smart enough not to jump off a cliff." He cocked his ahead. "Then again, she does eat bugs."

"It wouldn't really be that bad if she did fall off, would it?" I whispered and felt like the worst person ever for just saying it aloud. I could hear her in the tunnel, a little girl singing a song and coloring with chalk. "Never mind. I didn't mean it."

"You know what the worst part of it is?" Peter asked, still staring off at the cliff. "She grows on you. I know she's an abomination, and she's gonna end up hurting people and millions of defenseless cockroaches. But... she spent an hour learning to braid

Mae's hair last night, and when she concentrates, her face gets all scrunched up, and she sticks her tongue out the side of her mouth." He looked over at me and smiled, and when I didn't say anything, he shook his head.

"I don't know," he said. "You had to be there I guess."

"I guess."

"I never had kids," Peter said, somewhat abruptly. "Ezra did, and Mae did, obviously. I can't remember if I ever even wanted kids." He furrowed his brow. "When I became this, I never thought about it. I shut it out." He sighed. "The same way I tried to shut you out. I'm not very good at keeping things out, I guess."

"I'm glad you don't," I told him quietly, and he looked back at me, his eyes meeting mine in a way that used to take my breath away. It still did a little, but I tried not to show it.

"I'm going with for her too." He kept his eyes on me, but I knew he meant Daisy. "And I'm not totally miserable. I want you to know that. This isn't what I had planned or even what I thought I ever wanted, but... I'm happy helping Mae raise Daisy, in my own twisted way."

"Good." I swallowed hard, gulping down the sadness and relief that mixed inside me.

For so long, I'd been afraid that Peter would never be happy again. Not because I was so fabulous that I didn't understand how he could be happy without me, but because I thought he'd closed himself off to happiness. That he'd been hurt one too many times, and I'd contributed to that.

But he hadn't. In his own way, even Peter had found happiness with the choices I made.

"So, you're doing training?" Peter looked away from me. "What does that entail?"

"A lot of fighting, mostly." I rubbed my hands over my arms, trying to stifle the emotions I felt. "Um, like working on my agility and mastering my strength. Stuff like that." I shrugged. "I wish we worked more on tracking, though."

"Tracking is easy," he said.

"Maybe for you." I'd been tracking the killer for weeks and had barely come up with anything.

"For all vampires," he said. "Just bite them."

"What are you talking about?" I looked over at him.

"You can track whoever you bite, especially if you have an emotional connection," Peter explained, and he gave me a look. "Come on, you have to have realized that by now."

"No, I-" I furrowed my brow. I'd bitten both Jack and Bobby, so I tried to concentrate on them, to see if I could get any reading on them. I couldn't be more bonded with anyone than I was with those two, but I didn't feel anything. "I can't track anything. I have no idea what you're talking about."

"You can master it better if you try, but you'll really only feel it if they feel threatened," he said. "Like if they're hurt or in danger. But if you're with Jack and you see him get hurt, you probably wouldn't notice the tracking, because you're already witnessing it and feeling it. You understand what I mean?"

"I think so, but…" I trailed off, trying to think if Jack or Bobby had been in danger when I hadn't been around. Somewhat disturbingly, I realized that they hadn't, and Bobby had been in a lot of trouble lately. I was really, really bad luck for Bobby.

"That's how I found you," Peter said.

"What?" I pulled myself from my thoughts and looked up at him.

"That night that those vampires were following you, back when you were still mortal," Peter said.

I had walked downtown by myself to talk to Jane, and on the way back to my apartment, Lucian and Violet had jumped me. Peter had come out of nowhere and killed Lucian, thus saving my life.

"How did you know?" I asked.

"I had been around town. I came back for you, and I bit you." He lowered his eyes, and though he tried to hide it, I heard a tightness in his voice. "But I tasted Jack on you, so I… I left, but I stayed around town, deciding what to do.

"That night, when the vampires were after you, I felt it," Peter went on. "It's like a panic. The fear and adrenaline you feel, I feel. I can't see anything, but it's like phantom limb syndrome, except I can't feel a missing leg – I feel what you feel."

"Can you still?" I asked.

"Not so much," he shook his head. "Maybe if the fear was really strong, but that was a long time ago, and your blood has changed. It usually only lasts a few months, even when you care about someone a lot."

"So you just-"

I stopped cold and realized I knew exactly what Peter was talking about. I'd been thinking that I hadn't felt anything with Jack or Bobby, but they weren't the only two people I'd bitten.

I'd bitten Jane too.

"Oh my god." The color drained from my face, and my stomach knotted up. My heart stopped beating for a minute, and I could barely breathe.

"Alice?" Peter put his hand on my back and leaned in toward me. "Alice? Are you alright?"

"I felt Jane die."

"What?" Peter put his other hand on my knee and moved closer to me. "What are you talking about?"

"Jane, I bit her, when I saw her, and I knew I shouldn't have, but then she went to rehab, and I thought everything was okay, I thought everything was better." My words came out rushed, and tears tumbled down my cheeks more rapidly.

"You bit Jane?" He'd started rubbing my back, but I don't think it helped any.

"Yeah, I bit her and-and then in Australia-" My breath caught in my throat.

I remembered the terror I had felt when I woke up. The panic and fear surging through my veins. It'd scrambled my thoughts, and my heart wanted to hammer out of my chest. I had never felt that kind of intense fear before, and that's how Jane felt. That was Jane dying.

"Remember?" I looked at Peter, his worried expression blurred through my tears. "You came into the room, and I was freaked out, and I didn't know why, and I couldn't shake it. And I was mad that I felt that way! I was mad, and that was Jane!"

"No, Alice, you don't know that was Jane." He tried to reassure me, but I'm not sure that he believed what he was saying.

"No, it was! Jack called me later that night, and he told me she was dead, and I-" I cried harder, and I wiped at the tears with the palm of my hand. "I felt her die, Peter! I felt what she felt, and she was so afraid! She was terrified, and I didn't do anything!"

"You couldn't do anything." He wrapped his arm around me and pulled me close to him. I buried my head in his shoulder and sobbed. "You didn't know, and you couldn't do anything."

Peter stroked my hair and tried to tell me it was alright, but it wasn't. It wasn't just that I'd felt Jane die, and I hadn't done anything about it, although that weight of the guilt threatened to crush me. It was that I knew how scared and how horrible it had been for her to die.

Even though I'd known she'd been murdered, part of me had been able to hold out that it had been painless. If she'd been bitten before she died, she would've been unconscious, and she wouldn't have known what happened.

But now I knew. She had felt everything. She'd known she was dying, and it had been more horrifying than anything I had ever felt before.

Even after I stopped crying, I let Peter hold me in his arms. I should've pushed him away for a lot of different reasons, but I didn't have the strength for it. His arms were strong and safe, and I was afraid if he let go, I'd fall into a million pieces.

"What happened to Jane isn't your fault." He spoke into my hair, so his words came out muffled. He kissed the top of my head and stroked my hair back from my tear stained cheeks.

"It doesn't matter." I shook my head and pulled away from him. He left a hand lingering on my arm, and I let him. "She's dead, and I have to make it right."

"How?"

"I'll find a way." I swallowed hard and didn't look at him. I couldn't tell him my plans to destroy the bastard that had killed Jane. Peter would freak out as bad as Jack would, if not worse.

"Don't do anything stupid, Alice," he warned me.

"What me?" I laughed, and the flat sound echoed off the cavern walls. Suddenly, I felt ashamed of the scene I had made, and I wiped at my drying face. "Sorry. I didn't mean to do that. It just... hit me."

"You've got nothing to be sorry for," Peter assured me.

"Yeah, I really do." I wiped my hands on my jeans and stood up. "You've got your own stuff, and you don't need to worry about my shit."

"It's alright." He stood up with me and pushed up the sleeves of his shirt. I started to stumble out another apology, and he held up his hand. "Alice. It's fine."

I lifted my head, willing myself to look at him, and for a moment, I thought about Jack's apologies from earlier tonight. He felt guilty for forcing me into life because he knew the vampire life wasn't everything I'd hoped it would be.

Looking into Peter's eyes, I wondered if I'd feel the same way if I chose him instead, if our bond would've given my life the meaning I was so desperate for.

"Peter!" Daisy shouted, breaking my thoughts.

She dashed into the room, her skirt flying around her, and ran towards Peter. At first, I thought something had happened, but when she jumped at Peter, she screamed with glee and giggled as he caught her in her arms.

"What are you doing, kiddo?" Peter asked, holding her to his side.

"I finished my picture!" Daisy said.

Rainbow colored chalk smudges covered her pudgy cheeks and arms. One of her hands was balled into a fist. I thought she held a piece of chalk, but she pulled it away from Peter, like she was trying to hide it.

"What have you got there?" Peter asked, and she put her fist behind her back. "Let me see."

She shook her head fiercely, making her ponytail bounce. Peter reached around and pried open her hand, revealing a rather squashed cockroach. He wrinkled his nose and tossed the bug corpse away.

"Daisy, what did we say about bugs?" Peter reached for one of the towels I'd brought.

"That they're yucky," Daisy said, dutifully letting him wipe the bug guts from her hands.

"That's right," he said. "We need to leave them alone so you don't get sick anymore. Right?"

"Right," Daisy said, adding an overly dramatic sigh. "Do you wanna come see my picture now?"

Peter exchanged a look with me, checking to see if I was alright. I wasn't, not yet, but I could pass for it.

"I should be going anyway," I forced a smile.

"You have to look at my picture first!" Daisy shouted.

"Sure, of course," I nodded.

Peter carried Daisy out into the tunnel with me. Her floor mural had gotten much more extravagant while we'd been talking. The flying purple hippo had some sort of deformed frog companion, and there were random letters and stars and hearts all over.

Next to all that, she'd drawn a stick figure drawing of a guy, a woman with curly hair, and a little girl with curly hair. I assumed it was Peter, Mae, and Daisy, but I couldn't be completely sure.

"That's really lovely," Peter told her.

Daisy immediately launched into a story explaining exactly what happened in the picture, and she had him put her down so she could run all over pointing things out. As she talked, Peter watched her with a smile on his face.

I left as soon as I could, with Daisy waving and yelling goodbye long after I was out of eyesight.

Walking back to the car, it all hit me again. The distance between Jack and me that I couldn't fix. The way Jane had felt when she died. The fact that I had to live forever with the regrets from the choices I made.

I drove home and all I could look forward to was curling up next to Jack and falling asleep. I didn't care what problems we might be having, sleeping next to him was the only thing that would make me feel even remotely better right now.

Everyone was asleep when I get home, except for Matilda. She should've been in bed, but she was pacing the kitchen, whining. I gave her food, but she wanted nothing to do with it. I went over to the French doors, and as soon as I opened them, she darted outside, growling and barking.

"Matilda!" I yelled and stepped out after her. She ran around the lawn, sniffing in the snow with the fur on her back standing up. "Matilda, what's going on?"

But I heard it before she did. In the house behind me, something crashed, and Milo began to scream.

- 19 -

I ran so fast, my feet barely touched the ground, but I only made it as far as the bottom of the steps. Samantha stood in front of me, her hair smoothed back in a painful looking bun. Her eyes still looked deceptively innocent, but she'd traded in her pencil skirt for a black leather outfit that looked as if it'd been stolen from Olivia's closet.

Milo had stopped screaming, but he yelled at someone to get off him. I looked past Samantha at the top of the stairs, and I couldn't see Milo. I could only hear him struggling and the sound of his heart pounding, and worst of all, I could smell blood – heady and sweet.

"Hey!" Jack shouted. He'd just come out of his room, dressed only in his boxers, and his hair was messy from sleep.

"Take another step closer and we'll kill your human," Dane said, and Bobby whimpered. Jack didn't move, but I heard Milo grunting and fighting more. "Do you want me to kill him?"

"Just let him go!" Milo yelled, but I think he'd finally relented.

"What the fuck are you doing here?" I asked Samantha.

I wanted to push past her, but I didn't think I'd help the situation any. Milo was strong, probably stronger than me, and they had him. So far, Jack had been left out of the mess, and I didn't want to antagonize them into going after him. After Bobby, Jack was the weakest here.

"Looking for you." Samantha smiled, her lips a thin line of red. She stepped forward, off the bottom step, and I had to back up so she wouldn't run into me. "We've been following you. It's not that hard to track down a cherry red Lamborghini."

"You know them?" Jack asked, looking warily down at me.

"And you took the Lamborghini?" Ezra asked, his voice resonating behind me. I glanced back to see him standing in the dining room, holding back Matilda. She growled and gnashed her teeth, and if he let her go, she'd get herself killed up against Samantha.

"Why are you following me?" I asked, ignoring Ezra and Jack.

"If I let go of you, do you promise to be good?" Thomas asked Milo. Milo mumbled something in response, and I heard the sound of cracking bone, making Milo yell out in pain. "Answer me, or I'll do that to the human."

"Whatever you want, you guys can have it," Jack said. He took a step towards them, and Milo cried out again. "Stop it! Leave him alone!"

"What do you want?!" I yelled.

My mouth tasted like battery acid, and my veins surged with hot adrenaline. Every time Milo cried out, I felt a jolt through me so intense, it reminded me of bloodlust. Like an animal instinct, and I had to clench my fists to keep from ripping off Samantha's head.

"There's no need to yell." Thomas walked past Jack and descended the steps with a casual grace. He pushed the black hair from his forehead and noticed a bit of my brother's blood on his hands. With some disdain, he licked it from his hand, and I gritted my teeth to stop from tearing out his throat.

Dane followed a few steps behind Thomas, dragging Bobby with him. Dane held him by his throat, and he had him so far off the ground, Bobby's feet couldn't reach the steps. Bobby clawed and struggled to release his grip, but he couldn't.

Jack looked down at me, then turned back to tend to Milo. I could hear Milo's bones cracking as Jack tried to set them, and he let out a few more painful groans.

Ezra shoved Matilda in a nearby room, and she instantly began scratching and barking at the door. He walked towards me until Samantha cast him a glare, and he stopped a few feet back from us.

"What is this all about?" Ezra asked.

"We need to know what you're involvement is," Thomas said, resting his black eyes on me. "And why you have a human helping you."

"He's my brother's boyfriend!" I gestured to Bobby. Dane had lowered him enough where Bobby's feet could touch the ground and he gasped for air. "He doesn't know anything about anything! He's a moron!"

"She's right," Bobby croaked, and Dane tightened his grip around his throat, making Bobby's face turn purple.

"I will tell you anything you want! Just let him go!" I reached my arm out for him, but I didn't dare move forward. Dane was far enough away where he could snap Bobby's neck before I got to him.

"We will kill you if you lie to us," Thomas said. "You know that, right?"

"Yes!" I shouted, watching Bobby struggle to stay alive.

"Fine." Thomas shrugged, and Dane released Bobby. He collapsed onto the floor, breathing hard.

Even though they hadn't given me permission, I ran towards Bobby. I grabbed him by the arm and dragged him a few steps back from them. I couldn't really check on him because I didn't want to let my guard down, but I stood in front of him.

"Are you a part of a movement?" Thomas asked.

"A movement?" I shook my head. "Like a dance movement? What?"

"Don't get smart with us," Samantha narrowed her eyes. "We have no problem killing any of you. It's all part of our job."

"Look, I want to answer your questions. I just have *no idea* what you're talking about!" I told them as emphatically as I could. "You only speak in riddles. I don't know what you want from me!"

"We know you and the human are involved with the serial killer, and we have reason to believe that you have a child vampire as well," Samantha said. "Are you part of the movement to expose vampires?"

"What?" I raised my eyebrow and looked over to Ezra. His expression remained blank, not wanting to give anything away to them, but he had to know something. "I already told you. I'm not involved with the serial killer. I'm looking for him, but I'm starting to think you guys are the killers."

"Don't be absurd." Samantha rolled her eyes.

"We're here to catch him. It's what we do," Thomas gestured to Samantha and Dane. "We keep order in an order-less society."

Bobby coughed and got to his feet. He stood next to me. I glared at him, hoping he would take the hint and fall back, but he didn't.

"You guys are vampire hunters, right?" Bobby asked, rubbing his throat. In one synchronized movement, Samantha, Thomas, and Dane looked at him, and I stepped in front of him a bit more so my shoulder shielded part of him.

"They're more bounty hunters, actually," Ezra said.

"Bounty hunter is such a loaded term," Thomas said with exaggerated disdain. "Besides, we hardly ever work on commission anymore."

"So no one's paying you to be here?" Ezra took a step closer to us, his arms crossed over his chest.

"We're doing a service for the community," Samantha smiled thinly.

"Who called you?" Ezra asked.

"We're not at liberty to divulge that," Samantha replied, her tone getting icier.

"But you know several people that have our number," Thomas grinned. "The Commissioner has always been a big fan of our work."

"Oh!" Bobby gasped, and then lowered his voice to a whisper. "I told you the police were in on this."

"Bobby," I said through gritted teeth.

"Can we just get this over with?" Dane sounded exasperated, and he checked the neon green and pink watch on his wrist.

277

"Oh my god!" Bobby pointed at him. "That dude is supposed to be a vampire hunter, and he's got on a fricking *swatch*! There is no way these guys are for real!"

"Bobby!" I snapped.

"Whatever. I'm just saying this whole thing is messed up," Bobby insisted.

"If you don't shut up, *I* will kill you," I glared back at him, and he rolled his eyes, but he fell silent. I turned back to the supposed-vampire hunters. "I've already told you everything I know."

"What about the child vampire?" Thomas asked, and I fought to keep my expression neutral.

"The only child vampire we have here is Milo upstairs, and you just kicked his ass," I said.

I wanted to look over at Ezra to see how he reacted, but I knew that'd give something away. Milo had stopped groaning upstairs, and his bones weren't cracking, but I couldn't see him or Jack.

"I don't know if I should believe you." Thomas crossed his arms over his chest, staring at me with false contemplation. "I *want* to, but something about you just screams 'liar' to me."

"I don't know what I can say to make you believe me," I told them honestly.

"I tend to think that people are most honest under pressure," Thomas said, and Dane stepped forward.

"I have already told you everything!" I shouted and put my hands up. I'm not sure if Dane meant to hurt me or kill Bobby or what, but I didn't want to find out.

"Really?" Thomas asked. "Are you sure?"

"This serial killer, he killed my best friend Jane, and I've been hunting all over for him," I said hurriedly, thinking if I said it quickly it would make it more believable. "I know that the killer is a vampire, that he's branding the girls, and he wants to get caught. He wants people to know that it was a vampire, but I don't know why. He knew Jane, but I don't even know if it is a *him*. It could be a girl. Or it could be a group. Or it could be... anybody."

"You don't know why he wants to get caught?" Samantha looked at me seriously.

"No. I have no idea why," I said.

Samantha stared at me a moment longer, but my answer seemed to satisfy her. She looked over at Thomas, and finally, he nodded. Dane rolled his eyes and groaned, so I assumed it was good news for us.

"We won't be wasting any more of your time," Samantha said shortly.

"Sorry to bother you," Thomas added.

The three of them turned to leave. Dane hissed at Bobby as he walked past, and Bobby jumped in surprise, then scoffed at himself. As soon as they left out the front door, I ran upstairs to see Milo with Bobby hot on my heels.

Milo was shirtless, slumped against the wall. His eyelids were half-open, and one of his sides was swollen and red, looking strangely lumpy. His left arm hung at an odd angle, and his skin had turned almost purplish around it. The cheek below his eye was puffy and covered in drying blood.

"He's okay," Jack said when I fell on my knees next to Milo. Jack was crouched down next to him, watching him.

"Are you sure?" I asked, confused by how horrible a vampire could look after a fight. "What happened to him?"

"Milo? Can you hear me?" Bobby asked. He sat on the other side of Milo, afraid to touch him, and tears filled his eyes.

"You should let him sleep," Jack told him. "He had a lot of broken bones, and the more injuries he has, the longer it takes to heal. I gave him some of my blood to speed it up, and he should be alright soon."

"Should I give him my blood too?" Bobby sniffled and wiped at his nose.

"No, my blood is stronger," Jack said. "He will be fine. I promise."

"Oh my god." I let out a massive sigh of relief and ran my hand through my hair.

Milo had just had the shit seriously beaten out of him because of me, because I wouldn't let Jane's death go. It made me want to throw up, but when I remembered how Jane had felt when she died, I knew I couldn't stop.

"So." Jack turned to look at me, his voice cool and even. "What the hell have you been doing?"

- 20 -

After I got Milo comfortable in his room, I left Bobby to care for him, and I went downstairs to where Jack and Ezra waited for me. Jack had gotten dressed and paced the living room. The patio door was still wide open, letting in a cold wind and the morning sunlight. Some snow had drifted into the house, but nobody seemed to notice or mind.

I sat down on the couch, and Ezra sat on the chair across from me. Even though he knew what I'd been up to, the fact that I'd failed to mention the vampire hunters was a pretty big deal. Jack refused to sit down, and instead paced the room with his arms crossed over his chest.

"What do you guys want to know?" I asked, swallowing hard.

"Tell me everything," Jack said simply.

Taking a deep breath, I started from the beginning. I even told them about things they knew, like how I'd felt so helpless after the lycan attacked and I vowed to never feel that way again. I told them how it felt when I bit Jane, and how sad and lonely she was. How she called me from rehab and told me that was the only time she'd felt like someone cared about her.

I even told them what I'd learned from Peter, and how I felt her die. And about how I had decided I would stop the monster that had killed her almost right away, and everything I had done to find him. How I'd taken Bobby along with me, and he was the only one who knew exactly what I'd been doing.

Once I began talking, it all poured out of me, and I couldn't stop. I'd hated keeping this all from Jack, and I wanted him to know.

"And that's everything," I said at the end, staring up at them, and Jack stopped pacing.

When I told him everything I'd learned about the killer, all the information I had to help me catch him, I had been hoping he would get excited too, he'd want to join in the hunt.

But then I saw the way he looked at me. His blue eyes were like ice still, and he kept his emotions locked away from me, shoved down so deep, I could only feel him buzzing, like a livewire.

"Why didn't you tell me about the hunters?" Ezra asked, and I was relieved he spoke first.

"I don't know. I didn't…" I shook my head. "I thought you'd try to stop me if you knew."

"That's exactly why you should've told me." He sighed and leaned back. "I never should've told you anything. You're clearly not mature enough to handle any of this."

"That's not fair!" I shouted. "How was I supposed to know they'd track me down like that? Who the hell are they, anyway? And what did they mean when they asked if I was part of the 'movement?'"

"They're vampire hunters. They keep order, by any means necessary." Ezra rubbed his hands together and looked down at the floor. "It's my fault they're here."

"What? Did you call them?" I asked.

"No, I talked to the Commissioner after you asked me about the branding," Ezra sighed. "I told him I thought it might be a vampire. So he called in the hunters. They usually work for humans, dispatching of a problem people can't."

"So the police hired them?" I furrowed my brow. "But... I thought they weren't getting paid."

"I'm sure they are getting paid to catch the serial killer, but I think they're freelancing, too." Ezra glanced up at Jack, who had yet to say anything, and he leaned forward. "There is a movement among vampires to stop hiding. It's not a large movement. Most of us are content to live the way we do because it is much simpler. If people knew we existed, they'd hunt us, and even if they didn't kill us, it would be irritating."

"You mean like on *True Blood*?" I asked. "Where vampires 'come out of the coffin' and we all live as equals? Or try to, anyway?"

"No. These vampires don't want to be equal. They want to rule humans," Ezra said. "Humans are our food, and some vampires think they should be treated as such. Branded and kept in pens like cattle." He lowered his eyes, shifting in the chair. "The hunters wouldn't be out of a job, necessarily, but they would have less work. Most of what they do is keeping the peace for humans or keeping vampires a secret."

"Okay. So I get why they were so pissed about me because they thought I was working with the 'movement' to put them out of a job. But why did they care about Daisy?" I asked.

"Child vampires are unstable and volatile. Let one loose for a day, and the whole world would know about vampires," Ezra said. "And Mae let her loose in Australia."

"How did they even find about that?" I asked.

"Word travels," he shrugged. "The Commissioner might've mentioned something about the missing child, and it's common knowledge that Mae has moved out. Vampires have a lot of time on their hands to gossip."

"The hunters think she did that to attract attention," I said as it dawned on me. "And if everyone learned about vampires that way, with the serial killer and a crazy murderous child, humans would be terrified. They'll want to hunt us down and kill us, and that would give the 'movement' of vampires all the ammo they would need to round up the humans and turn them into cattle."

"Exactly," Ezra said. "The hunters are trying to stop that from happening. In this case, they are helping."

"But they're assholes!" I yelled and gestured upstairs. "They broke into our house, beat us up, threatened our lives! That's the good guys?"

"Alice, there are no good guys," Ezra said, giving me a hard look. "We're vampires, and no matter what we do or strive for, that fact doesn't change. We aren't the good guys."

"Yeah, I'm starting to figure that out." I bit my lip and leaned back on the couch.

"You've been busy figuring out a lot of things lately," Jack said, and I lifted my head to look up at him. His voice stayed even, but he had to fight to keep it that way.

284

"Jack, I'm sorry that I didn't tell you any-"

"Really? You're sorry?" Jack asked. "Were you sorry last week when I asked you what was going on when you said nothing? Were you sorry a few hours ago when I asked you directly what you were doing and you lied to my face? Were you sorry when I was beating myself about this distance between us because you've been sneaking around and lying to me? Is that when you were sorry?"

"Jack, I had to do this! I had to help her!" I leaned forward, pleading with him.

"She is dead, Alice! You can't help her!" Jack shouted. "You lied to me! You lied to Milo and put yourself in danger! You put Bobby in danger! What the hell were you thinking? He's human! He nearly died tonight! Because of you!"

"I know that." Bitter tears stung my eyes and I looked toward the floor. "Believe me, I know that. But I don't know what else I was supposed to do."

"After you kissed Peter last year, I begged you, I fucking *begged* you not to do that again!"

"I didn't kiss him again!" I shouted, looking up sharply.

"No, Alice." He smiled sadly and shook his head. "That's not what I meant. I asked you never to break my trust again."

"I'm sorry." My voice quavered, and a tear slid down my cheek. "I'm really sorry, Jack. I didn't think I had a choice."

"That's the thing with you. You never think you have a choice, but you always do." He bit his lip and shook his head. "But you wish you didn't." He looked away from me. "Sometimes, I think you wish you'd never met me, there had never been a choice between me and Peter."

"No, Jack, that's not true!" I stood up. "That's not true at all! I love you!"

"Oh, yeah, I know you do." He nodded, and his mouth twitched in a way that I knew he was holding back tears. "You love me so much, and that just *really* sucks for you. Cause if you didn't have that, you could just do whatever you wanted. You could be human or a little vampire Nancy Drew or hook up with any of my brothers. If only you didn't have to worry about me."

"Jack, no." I shook my head. "This is one stupid thing. This is a mistake. I did something stupid, but it was just something stupid. I know that you're mad because I lied, but I lied about something little. I didn't cheat on you. I didn't hurt anybody."

"You repeatedly lied to my face and snuck around behind my back, and I believed you. You're missing the point, Alice. I *can't* trust you anymore."

"No," I insisted. "I won't lie to you ever again. When you asked me not to break your trust, you told me it didn't matter. You told me you would forgive me of anything, and I'm not asking you to. I'm asking you to forgive me of this *one* thing. This one last thing."

"I did say that." His voice was so quiet, I barely heard it, and his blue eyes swam with tears. "But you know what? I lied too."

All the strength drained me from me, and I fell to the ground on my knees. Too much had happened, and hearing him say that felt like something had ripped open inside me. I couldn't even cry, it hurt too much.

"Alice." Ezra came to my side, putting his arm around me. "It's alright."

"What's going on?" Leif asked.

I heard him, but I couldn't see him. I couldn't lift my head. I wrapped my arms around my stomach, trying to hold in the pain. I had to physically hold myself, or I knew I would fall apart. I gulped down air, desperate to keep back the vomit that threatened to come up.

"What the hell did you do to her?" Leif got in Jack's face. "Did you hit her?"

"I would never hit her! And she's the one-" Jack pointed at me, then shook his head. "Never mind. It doesn't matter. You should just be happy, because now she's free to do whatever she wants!"

"Whatever you did to her, fix it! Apologize to her!" Leif shouted.

"*I* didn't do anything wrong!" Jack yelled back. "And what the hell is your deal? Why do you even care? If I break up with my girlfriend, why is it any of your damn business?"

"Because I'm her father!" Leif shouted.

- 21 -

I will say this for Leif – he managed to shock me out of my pain. I stared up at him, momentarily forgetting the horrible rift inside me at the thought of life without Jack. Leif sheepishly looked back at me, his dark eyes meeting mine.

"Sorry. I didn't want to tell you that way," Leif said, shoving his hands in his dirty pants pockets.

"Is this some kind of sick joke?" Jack asked, but all the anger had left his voice.

Somewhere inside me, I knew it was true. Maybe I had before he said it. Something had been there, a connection I had always felt with him but couldn't explain.

"You have Milo's eyes," I whispered. They were the same deep brown and reminded me of a puppy, the way Milo's always had.

"Actually, he has my eyes," Leif smiled and shifted uneasily.

"Wait." Jack looked between the two of us. "You guys aren't serious? Are you?" He turned to Ezra. "He can't be serious. It's not possible. Is it?"

"It is." Ezra still had his hand on my back, and he sounded reluctant to answer. "It's rare, but it's possible."

I tried to stand up, but my legs felt rubbery underneath me. Leif moved to help me, but Ezra was already at my side, beating him to it. I walked closer to Leif, and nothing had ever felt so surreal. I reached out to touch him. I expected my hand to go through him like he was a mirage, but it didn't.

My fingertips brushed against his cheek, and his skin felt smooth and cool, like my own. I gaped at him, and let my hand fall, unable to do anything except try to process this.

"You're my father," I breathed, and he nodded. "How old are you?"

"I was born 54 years ago, but I was only 22 when I turned," Leif said.

That made it all the more unreal. I was eighteen, and my father looked like he was only four years older than me. It was strange that I hadn't noticed how much he looked like Milo before. People meeting them together would think they were brothers.

"How did you find me?" I asked.

"I…" He lowered his eyes, and his cheeks reddened. "I wasn't looking for you. I didn't find you."

"What?"

"I didn't know you and Milo were my children until a few weeks ago," Leif swallowed and pursed his lips.

"How could you not know?" I took a step back, feeling betrayed by that statement.

Ezra moved in closer to me, in case I needed his support, but Jack stood off to the side of the room, unsure with how to react to any of this.

"You were so young the last time I saw you, and Milo wasn't even born yet." His dark eyes were sad and pleading. "I didn't even know I had a son. Your mother had just found out she was pregnant."

"You left us," I said softly and took another step back. "You left us, and I don't even remember you."

"Alice, I had to leave you." Tears filled his eyes. "I thought…" He rubbed his mouth and lowered his eyes. "I loved Anna very much, but we hadn't been together that long when she got pregnant with you. I didn't have time to think about what it would be like. And I loved you. I still love you so much, you and Milo. I left to protect you."

"How could you not know I was your daughter?" I repeated, louder this time. "How could you love me so much and not know?"

"Do you know how many girls I saw that I thought were you?" Leif asked. "Every time I saw a little girl, I'd wonder if that could be you. Every time I heard the name Alice, I wondered if it were you. Eventually, I just… I numbed myself to the idea."

"I don't even know what that means." I wiped at my eyes to stop tears before they fell.

"I didn't let myself think about you anymore, or worry about you or your mother or your brother," Leif said. "I knew I would outlive you, and I couldn't deal with that. I tried to blot you out of my mind."

"It was my birthday last month! And you didn't think, 'I had a daughter named Alice eighteen years ago today?' That never even occurred to you?"

"I didn't know you were eighteen, and I didn't..." He shook his head. "You look nineteen, but you're a vampire. You could've been a hundred for all I knew."

"What about Milo? You didn't put that together?" I asked.

"I didn't even know he was your real brother," Leif admitted. "I thought he was a brother like the way Ezra and Jack are brothers. He wasn't even born when I left, and the last time I saw you, you were living in Idaho. I had no reason to think..."

"Yes, I felt a connection with you, and with Milo," Leif went on. "But I didn't realize who you were until I heard you arguing with Jack a few weeks ago. And as soon as I found out, I knew I had to do everything in my power to make it up to you. I just hadn't found a way to tell you yet."

"I know you're a vampire but... why did you leave?" I crossed my arms over my chest and wiped at my eyes again.

"Your mother was barely nineteen when I met her, and I loved her the moment I saw her." Leif's eyes stayed on me, and he never looked away as he talked. "She didn't know I was a vampire. I meant to tell her, but she got pregnant with you right away. I couldn't tell her then because I didn't want her to do something drastic, like run away or have an abortion.

"I got her an apartment, and I stayed with her most of the time. I made up stories about work, but I took care of her the best I could," he continued. "I didn't think I could love anything more than I loved her, until you were born. I would've given anything to watch you grow up."

"You didn't though," I said pointedly, and he nodded.

"The day before I left, Anna was standing in front of a mirror," he said. "She had just started showing with Milo, and she had her shirt pulled up, rubbing the baby bump. I walked over to her and put my arms around and told her how beautiful she looked.

"She said, 'Don't lie. I've gotten so fat, and you haven't changed a bit since the day we met.'" He closed his eyes on the memory. "She laughed when she said it, but I knew then that I only had a few more years before it would be too noticeable. She would get older, and I would be forever young."

"So?" I asked. "Turn her. Or don't. Tell her you're a vampire. We could've moved before anybody noticed."

"I thought of that," he nodded. "I thought of turning her after she had Milo. I had wonderful fantasies of us running away together, living happily ever after. Anna and I young and beautiful forever, raising our children all over the world.

"But if I raised you that way, I knew you'd want this. I *never* wanted this life for you." Leif's smile only got more pained. "I wanted you to *live*. To have a real life. I couldn't give you that if I stayed. I didn't want you to end up like me."

"Well, good thing you left, because I totally didn't end up as a vampire," I said. "Oh wait. Yes, I did. I just grew up without a father."

"Everything I did, I did for you," Leif said emphatically. "You don't have to believe me, but it's true. I left when I did because I didn't want you to remember me or miss me. I wanted you to forget me and move on with your life."

"It didn't work, *Dad*!" I snapped. "I still missed you! When I was little, I used to cry myself to sleep, and Milo would ask me all these questions about you, and I would make stuff up to make him feel better. And Mom, she *never* got over you! She has been unhappy and bitter and... you left us alone with her!"

"I'm sorry." Leif's eyes welled with tears. "I didn't know. I didn't..." He looked down. "I was trying to protect you. I only wanted you to be happy.

"It destroyed me to leave you, Alice." Leif pursed his lips. "That's why I ended with the lycans. I thought they would kill me."

"Was Mom your one?" I asked. "The one you were meant for?" Out of the corner of my eye, I saw Jack look at me when I said that.

"Yes," Leif said quietly. "She was. She is."

I chewed my lip. I knew the ache of growing up with a father and why he didn't love me enough to stay. And I knew the horrendous pain of losing someone I loved. My fight with Jack was so raw, I could barely speak and breathe.

Yet Leif had chosen that pain willingly. He'd left my mother, my unborn brother, and me knowing how much pain it would cause him, and he did it to protect us. He had been willing to sacrifice himself for our happiness.

In the time I had known Leif, he'd been nothing but kind. He'd risked his own life more than once to help me and my friends. And until I found out that he'd abandoned me when I was an infant, I had really liked him.

"You're not gonna leave now, are you?" I asked.

294

"No, of course not," he shook his head. "I'm not going anywhere."

"Then we'd better tell Milo," I said.

Even though Milo was still healing and needed his rest, I woke him up for this. The swelling and discoloration of his skin had gone, but he moved slowly. I didn't tell him why he had to get up, but I managed to drag him downstairs. Bobby kept telling me I was being mean, so I elbowed him in the stomach, and he shut up.

I sat on the couch next to Milo, with my arm around him. I'm not sure if he needed it, but I knew I did. Leif pulled a chair in front of us and sat down, preparing to explain the whole thing. Ezra stayed in the room to oversee things, and that did make me feel better.

Jack tried so sit next to me on the couch, but I wouldn't have it.

"No," I told him. "You don't get to do that."

"Do what?" Jack asked.

"Try to be all supportive." I glared at him. "You broke up with me, remember?"

"What?" Milo asked, looking at me.

"Never mind," I said, and Jack moved to a chair on the side of the room, muttering something about how he could be supportive of Milo. "Leif has something more important to tell you, Milo."

Leif told Milo the whole story, and it went about the same way it had gone with me. Stunned at first, then disbelief, then angry when he remembered that Leif had left us. Milo took it better than I did, though. He had less anger about the whole thing, but that tended to be the case with everything.

"Wow," Bobby sat on the floor by Milo's feet and looked in awe. "You're so Luke Skywalker right now."

"Leif is not Darth Vader," Milo said, then he cocked his head. "Do I call you Leif? Or do I call you Dad?"

"Call me whatever you like," Leif shrugged. "I'm just happy to be a part of your life."

"I still don't understand." Milo's face scrunched up in concentration, reminding me of the way he looked when he'd still been human. "How... Well, just how?"

"Are you asking how I fathered you?" Leif asked carefully. "I did it the same anyone fathers a child." He looked uncomfortable and shifted in the chair. "I'm sure you understand the mechanics of reproduction."

"Yeah, I understand human reproduction," Milo said. "But I didn't think vampires could reproduce, not like actual offspring, fruit of their loins." He looked over at me. "Did you know they could do that?"

"No. Why would I know that?" I shrugged.

"I have seen it before." Ezra stepped forward from the side of the room. I think he'd been giving us space to talk over things, but his presence reassured me. "Only twice, but it's common enough that there's a term for it. Dhampyr."

"A what now?" I asked.

"The offspring of a vampire father and a human mother," Ezra explained, and Leif turned to watch him. "It does explain a lot of the peculiarities that we've encountered with you. Your strong connection and attraction to vampires, and in turn, their affinity for

296

you. Your ability to transform into a vampire with relative ease, and now, you're superior strength and control."

"Wait, wait," Bobby interrupted, snapping his fingers. "I've heard that before. That's like what Blade is, right? Wesley Snipes was a vampire hunter, but he was like super strong and badass from being a half-breed." He glanced back at Milo. "You weren't like that when you were human, were you?"

"No, I got my ass kicked all the time," Milo grimaced at the memory of his human self.

"So how come they weren't all like Blade?" Bobby asked, turning back to Ezra.

"Because it's a movie, Bobby," I said dryly. "Movies aren't the same as real life."

"It varies, from dhampyr to dhampyr," Ezra said. "From what I've heard, some are stronger than others, but the only constant is that they're drawn to vampires. Most end up as vampires."

"We're drawn to vampires?" I asked, and something about that made my stomach queasy.

"Yes, you are," Ezra nodded.

I didn't want to look over at Jack, but I could feel him staring at me. I still had my arm around Milo, and I held onto him tighter, this time for my own support.

My father was a vampire. I'd been born with part of that virus inside me, mutating my blood, so I was drawn to vampires. I'd been made to seek them out, and they sought after me, too.

What if that's all my connection with Jack had ever been? Or Peter? Some byproduct of a virus I'd gotten before I was born. Maybe I'd never really been bonded to either of them, to anyone.

Mae had told me something once, and I hadn't thought much of it at the time, but now it played over and over in my head. It'd been when one night when I was still mortal, and Mae had taken me out to cheer me up.

"I'm trying to understand your ancestry, because you and Milo are both so unique. I'm wondering if we've been looking at this all wrong. Maybe you weren't meant for Peter. Maybe you were just meant to be a vampire," Mae said, looking faraway. "We're just a means to an end for you."

"Alice?" Leif asked, leaning forward. "Are you alright?"

"Yeah," I said numbly, and my mouth didn't want to work. Nothing did.

"Are you sure?" Milo asked. "All the color drained from your face."

"No, I'm fine. I just… I had a *really* long night." I tried to force a smile, but I knew it fell completely flat. I stood up, relieved that my legs didn't give out under me. "I need to… I need to get some sleep."

"Do you need help?" Ezra asked, his brow furrowed with concern.

"Nope." I shook my head. "No. I'm absolutely…" I trailed off. I didn't know what I was.

Milo got up and tried to help me, but I refused to let him. He needed to stay and talk to Leif and sort things out. I couldn't sort anything out anymore. My brain barely worked.

It was after one in the afternoon, and I had yet to sleep. Last night had been the longest night of my life. I remembered feeling my best friend dying, we'd been attacked by vampire hunters, my boyfriend broke up with me, and I found out my dad was a vampire. It was all a bit much.

I staggered upstairs to the bedroom I shared with Jack, but I couldn't let myself think about him, or wonder where I'd sleep tomorrow. I couldn't even change out of my clothes. I just collapsed on the bed. As I drifted off, I just kept hearing Mae's words playing in my head over and over again.

"We're just a means to an end for you."

- 22 -

Wiping the steam from the mirror, I was surprised by how normal my reflection looked. I felt like I'd been in a train wreck, even after a night's sleep and a hot shower, but I looked just like I always did.

The breakup hurt even worse. I'd expected it to dull, the way the shock about Leif had, but it didn't. It throbbed painfully inside me, like a festering wound. I hadn't cried yet today, but I suspected that last night had completely dried me out of tears for a while.

I couldn't get Mae out of my head. What if she had been right? What if I'd just been meant to be a vampire? If I'd never been meant for Jack or Peter, had I ever really loved either of them?

I felt like throwing up every time I even thought about the fight with Jack last night, and my life looked like a giant vortex without him. That desperation for him, because of him, that had to happen because I loved him. I really and truly loved him. That couldn't just be a biological response ingrained in me so I'd become a vampire. Could it?

Not that it mattered anymore how much I loved Jack or not. He'd broken up with me.

"Alice," Jack opened the bathroom door without knocking.

"Jack!" I yelled. I had a towel wrapped around me, but I hadn't gotten dressed yet. When he walked in, I jumped and pulled the towel tighter.

"What?" Jack asked, surprised by my attempts at modesty. "It's not like I haven't seen you naked before."

"Yeah, well, you dumped me," I reminded him. "You don't get to see me naked anymore."

"You're in my bathroom," he countered.

"You still don't get to see me naked. Now will you get out so I can get dressed?"

He left the bathroom without further protests, and as soon as he shut the door behind him, I leaned against the bathroom sink and tried to catch my breath. I swallowed hard and told myself I could do this.

"So, Alice, I just..." Jack said from the other side of the bathroom door. "I wanted to talk."

I got dressed in a hurry because I wasn't sure how long he would wait. He tended to get impatient, and maybe what he wanted to talk about was something good. Like he realized how unfair he was being last night. Sure, I had lied to him, but it wasn't that big of a thing.

With my hair still damp, I stepped out of the bathroom. Jack stood by the end of his bed with his arms crossed over his chest, and he didn't really look at me when I came out.

Being close to him normally filled me with a warm, fluttery feeling. Not like butterflies, either. It happened after I'd turned into a vampire, after we had a blood bond. I could feel him, like a tether attached my heart to his. Without any effort on my part, my body always naturally tilted to his. My blood had become magnetized to him.

But not now. I only felt an ache, a dark cloud growing inside me, overshadowing our bond. A vice gripped my heart, clenching it too tightly for me to feel the invisible tether that held us together.

"What do you wanna talk about?" I asked, biting my lip.

"Um…" Rubbing the back of his neck, he shifted his weight. "I just wanted to make sure you were alright. After last night."

"You mean because you broke up with me over something really, really stupid?" I asked.

"It's not stupid, Alice." He sighed and shook his head. "And no, I didn't mean that. I meant, you know… about Leif and everything too."

"Well…" I wrapped my arms around myself, and my mouth felt dry. My stomach dropped, and I didn't even know how to answer his question. "Why?"

"Why what?" Jack looked up at me, but I wouldn't meet his eyes. I could feel him appraising me, making sure I was alright, and that hurt all the more.

"You don't get to do this, Jack." I ran a hand through my tangles of damp hair, and I put my hand on my side, pressing hard, as if I could hold the sadness in that way. "You don't get to break my heart *and* pick up the pieces."

"Alice." His entire face fell and his shoulders slumped as he stared helplessly at me. "I didn't… I don't want to hurt you."

"You're an even bigger liar than I am." I rolled my eyes to keep back the tears.

I hated being the in same room with him, feeling the way he felt. His own confused pain permeated through the air, like a thick fog, and I couldn't stand to feel it along with my own.

"How am I a liar?" Jack asked, his hurt expression growing defensive. "I don't want to hurt you."

"I know that!" I yelled, and I didn't mean to yell. I shook my head, and when I spoke again, I tried to lower my voice. "But you said you'd love me forever, and then I did something really dumb and relatively minor, and … I mean, let's be honest, kissing Peter was way worse than this."

"No, it wasn't." He chewed the inside of his cheek and furrowed his brow. "That was bad. But this… I asked you what you were doing. I told you I felt a distance between us. I was so honest with you, and you didn't correct me. You didn't… You couldn't trust me with this part of you."

"I just didn't want you to worry," I told him emphatically. "I didn't want to fight about this because we've been fighting about so much other stuff lately. I wanted to have one less argument."

"But that is the problem, Alice." He looked at me seriously. "We've been arguing, and there's been something going on with you. You're restless and distracted, and this whole thing is just a symptom of that. Something is going on with you that I can't fix."

"Jack, you don't need to fix me," I shook my head. "And yes, I know I'm going through some stuff. But that doesn't mean we should end this. We should work through it."

He smiled, one of his pained smiles that broke my heart even more. He lowered his head and ran his hand through his hair, and for a while, he didn't say anything.

"I've been trying so hard to be everything you wanted. To give you everything you could ever want. And you're not happy." He took a deep breath, and let his words hang in the air. "So now I'm going to be what you need."

My phone rang in my pocket, but I ignored it.

"What does that even mean?" I asked, and he shook his head.

"Answer your phone." He nodded at me and turned to walk away. I said his name, but he left the bedroom without looking back.

"Hello?" I answered my phone with a heavy sigh.

"Alice?" Olivia said.

"Olivia? Are you back? I've been looking for you."

"I need to talk to you," Olivia said, forgoing her usually rambled greetings. She sounded clear and clipped, and that made me nervous. "When can you get to my place?"

"When do you need me?"

"As soon as you can." Without waiting for my answer, she hung up.

I checked my phone to be sure it wasn't a dropped call, and it wasn't. I thought about calling her back, but if Olivia said she wanted me over there now, it was probably important. I didn't need to waste time making unnecessary phone calls.

"Hey, Alice, how are-" Milo was saying as he walked into my room, but then he saw me pulling on my shoes and stopped. "Where are you going?"

"Out," I said, then sighed and shook my head. After what happened with Jack, it would probably be better if I didn't keep anyone in the dark anymore. "Olivia called. She wants me to come over."

"What for?" Milo asked, narrowing his eyes.

"I don't know, but it sounded important."

"I'm going with," he said, and he'd been starting to master Ezra's tone when something wasn't open for debate.

"Don't you have school or something?" I didn't want him to go with me, not if Olivia'd gotten herself in trouble, but I couldn't very well tell him that. He'd only insist on coming with more.

"It's ten o'clock at night, on a Friday."

"Oh. Right." I nodded. "Well, then. Come on."

Since Milo came with, that meant Bobby had to tag along, not that I minded. For reasons I couldn't explain, I felt better about bringing Bobby along on dangerous excursions, even though he was more fragile. I cared about Bobby almost as much as I did Milo, so that wasn't it.

In a weird way, Bobby felt more like an equal to me. Milo would always be my kid brother who'd gotten shoved into lockers and needed me to look out for him. Bobby was more like... a sidekick.

Milo didn't see it that way. They'd apparently had some major fight about Bobby sneaking out with me, but thankfully, I'd slept through it. On the car ride to Olivia's, Milo made a point of telling me exactly how unhappy he was with me for putting Bobby in danger, even though they'd already forgiven each other and made up.

I hated how easily they always seemed to make up. I blamed Milo and his never-ending patience for that, and Bobby's unadulterated worship of Milo. Their relationship should've been almost as complicated as mine and Jack's, but it wasn't.

It was a Friday night, so the vampire club was even more packed than it had been the last few times. We went through V to get to the elevator up to Olivia's penthouse because it was usually quicker, and on nights like tonight, it could be rather tedious.

La Roux's song "Bulletproof" blasted over the dance floor, and even though I liked it, the decibel hurt. I hadn't gotten enough sleep or eaten lately, and a migraine loomed behind my eyes. The music only it made it worse.

I plunged into the sweaty bodies filling the dance floor and pushed my way through. I used to be delicate and careful, but now I'd shove anybody that got in my way. The crowd kept trying to swallow up Bobby, so I grabbed his arm and yanked him forward. Milo trailed behind him, fighting off anyone that might go after Bobby.

"Watch where you're going!" someone yelled at me, and I wouldn't even have stopped to look if he hadn't laughed. "You're following me, aren't you?"

"Hey, it's that douche!" Bobby said, almost cheerfully.

I turned back to see Jonathan with his shit-eating grin. He wore a leather jacket hanging open without a shirt underneath, and even if he did have perfect abs, it still looked tacky. He even had a silver cross hanging down around his neck, and I wanted to punch him just for wearing that.

"Do I have a reason to follow you?" I asked him.

Jonathan stood a foot or two in front of me, and the other people had stopped crowding around us. We were on the edges of a small circle where nobody danced, like we were about to dance off or throw down. Bobby and Milo stood behind me, adding to the feel that we were about to rumble.

"Only the same reason as everyone else." Jonathan's smile widened, revealing more teeth than he needed to.

"And why's that?" I asked.

"Cause you can't resist me, baby!" He spread his arms wide in a grand gesture, and Bobby scoffed. Jonathan's smile faltered, only for a moment, but it was enough where I knew he was pissed off.

He'd always given me the creeps, but it'd only gotten worse. The blood in my veins burned around him, like I physically couldn't stand to be near him. My stomach churned, and I just wanted to get away.

"We don't have time for this." I rolled my eyes and turned to walk away.

Bobby made a smart remark about resisting him, and he'd barely gotten it out of his mouth before Jonathan reacted. He flew forward, striking out at Bobby. I didn't move fast enough to stop him from hitting Bobby, but he only got in one punch.

I whirled on Jonathan, kicking him in the back of the legs so they buckled, and Jonathan leaned back and fell on his knees. With my left hand, I gripped his neck, closing my hand so tight on his throat that I felt his Adam's apple crack, and I punched him in the face as hard as I could with my right hand. His jaw felt like concrete against my fist, but it gave away, shattering underneath my knuckles.

I pulled my fist back to hit him again, but Milo's hand on my arm stopped me.

"Alice!" Milo yelled.

The bottom half of Jonathan's face looked like hamburger, and his blood streamed down over my hand. He gasped for breath, making the blood gurgle through his smashed mouth, but he didn't even try to fight me. His arms hung limp at his sides, and his head lolled back. His eyes were wide open, staring at me with that same dead shark-eye look always he had.

Even with that, knowing I'd be beating up someone that couldn't even fight back, and with Milo pulling on me to leave, I didn't lower my arm. My blood burned, searing my muscles, and my whole body felt electrified. I wanted to *destroy* Jonathan.

"Alice! Bobby needs to get upstairs!" Milo shouted. Based on his painful grip on my arm, he was using almost all his strength to drag me away, but I stayed cemented in place.

The crowd still circled around us, watching as I held Jonathan captive. If he'd been human, he'd probably be dead, and that sent a new chill down my spine. Without even trying, I'd almost killed him.

I let go of him, and Jonathan stayed kneeling. He leaned back, hanging in midair as if suspended by a string. His swollen bloody mouth curled, making some poor attempt at a smile, and I looked away. I couldn't stand the sight of him anymore.

Once Milo was sure I would follow him willingly, he let go of me. He looped an arm around Bobby, half-carrying him to the elevator. People gave us a wide berth as we walked, but nobody said anything to me, not even Milo.

"What the hell was that?" Milo hissed once we were in the privacy of the elevator.

"I'll be okay," Bobby had his hand over his eye, but some blood dripped down from it on his cheek.

His scent filled the small space so much, it was almost suffocating, especially since I hadn't eaten in so long. I paced the elevator and wiped my hand on my jeans, getting Jonathan's blood off of me.

"I know," Milo said. "But I wasn't talking to you, even though that was really stupid. I meant Alice. What the hell was that back there?"

"He hit Bobby," I mumbled.

But I knew that wasn't it exactly. I had been pissed that he hit Bobby, the same way I would be if anybody hurt him or anyone else I cared about. But it was something else. A rage I couldn't control had taken over me.

"Yeah, I know, but I thought you were going to kill him." Milo had his arm around Bobby, almost cradling him to his chest, and he kept his voice even.

It wasn't until I looked back at him that I realized that Milo was afraid. He'd seen something in me that had scared him.

"I told you I can take care of myself," I said.

"Don't be mad at her," Bobby told Milo. "She was just defending me. It's a good thing."

Milo sighed but didn't say anything. Bobby tried to convince him that his injury wasn't so bad and that I hadn't done anything wrong, so Milo just kept shushing him.

When the elevator doors opened, Olivia was standing in the middle of her penthouse. Her hair hung down her back, blending in with the long black dress she wore. In her hand, she had held a wine glass of fresh, cold blood, and my mouth watered a little.

"Alice, darling, is something the matter?" Olivia asked, stepping forward.

"I need to get him cleaned up," Milo said, helping Bobby off the elevator. "Do you have a bathroom I can use?"

"Yes, right around the corner, past the kitchen." Olivia pointed in the direction, and Milo led Bobby away. "What happened to your human?"

"What'd you need me for so urgently?" I asked, hedging her question.

I shoved my hands in my jacket pockets and walked around her penthouse. Nobody else appeared to be here, except for us, and I didn't sense any sign of danger. I still felt jumpy and anxious from the run-in with Jonathan, but my blood had started to cool, returning to its normal icy temperature.

"Do you want me get you something to drink?" Olivia asked. I stopped at the windows, looking down at the city lights, and I glanced back at her. "You look like you do."

"Yes, please," I nodded.

Olivia went into the kitchen and poured me a bag of blood into a wine glass. Milo came out of the bathroom, and she got him an icepack from her freezer, and he ducked back in the bathroom. She didn't eat, but she kept her place stocked for her human visitors, the same we kept ours stocked for Bobby.

"Here you are," Olivia smiled, handing me the glass.

"Thank you." I'd never drank blood from a glass. It looked elegant, and I took a sip of it, instead of guzzling it down the way I normally did.

"Something happened to you," Olivia said, studying me.

"It's not anything I need to talk about." I shrugged and took another a sip.

"Sit." She gestured to her couches. "Calm your nerves. Then we'll talk."

I sat down, and Olivia lounged on the couch across from me. She pulled her legs up next to her, letting the long silk of the dress flow around her. She twirled the stem of her wine glass between her fingers and watched me as I drank mine.

I tried to drink it slowly, but I really needed it. The blood rushed through me, filling me with the warm ecstasy. My body seemed to lighten. I felt buzzed, but that actually made me more alert than I had been before.

"Did you invite me over here to seduce me or something?" I asked.

Olivia wore a dress, and I'd never seen her in one before. Classical music played in the background, I think Mozart. The lights were dim, and she was plying me with blood in wineglasses.

"No, I wanted you comfortable," she smiled. "I have conquests much higher than you in my sights." I wondered if she meant Violet, but I didn't ask.

Milo and Bobby came out of the bathroom, with Milo leading him along like a Seeing Eye dog. Jonathan had punched him in the left eye, and Bobby held an ice pack over it.

"How are you?" I asked.

"Good as new." Bobby sat down on the couch next to me, and the ice pack shifted in the process, so he grimaced. "Well, almost good as new."

"So did you find out what the big news is?" Milo asked, sitting on the arm of the couch beside Bobby. He had his arm around him meant to look like a romantic gesture, but Milo was protecting him. He still didn't really trust Olivia.

"Not yet," I said. "Why am I here, Olivia?"

"Violet." Olivia leaned her head back, speaking towards the bedrooms behind her.

Milo tightened his arm around Bobby, making him wince, but Milo didn't loosen his grip. I have to admit that any information shrouded in secrecy and Violet tended to make me nervous too, but the blood was working against that. I felt almost serene.

The door to Violet's bedroom opened, but she didn't step out. Instead, a child of about eight or nine came out of the room. Her wavy brown hair hung neatly around her shoulders, and her skin was flawless and smooth. She moved in a slow, deliberate way, and she had poise like I'd never seen.

When she looked at me, that's when it really hit me though. Her blue eyes were ancient. They had none of the innocence and energy a child of her age would have.

"Oh my god." I gaped at her. "How old are you?"

"That's not polite," she said, her voice like a cold bell.

"Alice meet Rebekah, the oldest living child vampire I've met." Olivia smiled, and turned to face her a bit. "Can I tell her old you are?"

"I'm over a thousand years old." Rebekah sounded bored with the idea.

- 23 -

Rebekah didn't move at all. She had a stillness about her that I didn't know any living thing could master, and her eyes seemed to stare right through me, right through everything.

"She's like a porcelain doll, only way creepier," Bobby said in a hushed voice.

"I know, right?" Violet agreed. She'd come out of the bedroom, but I hadn't noticed her because I'd been too fixated on Rebekah. Violet twisted a strand of her hair and eyed up Rebekah warily

There was something tremendously unsettling about her. She looked like a child, and she clearly wasn't one. But it was more than that. I'd never see another vampire that looked less human than her.

"Rebekah, have a seat," Olivia told her, and with a resigned sigh, Rebekah sat on the couch next to her. "She's why I've been gone. I went to get her."

"Was she in trouble or something?" I asked, and I pulled my eyes off Rebekah. She had to think it was impolite that I stared, but I couldn't help it.

"No, I brought her here for you," Olivia said. "You told me about the predicament with your child vampire, and Rebekah knows how to control them. She's managed for centuries."

"I hardly even remember being a child," Rebekah said with some disdain.

"Yes, well, you're the only expert I know." Olivia smiled thinly at her, and Rebekah regarded her with her strange doll eyes.

Rebekah even dressed like a doll. Her dress was more of a gown, and too lavish and ornate for anything a child would wear today. It was as if a porcelain doll had come to life, or at least attempted to, since there didn't seem to be much life in Rebekah.

"I have helped some children over the years, although I'd rather not be doing it anymore." Rebekah crossed one of her legs over the other and laced her fingers on her lap. "Olivia pulled me from Prague for this, and here I am."

"Even you agreed it was time that you returned the favor," Olivia looked coolly at Rebekah.

"I honor all my debts," Rebekah said, holding her chin higher.

"What debts did you have to Olivia?" Bobby blurted out, and I elbowed him in the side. "Don't take me places if you don't want me to talk, Alice."

"No, it's quite alright," Olivia said and sipped her glass. "Young Rebekah had been living in England with her 'family' during the War of the Roses in the fifteenth century. Rebekah allied herself with the house of Lancaster in an attempt to control the throne of England, but that gamble didn't pay off. Rebekah's family was slaughtered in a battle, and she was left an orphan, or so it would seem."

"That's not entirely accurate," Rebekah cast a glare at Olivia, but Olivia waved it off.

"Rebekah was cast out of England, penniless and unable to fend for herself, at least not economically speaking," Olivia said. "I happened to be a courtesan in France, childless and widowed, and that fit Rebekah's needs perfectly."

"She turned you?" I sat forward, looking between the two of them.

"Indeed." Olivia looked over at Rebekah, her expression an odd mix of affection and loathing. "My maker is a child." Rebekah sighed at the use of the term 'child.' "We created an arrangement, after I'd been turned, of course. I would keep her safe, live as her mother in public while in reality I was nothing more than a servant."

"Don't be so dramatic, Olivia," Rebekah said tersely and leaned back on the couch. "We had a good life. Did I ever leave you wanting for anything?"

"You left me wanting my humanity," Olivia replied, surprising me with her depth of emotion. She rarely expressed anything deeper than hunger or annoyance. "It is a debt that you can never repay."

"After this, I will consider my debt paid in full," Rebekah told her.

"I worked for you over two hundred years, and this is only the second favor I have ever asked of you." Olivia's voice began to rise, but she shook her head and took another drink from wineglass. "But it's as you say. This is the last time I call upon you."

"Very well." Rebekah's lips curled up ever so slightly, revealing a hint of a smirk, and she turned to me. "Where is this child of yours?"

"Um, she's hiding out," I said. "I didn't know I was supposed to bring her."

"I'm certain it's for the best that you didn't," Rebekah said. "How old is she?"

"She's five," I said. "And she's been a vampire since November."

"I see." Rebekah pursed her lips and didn't elaborate.

"You can help her, though?" Milo asked. He'd loosened his grip on Bobby, becoming more interested in Rebekah and what she could do for Mae and Daisy. "You can make it so she stops killing people?"

"She's a vampire. Of course I can't guarantee that," Rebekah said. "I can help her learn control. It's a myth that child vampires never grow up. We don't, physically, but with time and practice, we gain the same emotional and mental maturity as our adult counterparts."

"She eats bugs and kills animals," I said, and everyone looked disgusted at that. "Can you stop that?"

"Yes," Rebekah nodded. "It's fairly common for child vampires to be unable to control their hunting impulse. In truth, vampires do crave more than blood. We were meant to kill. But with time, that urge can be dulled."

"How long does that take?" Milo asked.

"It depends." Rebekah tilted her head, thinking. "A decade before I'd let her live in a community with humans. Half-a-century until she matched your level right now. In a full century, you wouldn't be able to tell the difference between her or Olivia, as far as control goes."

"A decade?" My jaw dropped. "You're saying she should live on some deserted island for a decade?"

"I prefer somewhere colder, but yes," Rebekah nodded. "I've called in some acquaintances, and I have found us a place to live in Greenland. We should stay there, off the grid, for the next ten years."

"That seems like an awfully long time," Bobby said, echoing my thoughts exactly.

"For you, perhaps." Rebekah gave him a condescending smile. "For me, for the rest of us, it's a blink of the eye."

"It's longer than a blink of the eye for me," Violet muttered. She'd stayed to the side of the room, avoiding Rebekah. That child vampire must've creeped her out the same way she did me.

"So, what do you think?" Olivia asked me.

"I think its... amazing." I smiled gratefully at her. "I don't know how I'll ever be able to repay you."

"Right now, you needn't do anything," Olivia returned my smile easily. "But eventually, I'm sure that I'll think of something."

"So, Rebekah?" Bobby asked, and she rolled her eyes when he spoke. "What's it like being a child forever?"

"It's an endless hell," Rebekah said, accidentally betraying the emotion she felt. She hurried to erase it, though, so she turned to me. "I would like to leave in the next few days. Is that enough time to make arrangements with the child?"

"Um, yeah," I nodded. "It should be."

"With this settled, I'd like to excuse myself." She stood up and turned to Violet. "Violet, isn't there a human you've prepared for me somewhere?"

"He's not really 'prepared' for anything, but there's a guy in the room next to mine." Violet pointed to the door. "And he's open to… feeding you, I guess."

"Olivia, you really must get better help," Rebekah said as she walked around the couch, the hem of her skirt sliding across the floor. "One must have a reasonable chef on hand to prepare the food."

"Violet isn't help, Rebekah," Olivia said, watching her as she disappeared into the guestroom. "Rebekah doesn't understand that everyone in the world isn't her servant. Despite that, she does know what she's talking about, and she can help you, Alice."

"How do you prepare a human?" Violet interjected, staring warily at the bedroom door even after Rebekah had shut it behind her. "Am I supposed to salt them or something?"

"Rebekah prefers it when someone else opens them first," Olivia explained and pointed to her own neck. "Make an incision in the throat to get the blood flowing. Rebekah claims they bleed faster that way."

"That's interesting," I said.

"I was gonna go with disturbing," Bobby said.

"What the hell happened to your face?" Violet asked, referring the icepack Bobby had clamped to his eye.

"Got punched," Bobby shrugged.

"How bad is it?" I asked.

I hadn't actually been able to see what happened to him because he'd been covering it since it happened. All I knew is that Jonathan had hit him, and he'd bled.

"Not that bad." He took off his icepack. "It wouldn't have been bad at all if it weren't for his ring, but at least his ring missed my actual eyeball."

He moved his hand, and I finally saw his injury. Bobby kept talking, but I couldn't hear him anymore. I couldn't hear anything over the pounding of my own heart, and the blood rushing through my veins.

His eye looked swollen and red, but the bloody shape on his temple was unmistakable, even at an angle. I'd seen that mark before, looking nearly identical to this one. Though the mark I'd seen had been made with heat and not force. It looked like a U, but the scales had even left an imprint in Bobby's skin.

It was a dragon, the symbol for Dracula. The symbol for vampires. That ring had been used to brand the dead girls.

I stood up, but it felt like I was under water. Everyone's voice came out muffled, and I could barely stand up straight.

Every time I'd been around Jonathan, my blood burned. It was because I'd bitten Jane, and the blood left in my system reacted with the blood in his. It was like Jane had been trying to tell me he'd killed her, but I hadn't known to listen.

"He fucking killed her," I breathed, and my vision blurred red. I was getting hazy, like when bloodlust took over and I blacked out, but this was different. This was pure rage.

"Alice?" Milo's face appeared in front of mine, and he put his hands on my shoulders. "What are you talking about?"

"Jonathan killed Jane," I said. "I have to find him."

"What?" Milo blanched and tightened his grip on me.

"He did do it?" Bobby jumped off the couch and hurried over to us. "How do you know?"

"That mark-" I pointed to his temple. "That's the brand."

Olivia and Violet both chimed in to say things about Jonathan and serial killers and demanding to know what was going on, but I couldn't answer them. I could only feel what Jane had felt. Her terror and panic took hold of me again, and I pushed Milo's arms off me and staggered back.

"Alice, where are you going?" Milo asked, trying to follow me.

"I have to...." I shook my head. I had to find him.

"You smashed his face, Alice," Bobby reminded me. "He probably went home."

"No," I said. "No. He's hurt. He has to heal. He's feeding."

When Milo had been hurt, Jack had given him his blood to speed up the process. Vampire blood was more potent than human blood, but fresh blood would do the trick if he needed it to. And after what I'd done to him, he definitely needed it to.

I couldn't wait for the elevator, so I ran to the stairwell in the center of the penthouse. I'm sure someone tried to stop me, Milo had to have, but I didn't hear him and didn't slow down. I raced down the steps, leaping over several at a time, but I was still taking too long.

I looked over the banister, staring down the hole in the center of the stairs. The bottom floor plummeted twenty stories below me, but I couldn't wait.

I propelled myself over the railing, and my feet slammed into the concrete. One of my ankles snapped, hard. Part of the bone stuck out, so I pushed it in. I gritted my teeth to keep from screaming, and I focused on Jonathan and what he'd done. That made it much easier to forget the pain.

The back rooms of the club were an interconnected labyrinth where vampires fed. It could take me hours to find him, but it wouldn't. I stood by the entrance of the halls and closed my eyes, concentrating on his blood. I carried his blood with me, staining my pants, and I could track his scent.

I hurried down the halls, and my ankle threatened to give out, but I forced it on. I ended up running down three different corridors before I found him.

When I pushed open the door to the room, the first thing I saw was Jonathan slumped against the wall. His jaw still looked mangled, but it was clearly healing. Blood covered his face and chest, and his heart beat loud and strong. He was full.

The girl on the bed got my attention next. Her body lay at an odd angle, her spine bent awkwardly back, and her head twisted around. Blood from her neck dripped onto the mattress, but only because gravity made it. Her blood no longer pumped through her veins. Jonathan had his fill of her, and he'd finished her off completely.

"You son of a bitch!" I roared and flew at him. I grabbed him by his jacket and picked him up, then I slammed him into the wall so hard, his skull cracked on the concrete.

"Why are you always bothering me when I eat?" Jonathan asked, his swollen mouth attempting a smirk. "You're a very rude girl."

"You're going to die," I whispered, my face right in front of his.

"You can't save them, you know," Jonathan said wearily. "The humans. They will all die. You're not doing them any favors."

I pulled him back from the wall and threw him, so he landed hard against the opposite wall. His body clattered to the floor, and he laughed. He didn't even bother trying to pull himself up. He slumped against the wall and cackled at me, spraying blood as he did.

"Why Jane?" I asked. "Why her?"

"Because she was *mine*," he growled, pausing his maniacal laughter. "She was a piece of meat. And she thought she could decide when she left, that she was done, but that's not how this works. Humans think they can do anything they want.

"But Jane learned," he said, his smile twisting up. "I even got her to leave that place for me. All I had to do was call her and reminder her who I was and what I did for her. By the time she came back to me, she was begging for me to bite her. The way all humans should. *We're* the top of the food chain, and it's time they learned that!"

"But they won't," I said and it was my turn to smile at him. "I'm going to kill you, here, tonight, and everybody will think that a

324

human killed those girls. A stupid, weak human will get the credit for your work. No one will ever even know that you existed."

That got him. He jumped up and charged at me, slamming me back into the wall. I kicked him off me, and my broken ankle hurt like hell. He tried to punch me, but I dodged, and his hand collided with the cement wall. I stepped back away from him, towards the bed.

"You know, I'm stronger than you think I am," Jonathan grinned. "I've killed stronger bitches than you."

"I'm sure you have," I admitted.

The bed with the dead girl sat on an old metal frame. The legs were long and rusted, and I bent down and snapped one off with ease.

"What are you gonna do with that?" Jonathan laughed. "Poke my eye out?"

"Nope." I held it up, showing him the broken, pointed edge.

"If you think you can stake me with that, you're wrong," he grinned. "That'll snap before it goes through my ribs."

"I know."

My answer confused him, so he moved towards me. I kicked him in the chest, and he stumbled back. I rushed at him and threw him back against the wall. Pulling the metal leg back, I shoved it into his stomach, angling it up.

When I pushed it, it slid underneath his ribs. His eyes widened with surprise, but it was too late to do anything. I slammed the stake up into his heart, and he collapsed against me.

I took a step back and let him fall to the floor. His blood covered my hands, still warm and smelling of the dead girl. The pipe stuck of out his stomach, and his eyes stayed open, staring off at nothing. His hand had fallen on my foot, and I jumped back from it. He was dead, and I didn't want his corpse touching me.

I expected instant relief and gratification from this, and while there was some, I mostly felt sick. I had just killed someone, and even if it was someone that really deserved it, I was still a murderer.

I'm not even sure how I found my way outside. I moved in a daze, and I don't remember anything until I was walking on the sidewalk, a block away from the clubs. People were veering around me and giving me weird looks.

The cold felt wonderful, but I didn't know where I was going, so I just stopped. I closed my eyes and let the wind blow over me. The blood on my hand thickened as it began to dry, moving more slowly as it slid down my fingertips and dripped on the concrete.

"I found her!" Bobby shouted from somewhere nearby, and within seconds, Milo was at my side.

"Oh my god, Alice." Milo put his hands on my face, and I opened my eyes.

"I killed him."

"Are you okay?" Milo asked, and I nodded. "Let's get you home before you get picked up for being a crazy person."

Milo took off his own jacket and wrapped it around me, hiding the blood that stained my clothes. Bobby jogged up to us and tried to tell me they'd been looking all over for me, but he stopped when he saw my face. Milo led me to the car.

Before I got in the car, I put one hand on it, bracing myself. Then I bent over and threw up, my strange red vomit staining the snow all around us.

- 24 -

I took a long shower, but my skin still felt sticky from where Jonathan's blood had been. The water turned cold, and I finally got out and dressed slowly. When I came out of the bathroom, I found Ezra sitting on my bed.

"How are you feeling?" Ezra asked, studying me with his dark eyes.

"Fine," I lied and ran a towel through my damp hair.

"You went against my advice," he said.

"Yeah, sorry about that." I tossed the towel in the hamper and turned my back to him. I didn't want to see the disapproving gaze he gave me after that.

"I told you to call me," he went on. "But from what I understand, you ran away from Milo and Olivia and Violet. You had plenty of back up with you, but you went it alone."

"It was something that I had to do myself." I ran my fingers through my tangles of hair and looked back at him. "I had to take care of him."

"And?"

"And what?" I asked, surprised by the lack of judgment in his words.

"How did it go?" Ezra asked.

"I killed him." The words tasted bitter in my mouth, and I gulped them down. I wanted to throw up or cry at the thought of being a murderer, but I couldn't. I had done the right thing, and I wouldn't let myself shed a tear of Jonathan.

"I'm aware of that." Ezra looked away from me and smoothed out his pants. "Olivia called me after she cleaned up the mess. You owe her a debt of gratitude for that."

"I'll thank her tomorrow," I nodded. I did owe her, and I felt bad for leaving her with my mess. But I didn't have the strength to apologize for it now.

"He had a body in the room with him?" Ezra asked, and I nodded, biting my lip.

"If I'd stopped him when I saw him outside Jane's…" I shook my head and trailed off.

"You did the right thing in waiting." Ezra stood up and stepped over to me. He put his hand on my shoulder, and I looked up at him. "You didn't listen to me, but you handled yourself well. You've shown great strength and maturity, more than many other vampire hunters I've run into. I'm proud of you, Alice."

I wanted to thank him, but I knew if I did, I wouldn't be able to hold back the tears. I could only nod, and Ezra wrapped an arm around me, hugging me to him. I took a deep breath to keep from sobbing, and he held me until he was sure I'd be fine without it.

After he left, I went to bed, and thankfully, sleep came quickly for me. The glowing warmth spread through me, and I buried myself deeper in the pillows. I didn't want to wake up from the dream, back to the stark reality of the cold bed, but I couldn't fight it anymore.

I opened my eyes and blinked to be sure I wasn't still dreaming. Jack sat on the bed next to me, his brow furrowed, but he wasn't doing anything. Just thinking.

"Good morning," I said. I had no idea what he was doing, but it definitely made my heart beat faster.

"Hi. Sorry. I didn't mean to wake you. I just…" He licked his lips and stared at me. "I don't wanna be broken up anymore."

"I don't know what to tell you." I looked away from him and pushed myself so I was sitting up. "I don't even understand why you broke up with me."

"I thought that was the best thing for you." He leaned back, resting his head against the wall. "I felt like it was what you wanted."

"How would I want that?" I asked incredulously. "You know how I feel about you, and what I've fought to be with you!"

"And what you've given up." He sighed. "You gave up way too much."

"I didn't give up anything," I said. Unless he meant Peter, but I hoped we weren't going down that road again.

"You gave up being human," he said. "For me, it never seemed like that big of a deal. But for you, I think giving up death really messed with you."

"I didn't give it up. I can still die," I said, but he did have a point.

"And you're so young." He chewed his lip. "Compared to me, you don't seem that young, but you are. You didn't know what you wanted to do with your life, and that was okay when you were seventeen and had college to figure it out. But when you got immorality, you had endless time in front of you, and it's like you had no idea what to do. It's too much."

"Yeah," I agreed. "But there's nothing I can do about that. I can't undo this, and it's not like I want to die. I just… I've been trying to find something I'm passionate about, besides you. Something to fill my time with."

"No, I understand that. I got afraid that I was holding you back." He looked over at me. "This whole thing with Jane, when you were tracking down her killer, that was the most excited I've seen you about anything in a long time."

"It wasn't exciting," I shook my head. A knot in my stomach twisted when I remembered killing Jonathan. "Murder isn't fun."

"No, no, I know that." His brow furrowed. "Are you okay with all of that?"

"Yeah, I'm fine," I brushed him off. "I don't want to talk about that, though."

"Okay." He stared at me for a moment, then went on, "I know you're not into death, and I know you were motivated by revenge. But something about that really appealed to you."

"Yeah, I guess." I thought about it, trying to separate my feelings of grief over Jane to the actual act of searching for a killer. "I liked solving it and feeling like I did something that mattered. Jonathan was killing girls, and I stopped him."

"You did." Jack reached over and squeezed my hand. "I'm very, very proud of you for that. Do you know that?"

"Not really," I shook my head.

"You did something you believed in and helped people." He turned on the bed so he faced me and moved closer to me. "You don't need to hide that from me, okay? I mean, if this is who you are, what you're passionate about then... Good. I support you, one hundred percent."

"I don't think this is something I want to do," I said. "It was a onetime fluke thing. But thank you for supporting me, I guess."

"Anytime." He smiled and looked at me intently. "I love you, Alice. And if you can forgive me for reacting poorly the other night, do you still wanna spend forever with me?"

I smiled back at him but I didn't get a chance to answer. Peter knocked on the open bedroom door. Hanging onto the doorframe, he leaned into the bedroom.

"Sorry to interrupt, but Mae is freaking out," Peter said, but the smirk at the edge of his mouth led me to believe he wasn't sorry. "She says she can't find some sheets her mother gave her or something, and since Alice has been taking care of the laundry, Mae really wants to see you."

"Alice!" Mae shouted from downstairs, emphasizing his point.

"Tell her I'll be down in a minute." I sighed and got out of bed.

Peter lingered in the doorway for a moment as I grabbed a pair of jeans off the bedroom floor. I'd only worn a tank top and underwear to bed, but they were full-on panties that covered everything.

"Peter, why don't you go let Mae know?" Jack suggested, not unkindly, and Peter took the cue and disappeared downstairs.

"Sorry," I told him as I slid on my pants. "I mean, that we didn't get to talk."

"No, it's no big deal." He waved it off. "We've got time, right?"

"Yeah," I smiled.

By the time I made it downstairs, Mae had completely torn through the linen closet in the hall. She'd gone over to Olivia's to get everything straightened out with Rebekah, and afterwards, she came over here with Daisy and Peter to start packing.

They were leaving tomorrow for Greenland, but they'd left most of their belongings in Australia because they'd been forced to leave in such a hurry. Mae had gone on several shopping trips lately, but she still had things she wanted to get from the house before she left.

"Alice!" Mae yelled again, tearing an old quilt from the closet.

"I'm right here, Mae," I said walking up to her.

"Oh. Sorry, love." She pushed a curl back from her face and smiled at me. "I've just been so frazzled with all of this."

"It's alright. What did you need?"

"This blanket my mother gave me. It had roses on it." She held up the quilt, which did not have roses on it. "Have you seen it?"

"No, I don't think so," I shook my head. "Didn't you take with you to Australia?"

"No." She put her hands on her hips and sighed. "I don't think I could find it then."

334

"Are you sure it's even here? I mean, maybe you left it the last time you moved," I said.

"I thought for sure it was here." She shrugged helplessly, staring into the closet.

"Well, just make sure you pick up your mess when you're done," I teased, since she'd said that same thing to me a dozen times before. She shot me a look as I walked away, and it made me laugh.

I left her to finish sorting through what few undisturbed linens we had in the house and went to the living room. Milo had set up a game of Candyland on the floor, and he sat cross-legged across from Daisy.

"How's it going?" I asked, crossing my arms over my chest.

"Great." Milo shrugged.

"Where's Bobby?" I asked.

"I sent him away." Milo motioned to Daisy, who seemed more interested in making the colored pawns dance with each other than playing the game. "I think Ezra and Peter are working on getting money transferred for them to leave and all that."

"How does Ezra feel about them leaving?" I lowered my voice, and Milo shrugged.

"These dolls aren't as much fun as my *real* dolls," Daisy sighed. She spun around the blue pawn and stuck out her bottom lip. "I wish Mae would let me take them out."

"You're getting ready to move," Milo said, doing his best to sound cheerful. "Remember, Daisy? Mae talked to you about all the work you had to do."

"I'm sick of moving." Daisy spun the pawn harder, and it went flying under a nearby chair. Her face crumpled, like she might start sobbing over a missing pawn.

"I'll get it. Don't worry," Milo rushed to appease her. He crawled over to the chair and reached underneath it, feeling around for the pawn.

"He'll get it, Daisy," I said and put my hand on her back, and her lip quivered. "It's okay. You don't need to get upset."

"Is she getting cranky?" Mae asked from the hall. "It's been a few hours since she ate."

With his arm still stuffed under the chair, Milo arched his eyebrow at the words *a few hours*. Daisy was crabby because it'd been hours since she'd eaten. Even when I was brand new, I'd been able to go a day or two without any problems.

"Ouch!" Milo winced and yanked his hand back from under the chair.

Before I saw it, I could smell it. A shard of glass left over from the broken picture frame had been under the chair. In feeling around, Milo had managed to impale it in his forearm. Some blood seeped around the edges, already smelling sweet and strong, but when he pulled the glass out, it bled faster and harder. The air filled with the scent.

Daisy was on him before either of us could react. Her mouth clamped onto his arm, and Milo grabbed onto the back of her hair. He yanked her back, but she took a chunk of his flesh with her, which only made her more insane.

I bolted up and wrapped my arms around her waist, but she wriggled free. She was so small, she slid out, and launched herself at him. This time she went for his neck, and Milo couldn't even push her off. If he did, he risked tearing out his throat.

"Get her... off me." His words came out garbled, thanks to Daisy's teeth in his neck.

Mae ran in, yelling her name, but I wouldn't let her near them. I didn't trust her to do everything she needed to do save Milo.

I used the same trick Jack had used on me when I wouldn't stop drinking from Bobby. I wrapped my hand around Daisy's throat, squeezing as tight as I could so she couldn't swallow. Not that I could tell if she was even swallowing. Her bites seemed to be random attacks that had less to do with drinking blood than they did uncontrolled rage.

Daisy did stop biting him long enough to turn around and clamped her mouth on my hand. I moved back, dragging her with me so I could get her away from Milo. The wound in his neck poured all over the floor, and he pressed his hands to it, trying to stop the flow.

I wrapped my arms around Daisy, pinning her to me in hopes she would calm down, but she only seemed to get crazier with bloodlust. She clawed at my arms. Her little fingernails were like steel and raked through my skin, and she bit me anywhere her mouth could reach.

"Daisy, honey, calm down!" Mae begged her with tears in her eyes.

"Do something about that child *now!*" Ezra boomed, standing at the side of the room. "Or I will."

"Alice, let me have her!" Mae held her hands out to me.

Daisy bit my arm so hard, her teeth smashed into my bone. I winced, but I looked uncertainly at Ezra. I wasn't doing a great job of holding her back, but at least when she was biting me, I knew she wasn't hurting anyone else.

Then Daisy reached up and sliced the underside of my chin open with her fingernails. She tried to wiggle up, so she could get to the blood, and that's when I let her go.

"Daisy!" Mae yelled, but Daisy ran past her.

Ezra and Peter blocked the doorway to the next room, and I stood on the other side of the room, so Daisy had nowhere to go. She ran to the corner and turned to face us, her face contorted in her demon smile as she snarled.

While I'd been trying to contain Daisy, Jack had come down, and he sat crouched over Milo, holding a blanket to his neck. The scratches and bites that covered my upper body stung and tingled as they tried to heal.

"Daisy, love." Mae held her arms out to her and walked slowly towards her. "You need to calm down, sweetie. Everything will be alright."

"No!" Daisy snarled, with blood dripping from her mouth. "No! It won't! I'm hungry! I'm so *hungry*!"

"I can feed you, love," Mae told her softly.

Mae reached out for her, and Daisy swiped at her. Daisy had begun to sob, but her bloodlust hadn't relented. Mae grabbed her, wrapping her arms around her tightly to hold in her place, but Daisy fought her mercilessly, biting and kicking and clawing.

"Daisy, love, please calm down." Mae tried stroking her hair, and Daisy nearly bit off one of Mae's fingers. "Daisy!"

"I'm hungry!" Daisy wailed as tears mixed with blood staining her cheeks. "It hurts! It *hurts*!"

She threw her head back and began to scream. This wasn't the scream of a child having a tantrum. This was a child in incredible, intense pain from being hungry, and she could do nothing to satiate it.

"Mae." Ezra walked over to her, watching as Mae struggled to control Daisy, and he crouched down next to them.

"She's not usually like this," Mae insisted, looking up at him with tears in her eyes. "This is the worst I've ever seen her, but…"

"Mae," Peter said gently. "That's not true. She's like this all the time now."

"It hurts!" Daisy cried, but her fit seemed to be lessening. She had stopped biting Mae, but she kept kicking and wriggling.

"Mae, she's in pain," Ezra told her quietly, his dark eyes rested on her.

"If I feed her…" Mae trailed off.

"When was the last time she ate?" Ezra asked.

"Three hours ago." Mae swallowed hard and looked down at the sobbing child in her arms. She screamed and thrashed because of how much pain she was in, and even if Mae fed her now, it would only hurt again in a few hours.

Nobody understood how it felt exactly for a child to be a vampire. By the way Daisy acted, I suspected she felt pain even worse than I did when I was starving. It had to be more than a lack of control that made her react like that. She was in agony.

"Daisy." Mae held her close to her, hugging her more than restraining her, and stroked the damp curls on her head. "Daisy, love, please…" Mae squeezed her eyes tightly as tears slid out.

Daisy's fight picked back up, and she reached out for Ezra, trying to claw at him. She snarled and almost lunged from Mae's arms, but Mae held fast to her. In response, Daisy sunk her teeth into Mae's shoulders.

"Daisy, I love you." Mae whispered.

She kissed the top of her head, stroked her hair, and then as she held Daisy in her arms, Mae reached up and twisted her neck sharply. The cracking sound that her neck made as it snapped was barely audible, but I jumped when I heard it.

For a moment – barely even long enough to take a breath – everything was so eerily silent, it didn't seem real.

Then Mae began to wail, and it was a sound unlike any I had ever heard before. Rocking the dead child in her arms, Mae wept with everything in her. Ezra tried to put his arm around her, and at first she pushed him off, screaming at him that she hated him, but finally she relented, letting him cradle her.

Milo had lost enough blood where he was on the brink of blacking out, so Jack ran to get him blood. I sat next to him, holding the blanket on his neck, and watched Mae fall apart. Milo drank quickly, and then Jack carried him upstairs so he could rest.

My own wounds had already healed, but dried blood covered my skin and clothes. I should've went upstairs to change or hide out, but I sat on the steps off the living room, listening to Mae.

For a while, I didn't think she would ever stop crying, but eventually, she began to lose her voice. She made small croaked sobs and sniffles. I heard Ezra murmuring things to her, but she never responded.

"Alice?" Peter asked, and I looked up. I'd had my head resting on the wall, leaning and listening. He stood in front of me at the bottom of the steps, his green eyes moist.

"Hi," I said softly. I didn't want to disturb Ezra and Mae, even though they were both far enough away and so lost in their own pain that they would never notice me.

"What are you doing?" Peter asked, and I shook my head.

I had no good answer for what I was doing. I just... I felt like I should hear. Like this was my fault somehow, and it hurt listening to Mae cry like that, so I should listen. As some kind of punishment.

"Mind if I join you?" Peter asked taking a step up towards me.

"No, of course not." I gestured to the empty space on the stair next to me, and he sat down. "How are you doing?"

"I don't know." He shook his head, but his eyes were still wet and red. Daisy had gotten under his skin, and he hadn't want to see anything bad happen to her. "I knew it would end this way, but..."

"I'm sorry." I put my hand on his back, leaving tacky bloodstains on his shirt, but I doubted he'd mind. "I know you liked her."

341

"It is better this way," he said thickly and looked down at his hands. "Her life would've been torture. She was going to keep hurting people, killing them, but I think Mae would've stomached that. It was just... she was in so much pain."

"Yeah?" I asked.

"Yeah." He nodded and swallowed. "Daisy would wake up at night, screaming in pain. The hunger is too intense for something that small. They can't..." His mouth twisted as he fought off tears.

"I'm still sorry this happened," I said.

"Me too." Tears streamed down his cheek, and I put my arm around him, pulling close to me.

Peter cried softly in my arms, and I wouldn't have known if it wasn't for the shaking of his body as he held back sobs. I ached for him, and I wanted to take away his pain.

"I'm sorry," he mumbled when he got himself under control a bit.

"Don't be sorry." I pushed the hair back from his face, and he sat up more but still remained close to me.

When he looked at me, his green eyes meeting mine, I'd never seen him look more wounded. With my hand still on his face, I leaned in kissed his cheek, meaning to kiss his tears away. His skin warmed under my lips, sending a familiar thrill racing through me, and I leaned back.

I wiped my thumb along the spot I'd kissed him, erasing it, and his eyes held me the way the once had. Captivating and entrancing, for a moment, I didn't breathe. I didn't want to. I just wanted to lose myself in Peter, and forget about everything else that hurt so much lately.

But I did remember, and I exhaled deeply, knowing this moment had to end.

"You'll be okay, won't you?" I asked, dropping my hand back to my lap.

"I always am." Peter attempted a small smile, and his effort made me smile.

"I do love you, you know?" I asked him, and he nodded.

"You just love him more."

"But that doesn't change the way I feel about you." I reached over and took his hand in mine. "Nothing can. And I don't want anything bad to happen to you."

"You're worried I'm going to do something stupid?" Peter arched his eyebrow, and his smile widened.

"You tend to do that when you're hurting," I said.

"Don't worry, Alice. I know that you'll always come chasing me down, and I won't do anything to risk your safety again."

"So..." Jack interrupted, and I looked up to see him standing at the top of the steps, staring down at me sidled up next to Peter, holding his hand. "I just thought I'd let you know that Milo was doing good."

"Thanks, Jack." I let go of Peter's hand and stood up, but I didn't rush. I hadn't done anything wrong, and I had nothing to hide. "I should go get cleaned up."

"Yeah. Do what you want." Jack walked down the stairs, brushing past me and Peter.

"Where are you going?" I asked.

"Out," he said without looking back. "And I'm leaving on a business trip tonight, so don't wait up."

"Jack!" I called after him, but he didn't answer.

- 25 -

Ezra buried Daisy in the backyard, under the willow tree. After that, he decided that we'd had enough of it here and put the house up for sale.

The next few days, Mae was inconsolable. She moved like a zombie, and Ezra had to physically prompt to her do anything. She was pale and listless, and I'm not sure that even Ezra was convinced that she would ever get better. But no matter, he would stand by her through this.

Milo decided that we needed to visit our mom and that Leif needed to come with us. I was against it, but Milo eventually wore me down. She was our mother, and she had loved us the best she could. She didn't deserve to be alone, abandoned by everyone she loved, without knowing why.

More than that, maybe she didn't need to be abandoned anymore. Milo wanted to come clean with her in hopes that we wouldn't have to hide from her.

Before Leif came in, Milo and I sat with her alone in our old apartment, and Milo told her the whole truth. About where we'd been and that we were vampires.

At first, Mom got angry, asking why we were being so cruel to her. Then Leif came in, and all her defenses melted. He told her she looked as beautiful as she ever did, and by the look in his eyes, I think he meant it. They both cried and kissed, and after that we talked. We talked for hours, having the first real open conversation we'd ever had.

She cried a lot, and I'd never really seen her cry before. She apologized for always running away from us, and said she was a coward. Milo and I reminded her too much of Leif, and she'd been trying to out run the pain from that, but she never could.

When Milo and I left, Leif was still there. By the way they were interacting, I doubted he'd leave any time soon. They had a lot of years to catch up on.

That reunion made me feel a tad bit better about everything else going on. Jack still hadn't talked to me much since he'd been on his business trip. He responded to a couple text messages, but never initiated them.

Although, in that defense, he said the trip was really busy since he was doing it all by himself, and Ezra was supposed to be the one to handle it. But Ezra was busy taking care of Mae, and Peter was mourning in his own Peter way.

I tried not to think about anything and went about putting the house in order. I wasn't sure how long it would take to sell, or where we would go once it was sold, but I wanted to be prepared.

As I was going through my clothes, sorting them out to pack and to get rid of, I opened my underwear drawer in the closet. I decided I had way too many, and I picked up a handful to throw away. I lifted them up, and something caught on the drawer.

A diamond encrusted heart-shaped locket, Peter's gift to me for my eighteenth birthday. I detangled it from the panties and my drawer, and I held it up, watching as it spun and light shone off the diamonds.

It was very beautiful, and I loved it, even though I had no idea where I'd ever wear something that extravagant. I clasped it behind my neck and went over to the mirror to admire how the necklace looked on me. I'd never tried it on before, and it did look stunning, resting right above my cleavage.

But I would never wear it. No matter how lovely it might be, it wasn't for me. I unhooked the locket, and I set it with the stuff to get rid of.

Peter hadn't been taking Daisy's death much better than Mae. He'd spent the whole time locked inside Ezra's den with the lights off, listening to classical music.

Bobby had a big art show opening at the college, and I made Peter go with me to get out of the house for a while. Bobby had done some really amazing charcoal sketches, and even Peter commented on his talent.

But it wasn't long before the crowd started getting to him. Not the blood, but all the chatter. Too many people talking too much. We stayed long enough to see Bobby's work and tell him it was fantastic, then we left to let him and Milo deal with the crowds all night long.

"It's good to get out of the house sometimes," I told Peter as we walked out of the college.

"I guess," he shrugged. "I prefer sitting in the den listen to Joseph Hadyn."

"You and Ezra are so much alike sometimes, it's not even funny," I rolled my eyes.

"Well, we have lived together for nearly two-hundred years," Peter pointed out. "We ought to have some things in common."

"Yeah," I said and pressed my hand to my stomach. The strangest wave of nausea hit me, and I stopped, waiting a moment until it passed.

"Are you okay?" Peter asked, pausing to wait for me.

We stood in the middle of the sidewalk as art students and their friends and family brushed past us. Peter put a hand on my arm and ushered me off to the side so we weren't blocking traffic so much.

"Yeah, I'm fine," I nodded.

"You're sure?" he asked.

"I'm fine," I insisted, and the queasiness had passed, so I thought I really might be.

Twice more on the short drive home, I felt that same weird nausea pinching my stomach. I rolled down the windows, hoping the cold night air would help, and it did help, a little bit. Peter asked me about it, but I didn't want to talk, so I turned up Julian Plenti on the stereo so I wouldn't have to.

As soon as he pulled into the garage, Peer jumped out of the car and ran around to help me out. I tried to brush him off, but I doubled over when I stood up. The nausea was so intense, I almost threw up all over his shoes.

"What's wrong?" Peter wrapped his arm around me and helped me hobble to the house.

"I don't know." I shook my head. "It just… hit me. Maybe I have the flu."

"Vampires can't get the flu," he said and pulled open the door to the house. "Oh fuck."

"What?" I lifted my head, but when I saw the kitchen, I understood.

The house had been ransacked. Broken appliances and a dining room chair were splintered all over. Blood stained the tiles, splattering red on everything.

- 26 -

I ran into the house, pushing past Peter, and I found the source of the blood lying in the corner of the kitchen. Matilda's fur had been soaked red, and she whimpered up at me, thumping her tail on the floor. I wanted to crouch down next to her and tell her everything would be alright, but I couldn't.

"Ezra!" I shouted, holding my stomach to fight the pain growing inside me. "Mae!"

"I'm looking!" Peter ran ahead, and I went after him.

He went upstairs, and I searched the downstairs. Every room I went through looked like it had been demolished. But I never found anybody.

"Nobody's here," Peter said, running down the stairs to me.

"Maybe they weren't here." I ran a hand through my hair and tears stung my eyes.

"I think their cars were gone in the garage," Peter said, rushing back to the garage. He pushed open the door to check, but he paused there.

"What?" I asked.

"The Lexus is gone." He looked back at me. "But the Delorean is here."

"Jack was supposed to come back tonight," I remembered, and the pain in my stomach intensified. I put a hand over my mouth to keep the sob back. "Oh my god, Peter, what if he was here?"

"Call him," Peter commanded pulling out his own phone. "I'm calling Ezra. Maybe they went somewhere together."

I pulled my phone out of my pocket, and Matilda whined. Kneeling down next to her, I listened to the phone ringing in my ear over and over again. While I listened to Jack not answering his phone, I stroked her wet fur, trying to comfort her.

Peter called Ezra, and I heard him talk excitedly when Ezra answered. But Jack never answered. Somewhere in the back of my mind, I knew he wouldn't.

"Ezra and Mae are safe. They went to the headstone of her other child." Peter hung up his phone, and then he saw my face. "Jack didn't answer?"

"No." I swallowed hard and stood up. "Where is he?"

The nausea hit me again, much harder this time, and it sent a shooting pain all over my body. I bent forward and collapsed on the ground on my knees. The pain had gotten too intense for me to stand.

"Alice!" Peter crouched down next to me and put his hand on my back.

"Oh, hell." I gritted my teeth to keep from crying out.

"When was the last time you bit Jack?" Peter asked me, and I shook my head.

"I don't know," I managed when the pain subsided a bit. "What does it matter?"

352

"That pain you're feeling, do you think that could be Jack?"

"What?" I looked up at Peter.

"Maybe you can use it to track Jack." He put his arm around my waist. "Come on." He stood up, pulling me with him.

"The pain?" I held my stomach. "That's coming from Jack? He's feeling that much pain?"

"Don't think about it." Peter put his hands on my shoulder and looked me in the eyes. "If you wanna find Jack, you need to focus on him. You can tell where he's coming from."

"How?" I asked.

"Think about him. Not the pain, *him*."

I closed my eyes and thought of Jack. The pain jolted through me again, and Peter squeezed my shoulders, keeping me here, in the moment. I thought of Jack, his smile, his laugh, and the tether that kept us connected... and then there it was. I could feel it – *him* – pulling me.

"I don't know where he is, but I can take us there," I opened my eyes. "We have to go."

"I'll drive."

As we ran out the door, I promised Matilda we'd come back for her as soon as we could. I sat in the passenger seat of the Lamborghini, holding my stomach to keep from throwing up, and I told Peter where to turn. I couldn't tell him directly where to go – it was just a pull in a certain direction.

We were almost there when I realized we were going to the tunnels where Peter, Mae, and Daisy had stayed. Jack had been taken underground.

"Do you know what he's doing there?" I asked Peter as he pulled up next to the bridge.

"No," he shook his head. "There shouldn't be anybody here at all. If Leif has been staying with your mother... The tunnel should be empty."

The pull and pain got stronger when we reached the tunnels, and I ran down them as fast as my legs would carry me. Peter called for me to slow down, to wait for him, but I couldn't. I knew how much pain Jack was in, and I had to get to him.

Before I reached the cavern where Peter had been staying, I could hear Jack's screams echoing through the sewers. My skin crawled, and adrenaline pulsed through me. Something else, the animal part of me, started taking over, blocking out the way Jack felt. It even blotted out my connection to him, but I didn't care. I needed to be strong to help him.

I peered around the entrance of the cavern to see what I was up against, and it made my blood run cold. Thomas, Samantha, and Dane – the vampire hunters – had ransacked the cavern too. All of Peter and Mae's things had been flipped over and torn apart.

Samantha had cut open Mae's mattress, and she dug through it. Dane stood at the edge of the cliff, holding a chain in his hands. The chain had been looped through an old pulley system in the ceiling, and Jack hung from the other end of it, right over the edge of the cliff. His hands were bound with chains, and he had blood all over his body. His head hung down, and his body was limp.

Thomas stood off to the side of him, leaning on a walking cane. Or at first I thought it was a walking cane. Then I realized it was a long metal poker, and the end on the ground still glowed orange. They'd set fire to Leif's books, and the smoke from it stung the air.

"So, you're still saying that you don't know where the child is?" Thomas asked. He picked up the poker, twirling it in his hand like a baton.

"No, I've already told you she's dead," Jack said, and Dane yanked on the chain, making Jack bounce up and down. He grimaced, and his shoulders had already been popped from their sockets. His wrists looked like they'd been crushed, and blood seeped down his arms.

"We need to find the child," Thomas said firmly. "I don't think you understand how serious I am."

"No, I do... I just..." Jack closed his eyes and winced. "I can't help you."

Thomas held the poker over the flame from the books, waiting until the end was glowing bright yellow, and he took it out. He stepped toward Jack, raising the poker, and I couldn't take it anymore.

"Stop!" I shouted and ran inside.

"Alice." Jack looked at me, and his eyes were wide and terrified.

"Well, well." Thomas grinned and twirled the hot poker again. "Maybe she can tell us something."

"No!" Jack shouted. "She doesn't know anything! Leave her alone!" He struggled against the chains, bucking so hard at them that it had to cause excruciating pain. "Alice! Get out of here!"

"Do you have the child?" Samantha asked. She stood up from her task of butchering the mattress, still holding the knife in her hand, and stepped towards me.

"No," I said. "But I know where she is."

"Alice!" Jack yelled. "No, don't listen to her! She doesn't know anything! The child is dead!"

"Oh, be quiet." Thomas sounded bored. While looking at me, he jabbed the burning poker backwards, right into Jack's abdomen, and he twisted it.

"Stop it!" I yelled. "Stop it or I won't tell you where she's at!"

"Tell us where she is, or we'll kill him," Thomas countered.

"I don't think she knows anything," Samantha sniffed. She stepped closer to me, cocking her head and breathing me in. "I think she's lying."

"I think you're a stupid bitch," I said.

Her eyes widened, which was probably the biggest reaction I would get out of her. I raised my right arm like I meant to hit her, and when she dodged to the side, I kicked her with my leg, connecting right in her stomach.

As she went to the ground, Samantha tried to swipe out my legs from under me with her knife, but I jumped. She hit the concrete but did a backflip back up, landing on her feet.

She kicked me in my hip, but I grabbed her leg, twisting her around. She jerked the knife back, stabbing me in the stomach, but I ignored that and grabbed her hair and yanked it back.

"Fighting like a typical bitch," Samantha grinned wickedly at me.

"I'm just getting started." I pulled the knife from stomach, and I sliced open her neck.

I let go of her, and she wrapped a hand around her throat, trying to stop the blood flow. I turned the knife sideways, and while she held her throat, I stabbed the knife into her chest. It slid in between her ribs and right into her heart.

She stared at me for a moment, and she didn't fall, so I twisted the knife, making sure she was dead. Her eyes rolled to the back of her head, and she fell back on the concrete.

"That was unexpected," Thomas said.

I wiped her blood off my hand, trying to make it less slippery, and then I threw the knife at Dane. It only hit him in the shoulder, not enough to really hurt him, but it startled him into letting the chain go. I thought it might, so I started racing forward as soon as I threw the knife.

When I got close to the edge, I jumped. One foot landed on Dane, and I used him as leverage to jump up higher. It also had the side effect of knocking Dane forward, and he fell over the side of the cliff. I heard him yelling as he fell, but I never heard him hit the bottom.

I grabbed the end of the chain just before it slid through the last pulley, stopping it a split second before Jack plummeted down after Dane. The force of Jack falling pulled the chain hard, and it slammed me into the ceiling.

I almost lost my grip, so I looped the chain around my wrist twice. I used my body as an anchor, preventing the chain from slipping through the pulley, and Jack from falling down the endless hole.

Thomas didn't get to stop us because Peter came in, and he started fighting with him. Thomas turned out to be a much better fighter than his friends, but Peter wasn't too bad himself. He bounced off a wall to kick Thomas in the head, but Thomas recovered quickly.

Bracing my feet against the ceiling, I tried pulling the chain up. Jack wasn't that heavy, but I had one wrist bound to the chain, so I had to do it one-handed. Plus, I had to do it hanging upside down, and the angle I pulled it from made it hard to slide through.

"Alice." Jack stared up at me, his feet dangling over a black, bottomless pit.

"Hold on, Jack. I'm getting you." I strained on the chain.

The chain cut into my wrist deep, making blood pour down over my arm and the chain. The chain was slick, and it began to slip through my hands. It would deglove my hand soon, and if it did that, the chain would slide free, off my hand, through the pulley, and Jack would fall down...

"Alice, don't!" Jack yelled.

"No, I'll get it!" But as soon as I said it, the chain slipped.

I'd pulled Jack up higher, so when the chain slipped through my hand, he fell harder and faster. That put more pressure on my wrist when the chain pulled taut.

The force of it slammed my hand into the pulley, and I heard Jack cry out. The chain had to be nearly tearing off his own hands and arms.

"Alice, listen to me. You have to stop. You can't pull me up, and if you try, you'll just lose your hand and end up falling down with me."

"I can save you," I told him. "You have to trust me."

"No, you need to free your wrist and swing back on the cliff," Jack said. "We both don't need to die for this."

"No! If you die, I die! You asked me to spend forever with you, and I'm going to! "

I strained harder, pulling the chain farther up. I only had to get it up far enough where Jack could swing over, and put his feet on the cliff, and that was only a few more feet. Peter was too busy fighting off Thomas to help, so I was left struggling with Jack on my own.

I almost had him. His head was over the top of the cliff, but the chain slipped again. This time it was too much. The chain crushed my wrist. I heard the bones snap when it hit the pulley, and the chain pulled at my skin.

I was losing blood, which only made me weaker, and the blood left the chain impossibly slippery. I couldn't get a grip on it again. It didn't matter how strong I was. The blood made it too slick, and the chain was going to slip off.

"Alice," Jack said, but I kept pulling at the chain. I couldn't get any traction, and my hand kept slipping. I wasn't moving him at all, but I kept trying to pull and pull as tears stung my eyes.

"Jack, I love you, and I'm not giving up on you!" I hung upside right above him, my feet pressed to the ceiling and my wrist wedged in the chain against the pulley. He was looking right in my eyes, and he knew.

"I'm sorry for everything I said to you the other night. I didn't mean any of it. I was just trying to protect you," Jack said, his voice thick. "I wasn't even mad, and I can forgive you of anything. I always would. I love you. More than anything else in this world or the next."

The only thing I could see were his blue eyes. They were the only thing I wanted to see. They never wavered, not even when the chain slid off my wrist.

- 27 -

I hit the concrete hard. I had wanted to fall over the edge of the cliff, following Jack down, but I'd been angled just the right way so I landed on my back on the ground. I stared up at the bricks on the ceiling, and for a minute, I couldn't feel anything.

I heard Peter grunting. Somewhere in the back of my mind, I knew I should help him, but I couldn't bring myself to do it.

With some effort, I turned my head to see Peter crouched over the edge of the cliff next to me, the chain in his hands. It took me a second to realize what I was seeing. Hand over hand, he pulled the chain up, and within a few seconds, he heaved Jack up over the edge.

"Jack!" I screamed and crawled over to him.

With his hands still bound and his chest and stomach covered in wounds, I dove at him. I pressed my lips to his, kissing him. I brushed back the hair from his forehead and sobbed.

"I love you, I love you, oh my god, I love you," I repeated over and over between kisses.

I had thought that I had truly lost him, and there was a desperation to the kiss that he matched with equal fervor. I wrapped my arms around his neck and held him to me, breathing him in, tasting his lips, relishing his heart pounding against mine.

"I'm okay, Alice," he smiled, looking me in the eye.

"I'm sorry for everything I've put you through," I said. Tears of relief streamed down my face, and Jack just smiled at me. "I've never stopped loving you. Never. And I was wrong. You're all I need to be happy. You're all I'll ever need."

"I'm not all you need, and I don't even want to be. I just want to love you, for the rest of my life, and as long as you let me do that, we'll be okay."

I leaned to kiss him again, but he stopped me.

"I hate to do this, but would it be okay if we popped my arms back in their socket before we made out?" Jack asked, and when I apologized, he laughed, sending the same dazzling tingles through me that he always did.

"Need help?" Peter asked, crouching down next to us.

I got over the shock of seeing Jack alive and looked over Peter for the first time. He'd sustained a few blows himself, but Thomas was the one with a metal poker through his heart in the corner.

Jack grimaced as Peter shoved both his arms back in place. Peter got to work getting the chain from around Jack's wrists. He might've dislocated Jack's thumb in the process, but he got the chain off.

He sat up, rubbing his battered wrists, although they didn't look as bad as my completely wrecked hand. Peter tossed the chain off the cliff, still crouched down in front of us, and Jack looked at him.

"Hey, Peter?" Jack said, popping his thumb back into place.

"Yeah?" Peter turned to him.

"Thank you." Jack met his eyes, and they looked at each other for a moment. Peter swallowed and nodded.

"We should probably get you guys out of here," Peter said, standing up. "Your girlfriend needs to get that hand fixed."

"Holy hell." Jack noticed my hand for the first time.

It looked like a bloody piece of meat. The tingling heat had taken over, scrambling to heal. I'd actually lost a lot of skin, and I wasn't really sure how it would grow back.

Peter grabbed a towel, and I wrapped my hand in it. He helped both Jack and I out to the car, and Jack explained how he'd ended up there in the first place. He'd gotten home to find the vampire hunters demolishing the house, and Matilda in the process.

Apparently, they were obsessed with finding Daisy. They were certain she was part of the movement and sent to expose vampires. The hunters would do anything to stop that, and nothing Jack could say would convince them she was dead. If he'd been there when she'd been buried, that might've helped.

Samantha had seen the Lamborghini parked outside the tunnels before when they were following me, and she insisted that Jack take them down there. When they still didn't find Daisy, they resorted to torturing Jack for information, and that's when I had walked in.

On the car ride back to the house, I called Milo to tell him to come home. Ezra and Mae were already waiting, and something about the crisis had set Mae back into motion. She wrapped my hand in gauze.

The skin would grow back in a few hours, but I didn't want a bloody hand until then. Ezra took care of Jack, checking his wounds and forcing him to compensate for his blood loss.

As soon as Milo and Bobby arrived, Jack sent them back out to take Matilda to the emergency vet clinic. Ezra thought she had a few broken bones, but he figured that she would be alright, once she had proper medical care.

After Mae finished tending to me, I headed upstairs to lie down. Jack was already up there, and I could hear him arguing with Ezra. Ezra told him that he needed to let the blood work, and Jack kept insisting that he should be at the vet with Matilda, even if he did have bleeding wounds all over.

Peter was in the dining room, picking up the mess the vampire hunters had left, and I stopped.

"How are you?" I asked.

"Better than you." He looked down at my hand. "How is that doing?"

"I'll live," I shrugged.

"Glad to hear it," he smiled, and he looked at me. His emerald eyes met mine, and though they didn't captivate me the way they once had, they still held my attention.

"Thank you, Peter," I said softly. "For what you did tonight."

"You know, I didn't save him for you." He looked towards upstairs, where Jack was. "He's a good guy, and the world wouldn't be as nice a place without him in it."

"I know," I smiled. "But thank you anyway."

I went upstairs, and Ezra stood in the bedroom doorway, blocking Jack from making an escape. He sat on the bed in his boxers. Most of his cuts had healed, but some were still raised and red. A bad one his stomach still bled.

"Mattie's gotta be terrified without me!" Jack said.

"Milo and Bobby are with her." Ezra sighed and looked back at me. "Maybe you can talk some sense into him."

"I'll try," I said.

He left us alone, and I walked over to Jack. I could see him working up some argument about how he needed to leave, but I climbed on his lap, straddling him. I kissed him on the mouth, so deeply I could feel his blood pulsing through his lips. His arms went around me, pressing me close to him.

Maybe I had never been meant for Jack or Peter. Maybe I had only been meant to be a vampire. That thought had terrified me before, but I realized it was better this way. When I held Jack to me, feeling how much he loved me and how much I loved him, I *knew* it was real.

I loved Jack because of every little thing about him. The way he laughed, the way he made me smile, the way he'd stay up until nine in the morning watching zombie movies he'd seen a hundred times, and the way he could never hold a grudge.

I loved him because I loved him, not because it was fate or destiny or in my blood. We had chosen each other, and that felt more powerful and more magical.

Matilda came back home with three broken ribs and a broken back leg, but she was slated to make a full recovery. Jack babied her like crazy since she'd been injured protecting him, but I didn't blame him.

After things had settled down a bit, I sat down with Jack and told him exactly what I wanted to do. After everything that happened with the vampire hunters, I felt like I had to do it.

People and vampires were being hurt and tortured, and I wouldn't stand by and let that happen.

Jack wasn't thrilled about it, but he was supportive. I drove to Olivia's with his blessing, and that was all that mattered.

I arrived at *V* in the early morning hours when the club was empty. That's the time they received deliveries of alcohol for the drinks for the human bar. The club always looked bizarre and cavernous when it was empty, but I supposed that was true with all clubs.

Olivia sat at the bar next to the dance floor, going over her inventory checklist. Violet was behind the bar, helping the delivery guy stock up. They were at the opposite end, far enough away where they couldn't hear me talk to Olivia.

"If you're looking for Rebekah, she left last night, since you didn't need her anymore," Olivia said, and I got up on the stool next to her. "Though, lord knows why anybody would willingly spend time with her."

"No, I'm not looking for her," I shook my head.

"Then what can I do for you, doll?" She lifted her head and smiled at me.

"Those vampire hunters that were here, they were bad people," I said, and she nodded. "They didn't do what was best for vampires or humans. They only cared about money, and they were monsters. We never did anything to them, and they tortured us."

"I'm sorry to hear that," Olivia said, and I knew she meant it. "That's not how they should be. That's not how I was, and I've always hoped that hunters could live on the side that benefits both humans and vampires."

"Ezra told me that because we're vampires, there are no good guys. But I don't think that's true. I want to be one of the good guys," I said. "I want you to train me to be a vampire hunter."

"Honey, it would be my pleasure," she smiled.

Other titles by Amanda Hocking:

My Blood Approves series

My Blood Approves

Fate

Flutter

Wisdom

Letters to Elise: A Peter Townsend Novella (Christmas 2010)

Trylle Trilogy

Switched

Torn (coming September 2010)

Ascend (coming January 2011)

Connect with Amanda Hocking Online:

Twitter: http://twitter.com/amanda_hocking

My blog: http://amandahocking.blogspot.com/

Facebook Fan Page: http://www.facebook.com/amandahockingfans

Made in the USA
Lexington, KY
06 October 2011